D1527930

STICK-SLIP

A NOVEL

CHRISTOPHER SCHOLZ

ISBN: 1497349516
ISBN-13: 9781497349513

Library of Congress Control Number: 2014908361
Createspace Independent Publishing Platform
North Charleston, SC

To Yoshiko

Author's Note

This story takes place in the near future. How near is anybody's guess.

PREFACE

Prominent in the folklore of the native coastal peoples of the Pacific Northwest, ranging from Vancouver Island down to northern Oregon, are the legends of Thunderbird and Whale. Whale was a malevolent sea monster and Thunderbird a gigantic bird that created the thunder and the rain. They were antagonists, and from time to time Thunderbird would attack Whale, grasping him in his enormous talons and carrying him off to the mountains. There they would have a terrible fight, causing fearsome shaking of the ground. When they fought at sea, great waves would crash against the coast, causing vast flooding. According to one such tale, "There was a shaking, a jumping up and trembling of the earth beneath, and a rolling up of the great waters."

Accounts of the most recent of these battles have been collected from many locations along this coast. They describe a shaking in the night, followed by great waves engulfing villages along the shore. People were swept eastward up the rivers by the great flood, or westward out to sea, never to be seen again. Afterward canoes and other objects, and sometime people, were found in the tops of high trees.

In the twelfth year of the Genroku era, AD 1700 by the Western calendar, a great tsunami struck Japan, flooding villages over 1,000 kilometers of coastline, from the Sanriku Coast on the Pacific side of northern Honshu to the Kii Peninsula south of Kyoto. Meticulous records of this event were entered into the chronicles of the Tokugawa shogunate. Because there had been no earthquake that could be associated with this tsunami, it became known as the orphan tsunami. Its source would remain unknown for 300 years.

The people of European descent who came to settle the Pacific Northwest beginning in the middle of the nineteenth century knew nothing of any of this.

In 1986 Brian Atwater, a geologist with the US Geological Survey, was canoeing in Willapa Bay, just north of the Washington-Oregon border. It was a low tide that day, and he noticed cedar stumps protruding from the exposed mudflats. This rang a bell for him because he had recently heard a report about the great 1964 Good Friday earthquake in Alaska, in which portions of Cook Inlet had dropped five feet with respect to sea level. This prompted him to return to this place to investigate further. He dated the tree stumps and found that the time of the drowning of the "ghost cedar forest" was about 300 years ago. The same submergence event was found to be recorded at other places along the coast, and deeper excavations showed repeated submergences of the shore every few hundred years or so going back into the more distant geological past. The submerged forests and marshes were found to be typically overlain by layers of sandy debris, which he and his colleagues interpreted as the detritus swept in by a tsunami that followed each great earthquake.

Soon other scientists joined in to help complete the solution to the puzzle. Ethnologists were prompted to reexamine the tales of the native peoples and in so doing were able to establish the date of the most recent such event as the winter of 1700. Japanese scientists carefully reexamined the old records of the orphan tsunami. They were able to reconstruct its source as the Pacific Northwest. To account for the size and extent of the tsunami in Japan, they concluded that the earthquake must have ruptured the entire length of the Cascadia Subduction Zone, from central Vancouver Island in British Columbia to Cape Mendocino in Northern California. The date of this earthquake was established as January 26, 1700, and its size was estimated as magnitude 9, about fifty times more powerful than the earthquake that destroyed San Francisco in 1906.

So it was that the people of the Pacific Northwest belatedly came to know of the existential threat that they live under: a peril that might strike without warning at any time.

SEPTEMBER 7

Birkett Valley

Far below bright scintillations danced over the deep blue Pacific, illuminated obliquely in the late afternoon sun. A sudden groundswell stretched the ocean surface, which flashed a mirror-sharp glare. The broad bulge in the sea surface raced to the north, following a tearing uplift of the underlying seafloor. The trailing edge of the bulge collapsed in the center to form two forks of a wake that moved outward, one westerly toward the central Pacific and Hawaii and the other toward the coast of North America, just visible as a dark smudge on the eastern horizon.

Carl woke with a jerk and leaned over to fumble for the clock on the bedside table: 5:10 a.m. He muttered to himself and rolled his lanky frame out of bed. He slipped on his robe and padded down the hall to the kitchen, flicked on the light, and began his morning ritual, putting the kettle to boil and getting out the coffee paraphernalia. He waited in front of the sink, staring out the window at the predawn darkness, deep in thought.

He heard a rustle and turned as his wife, Sally, slipped into the room.

"Morning," he said ruefully.

She sat down at the kitchen table. "Same dream again?"

He nodded.

"You know, Carl, you're going to have to talk to some people about this."

"I know, I know. I'll call Mark this morning to see if he can get some people together down at the university. I'll lay it all out for them and see what they have to say." He poured their coffee and sat down opposite her.

"Carl," she said gravely, "are you really sure about this? I mean, this isn't just one of your cute little scientific theories. This is really bad stuff. If you're really right about this, it's going to one hell of a horrendous disaster. I have trouble even imagining how bad it could be."

"I don't know, Sally. Right now it's not much more than a hunch. I mean, it's still pretty speculative. But I've got a nasty feeling about it just the same. I'm just hoping that somebody can pick a hole in my story— show me that my intuition is off or I've made a mistake somewhere."

"By God, I sure hope so."

"No kidding! It's ironic, but when I first made the discovery, I got so excited. It was the full eureka rush—like a little kid on Christmas morning finding something under the tree totally wonderful and unexpected. Cool. I was pretty high until the implications whooshed in like an Arctic wind. I thought, 'Oh, shit, this had better be wrong!' So I checked everything over again and again. I kept coming up with the same answers. So now I'm hoping there's an out somewhere—some escape clause in the theoretical fine print. Or maybe I've just made a dumb-ass mistake somewhere—it wouldn't be the first time I've screwed up like that. Sometimes my intuition gets out of whack."

He gave her a wry grin. "I gotta say, though, it feels pretty odd to be rooting so strongly against my latest discovery. It's a really strange emotional mix."

"I can imagine, Carl. But in the meantime, drink your coffee and try to calm down. It won't help to have a nervous breakdown over it. Let's talk about refinishing the back deck or something equally mundane."

◆　◆　◆

Mark was very helpful. Without asking too many questions, he managed, in pretty quick order, to get almost everybody on Carl's list to agree to a meeting at his lab two days later. It was just luck that so many of them happened to be in town at the same time. Carl settled down in his office to pull together all the figures and backup arguments he would need to present at the meeting.

As he assembled the evidence, he reviewed the sequence of events that had led to his discovery. At the time he had been noodling around with the GPS data on SSEs in Cascadia. SSEs, shorthand for slow slip events, episodically occur deep along the frictional contact between the tectonic plates at subduction zones, those tectonic plate boundaries where an oceanic plate descends at a shallow angle beneath a continental one. In Cascadia the SSEs reoccur every fourteen months like clockwork, each one producing a slip of a few centimeters over a period of a few weeks on a strip of the plate boundary from thirty to forty kilometers below the surface. These slow slip events occur just below the part of the interface between the plates that is normally locked by friction. That frictionally locked section is the buttress that resists plate tectonics, causing the adjacent regions to take up the inexorable convergence of the plates by elastically deforming like gigantic springs. When, after many centuries of this growing compression, the frictional resistance of the locked section finally gives way, the continental plate slips out and over the oceanic one with a violent lurch. This produces one of a species of giant earthquakes that are by far the largest anywhere on the planet and that, because they also produce uplift of the seafloor, generate huge tsunamis.

SSEs were discovered when the first continuously monitoring high-precision GPS stations began operating in the Pacific Northwest in the early years of the twenty-first century. Those instruments can measure movements of the earth's surface to millimeter precision, and their deployment provided, for the first time, the resolution needed to detect such fine stirrings at depth. Since their discovery seismologists have been closely monitoring the SSEs, trying to find out what they signify. Seismologists are very wary of them: some have suggested that one of those little slip events might one day awaken the sleeping beast above and trigger the next megaquake, but that was all speculation—nothing more. Or so it was thought.

The SSEs propagate within their narrow channel at speeds of ten to twenty kilometers per day to the north or south along the length of the subduction zone, like little zippers letting out precise allotments of plate tectonic motion to load the locked region just above. Carl had been using the GPS data to study the propagation paths of the SSEs to see if he could find any pattern in their starting points or propagation directions. He hadn't had any particular theory in mind that he was trying to test; it was just an exploratory study—a fishing expedition. If anything interesting should pop up, it might jog his intuition into some new insight about what controlled the SSEs.

Since he had retired, he could entertain his scientific curiosity without any obligations to funding agencies, students, administrators, or department heads. There were no longer any deadlines to be met, nor was there a sense of any necessity to produce papers or reports. He had given up his professorship at a major research university, in what his surprised colleagues had called his prime years, to get away from the funding cycle rat race that had spoiled science for him. He had returned from the East Coast to the land of his roots in the coastal mountains of Oregon and in the subsequent few years had gradually regained a free and untrammeled style of doing science that he hadn't enjoyed since his grad student days. Science had become fun again.

But what he had found that day would forever put an end to that tranquility. He vividly remembered the moment when everything had changed for him. He had assembled all the displacement-time GPS plots for last summer's SSE on the screen of his computer workstation in a sort of space-time sequence of snapshots as it had slowly propagated from southern Washington down to central Oregon, its progress recorded as it went by one GPS station after the other. Each trace showed the displacement of the ground over a period of a few days, forming a curve like an ascending ski jump. But his eye had caught a nuance in the shapes of the curves, a subtle flattening in the middle of the ski jump, which seemed to gradually evolve as the SSE progressed. On a hunch he had clicked on the first derivative icon in the analysis menu, and everything had been converted to velocity-time plots. The early ones in the north, near the early stages of the growth of the SSE, showed the typical bell-shaped curves that he had expected—a gradual acceleration of slip rate, followed by a smooth deceleration. As the SSE progressed in time, the crown of the bell developed humps on either edge with a shallow depression between them, like a Bactrian camel. Further on the humps gradually crawled closer and sharpened, resembling horns.

When he saw that shape, a frisson of faint recognition had run through him. He highlighted one of the better-developed horned profiles and clicked on the spectral analysis button. The spectrum appeared in a box at the corner of his screen. It had two peaks, one at half the frequency of the other; or to put it the other way, the other had twice the period. He caught his breath. A sudden clarity opened with a blazing jolt: it exhibited *period doubling*. *Ah so desu ka*. Something new had just popped out of nature's cabinet of curiosities. He highlighted another profile and analyzed it. Same thing. And another. Ditto. The SSE was no longer simply periodic. The SSE had entered a new regime—the one characterized by period doubling. But what was this development telling him?

He remembered leaning back in his chair, his mind zipping back and forth from one connection to another. No one had ever seen period doubling before in this situation. Period doubling was mainly known from chaos theory. You could find illustrations of it in the scientific literature in which it was generated with computer models of nonlinear dynamical systems. But the chances of seeing it in reality were very slim indeed. It is the last stage of one of the classical routes to chaos and normally inhabits a very narrow region in phase space. In the real world, it would be easy to miss this transitory way station on the road to instability. Seeing it would be like seeing the green flash in a sunset. In this case, though, it seemed very clear. In the system he was looking at, the instabilities that define the cycle are the mega-earthquakes that occur along the plate boundary. The recurrence time between those rare events is measured in centuries. In this new world in which a network of GPS stations report their locations to millimeter precision once a minute, you could clearly observe the period-doubling regime, as he had just found out. You just had to look at the data in the right way to recognize it. Once you had seen it, it was as plain as day. You also had to be looking at just the right time—just on the eve of the catastrophe. Because that is the only time, according to theory, that period doubling should appear.

That realization flooded him with a sense of deep dread. If what he saw was what he thought it was, he had stumbled upon a hidden back channel into the future. With that he envisioned the horrors it held for the people of the Pacific Northwest. The appearance of period doubling meant that the system was hanging on the very edge of the abyss. Teetering. That was what period doubling signified: teetering on the edge of the cliff. The next SSE would most likely push the tectonic engine over the brink, where it would suck up all the pent-up strain energy stored in the tectonic plates and unleash it in a gigantic earthquake that would radiate all that energy back out as seismic waves of enormous power. Once it started, there would be no telling how far the earthquake would run. But he could vividly envision what kind of havoc it would wreak. And, in many ways worse, he could imagine the destructive power of the tsunami that would follow just behind it. The expected arrival of the next SSE was just eleven months off.

September 9

Birkett Valley, Corvallis

Carl stood on his front deck, staring into the distance. Beyond the hemlocks and Douglas firs that enclosed his home clearing loomed the succession of peaks and ridges of the Drift Creek Wilderness, the inner keep of the Siuslaw National Forest. It was a view that never failed to calm and inspire him. He and Sally had built their ridgetop aerie over fifteen summers after he had bought the property from his cousins. The property was an old patented mining claim dating from the 1890s that his Uncle Jimmy had picked up for a song in the early fifties and turned into a camp. Jimmy hadn't done much more with it than bulldoze away the miners' shacks and park a trailer on the site. Carl had spent many a summer of his youth living with his cousins in a tent out back of that old Airstream. With so many memories of roaming the surrounding mountains and canyons, this place had somehow become more connected to his roots than his own childhood home in the flatlands and rolling hills of Yamhill County down below.

When Jimmy died, his sons, having long ago migrated to distant cities, showed little interest in keeping the place, so Carl had snapped it up. He and Sally had built this place, a solar-powered, off-the-grid bastion of privacy, with a custom-designed study for him and a studio for Sally, who was a poet and novelist with a small but devoted following. There was also a terraced garden descending the slope out back, where they shared their passions for growing vegetables and tending a rock garden of shrubs, descending vines, and flowers.

With a glance at his watch and a grimace, Carl checked in his pocket for his memory stick, picked up his laptop, and walked down the steps to his battered old narrow-eyed Land Rover. He cranked it over until it started with a wheezy cough and stutter. At the end of their long driveway, he pulled out onto the gravel Forest Service road that was their link to the outside world. Fifteen minutes of winding mountain road later, he hit the tarmac of the county road and quickly passed through the hamlet of Birkett Valley, an old logging town that now consisted of little besides a few ramshackle houses, sheds, and a combination general store/post office that served as a community center for residents from miles around. Ten miles farther on, he turned east onto the state highway and drove down the long slope toward the Willamette Valley.

Carl drove in autopilot mode, thinking about what he needed to say at the meeting and how to say it. He had been stewing about it all morning. As the traffic began to build up, he shook his head and decided to give up trying to rehearse it. *Just play it as it goes*, he thought, clearing his mind.

Mark Weisenberg's office on the third floor of the Earth Sciences Building had, on one side, a nice view overlooking a grassy campus quad but otherwise was a jumble. Stacks of journal articles and manuscripts covered the table that filled the center of the room. Chairs of several styles were clumped haphazardly around the table, several serving as additional piling places. Behind the table was a narrow space backed by a whiteboard covered with partially wiped out diagrams and mathematical scribbles. Mark himself was barely visible behind a desk holding two oversize computer monitors. He waved over the top of them.

"Ah, the mystery man arrives." He bounced out from behind his desk. "Hello, hello, Carl. It's nice to see you again. It's been a while. Now I suppose we get to find out what brings you down from your mountain fastness?"

"Hi, Mark. Thanks for organizing this. It's great you could arrange a meeting on such short notice."

"No problem at all. We see you so seldom around here that it's always a pleasure. Particularly with you being so cagey about what you want to talk about. I'm intrigued—it sounds like it ought to be great fun. Come along; we're just gathering down the hall in the seminar room."

In the seminar room, half a dozen people were seated around the long table that occupied the center of the room. Mark bounded to the front and, unconsciously stroking his scraggly goatee, began the introductions.

"Good; everyone's here, except for Shuichi Kato, who's off on leave in Japan. As most of you know from my messages, Carl Strega, who is this fellow standing here, called for this meeting. He told me it was urgent but refused to say any more. So I'm as curious as anybody to find out what it's all about.

"For those of you who don't know him, Carl is well-known in the geophysics community for his trailblazing work on earthquake physics. A few years ago, he took early retirement and came back here to his home state of Oregon to settle down in his ancestral fiefdom, which I'm told is somewhere up in the Siuslaw. He has a visiting adjunct position here in Earth Sciences, so we see him from time to time. So are you all set up, Carl? I'll turn it over to you."

Carl looked up from connecting his laptop to the projector. "Thanks, Mark. And thank you all for coming. For starters, why don't we all get acquainted? You all know Mark, so I'll start off by introducing José Soromenho, just there to my left. José is from Physics by way of Brazil; he studies nonlinear dynamical systems. José, the bearded gentleman across from you is Hugh Duckworth, our leading expert on the history of tsunamis of the Pacific Northwest. And I don't know the young people. Please introduce yourselves."

The young woman next to José raised her hand. "Hi; it's Anastasia Reznikova. I'm a postdoc with José."

They continued around the table: Gregor Patz, José's grad student, and two grad students of Mark's, Kiersten Lunqvist and Jason McAlistair, each introduced themselves.

"Before I begin I would like to ask something of you all that is a bit unusual. I would like this meeting to be kept confidential. That is, I don't want any of you to discuss what will be described here with anyone who is not in this room. My reason for this will become apparent shortly. If anyone is uncomfortable with this request, I ask you to please leave the room now." Carl gaze surveyed the small audience. He found only a few quizzical looks. "OK, I guess everyone agrees."

He turned and clicked on the first slide. "For the sake of the physicists present, I'll start with the basics of the tectonic situation we face here in Cascadia. This map shows the Cascadia Subduction Zone, which is the boundary between two converging tectonic plates. The offshore oceanic plate, called the Juan de Fuca Plate, meets the continental North American Plate at a deep-sea trench that lies about 100 kilometers offshore and runs from central Vancouver Island down past Washington and Oregon to Cape Mendocino in Northern California, a distance of about 1,100 kilometers.

The oceanic plate, the Juan de Fuca, is moving to the east relative to the North American Plate at a rate of about four centimeters per year. The convergence between the plates is accommodated by the oceanic plate sliding at a shallow angle beneath the continental plate, a process known as subduction. When the subducting plate reaches a depth of about 150 kilometers, it reacts with the mantle to form magmas that rise and erupt at the surface, forming the Cascade chain of volcanoes that are shown on the map by the red triangles.

"The next slide shows a schematic vertical cross section of the interface between the plates. The oceanic plate descends from the trench at a shallow angle beneath the continent. The shallowest part of the plate interface, from the trench down to a depth of about thirty kilometers, is normally locked by friction so that the continuous convergence of the plates results in their elastic deformation. This stored elastic energy is released every few hundred years when the friction lets go and ten meters or so of slip occurs suddenly on the interface, resulting in a great earthquake. This is why we call this part of the plate interface the seismogenic zone. These kinds of subduction zone megaquakes are by far the greatest earthquakes in terms of their energy release and physical dimensions. And, because they produce uplift of the seafloor, they also generate great tsunamis. The latest one of these to occur in Cascadia was in 1700. It ruptured the entire length of the plate boundary and was about a magnitude 9. It also produced an enormous tsunami that caused extensive damage as far away as Japan." Carl glanced at the physicists. "Just ordinary stick-slip friction so far.

"At greater depths, below forty kilometers, the two plates slide smoothly and silently past one another at the plate-tectonic velocity. Between these two regions there is a transitional region, between depths of thirty to forty kilometers, where something interesting happens." He clicked on the next slide. "This slide shows ten years of data from a continuously recording GPS site in northern Washington. The plot looks like an upwardly sloping saw blade. As the oceanic plate converges, the upper, continental plate is elastically deformed so that points on it gradually move to the east. In the plot time is the horizontal axis and motion to the east is the vertical axis. The upward slope on the plot indicates this continuous eastern drift. This is punctuated every fourteen months by the point slipping partly back to the west, which produces the teeth in the blade. The eastward migration indicates the steady accumulation of elastic strain, and the sawteeth are back slips. These take place over a span of two or three weeks and are caused by episodes of two to three centimeters of slow slip occurring on that transitional strip just below the seismogenic region. We call these slow slip events, or SSEs, for short. At the bottom of the slide are shown the signals recorded by seismometers during the same period. It shows that a burst of seismic

20

activity occurs during each of the slow slip events. This seismic activity is not from earthquakes. It is a kind of low-level seismic noise that seismologists call nonvolcanic tremor. Because they like to emphasize all things seismic, seismologists call the whole business ETS, for episodic tremor and slip. It turns out, though, that the tremor is a secondary phenomenon. It is the rubbing noise of the slow slip events.

"OK, that's the background. Now we get to what I brought you here to tell you about. The slide I show now is a screenshot from my computer of the latest slow slip event, which occurred three months ago. From lower left to upper right are the displacement-time profiles for a group of GPS receivers that recorded the passage of the SSE as it propagated along that transitional strip at about ten kilometers per day from northern Washington to central Oregon. You can see they each show a gradual rise over a period of a few days. Plotted next to those are their time derivatives, the velocity-time profiles for each station. The velocity plots at the lower left, during the earlier stage of propagation, show a bell-shaped curve, which is typical for SSEs. However, as the event propagated further, its shape gradually morphed into one with two peaks, like horns, which became more pronounced as time went on. The little boxes next to those plots show their spectra. The bell-shaped curves have a nice central spectral peak, but the horned strain-rate profiles are bimodal, with two peaks, one having a period twice that of the other."

A low whistle came from the left side of the audience.

Carl glanced over. "So—I gather that José has already twigged. For the rest of you, let me try to explain what I think is the physics going on here.

"This SSE behavior is a mode of frictional sliding that was known from laboratory experiments on rock friction long before anyone ever installed a continuous GPS device above a subduction zone and observed it for the first time in nature. The rock mechanics people called it oscillatory stable sliding. We usually think of friction as having two modes of sliding. In one mode, called stable sliding, when the pushing force on an object equals its frictional resistance it will begin to slide stably at the same speed as the pushing speed. In the other mode, called stick-slip, slip will occur in a sudden jerk when friction is overcome, which drops the force so that the object sticks again until the force is built back up again to the friction level. In the stick-slip mode, the slips are dynamic instabilities, and in this case, an earthquake is the result. The oscillatory mode of friction occurs in a narrow window between these two more common modes. If we look at the phase diagram for rock friction, on the next slide, we see that this oscillatory mode of behavior occurs in a narrow region of phase space just at the boundary between the stable sliding field and the unstable, or stick-slip, field. To translate this to the subduction zone situation, the SSEs are in the oscillatory stable sliding mode and occur in a strip just below the seismogenic zone, which is in the unstable stick-slip mode, and above the deeper region, which is in the smooth stable sliding mode.

"Every time an SSE occurs, it increases the stress at the base of the neighboring frictionally locked zone. So what has worried people ever since SSEs were first discovered is that one of them might trigger the next megaquake. The question has always been, 'Well, OK, but how do you tell which one will be the critical one that sets it off?'

"If I zoom in on the slide, you can see that inside the oscillatory sliding field there is an even smaller field just at the edge of the unstable field. This field is so narrow that it is extremely difficult to explore with laboratory experiments. Ordinary laboratory testing machines are usually just too crude to work at such a fine scale. As a result this field has been mapped out largely with computer simulations of the rate-state variable friction laws that were derived from laboratory data and are the basis of modern earthquake physics theory. The next slide shows a computer simulation of a typical slip event in that field. Look familiar? It's the two-horned monster. This is the period-doubling field. What we found in last summer's SSE is the first time this has ever been observed in nature.

"So my interpretation of our sighting of a period-doubling event, if that indeed is what it was, it that it is signaling that we are at the very end of the seismic cycle. How close are we? I'm guessing very close. My gut instinct is that the next SSE, which is scheduled to occur next August, will be the trigger of a major Cascadia earthquake. Or maybe not. It's going to take a lot more work to be sure about any of this."

He looked around at the now hushed group. "So I am hoping that someone here will find a fatal flaw in this story. José, what do you think?"

"Well, I don't know. It certainly does look like period doubling, doesn't it? But I don't know your system." He shrugged and spread his arms. "In some systems this can lead to a cascading sequence. In others you get intermittency behavior—there's a sudden jump from one stable state to another. That seems to be what you're implying, no?"

"Yes, exactly. In this case the two states are what are called, in high school physics, static and dynamic friction. The first is larger than the other, and when the jump occurs, it is so sudden there is a dynamic instability—it propagates at the speed of sound like a running crack. Voila—you have an earthquake."

Carl turned toward the far side of the table. "What about you, Hugh? You've been sitting there quietly. I expected you to jump up and tell me this is impossible. Isn't it true that a big one in Cascadia isn't due for another couple of hundred years?"

Hugh Duckworth twiddled his beard and pursed his lips. "I suppose you are referring to the famous 500-year recurrence time between the big ones. That number was obtained by taking the number of full-length plate boundary earthquakes in the paleoseismic record since Mt. Mazama time and dividing it into 7,700 years." He directed an aside to the physicists: "Mt. Mazama was the volcano that exploded in a violent eruption 7,700 years ago and left the Crater Lake caldera. That eruption resulted in a deposit of volcanic ash over the whole of Cascadia that is used by us Quaternary geologists as a standard time reference." Turning back to Carl, he said, "That number is pretty misleading. The time intervals between successive megaquakes range from about 150 to 900 years, so saying that the average is 500 is next to meaningless. Not only that, but there are other earthquakes in between that rupture only half or a third or so of the length of the plate boundary. They are magnitude 8.4s or 8.6s, what have you, but they are also plenty dangerous. They also produce big tsunamis. If you include them, the average repeat time is more like 240 years. So I am afraid that my answer to your question is that it's quite possible for a big earthquake to occur next year. Of any size."

An uneasy silence settled over the room. Anastasia raised her hand and stood. "This is so scary. Why you want to keep this secret? Why you not want to tell people about this? It is important for the people to be warned. So to do something, no?"

"Yes, of course, Anastasia. But right now everything is still pretty iffy. A lot of this is just guesswork on my part, and we don't want to cry 'Wolf!' or 'Fire!' or whatever cliché applies. There are some important issues yet to be answered that will require a lot of work before we can even think about sharing any of this with the public.

"Which brings me to the important point. I am going to need some help on this. Two problems. Firstly if what I am looking at is really period- doubling then theory also predicts some other properties of the SSEs. Checking this out requires tracking the SSEs with tremor, so this problem needs seismologists. Secondly the system needs to be modeled and simulations run to check out my intuition that the period- doubling foreshadows an earthquake, and if so, how imminent that might be. This needs physicists. I haven't the time, facilities, or know-how to tackle these problems on my own in the time available. So I am asking for help. So please think about this and about the problems I've posed. Anybody who is interested in joining me on this project, please send me an e-mail.

"I give fair warning, though. This work is obviously time-sensitive, so the pressure to get results will be intense and will only increase as we approach the expected occurrence date—next August. There's no place here for less than a total commitment. The other downside is that this is a high-risk project. If, as is likely, it turns out to be a dud, it will have been a colossal waste of time for all involved. Worse, because the scientific community in this country has always been quite disparaging about earthquake prediction research, working on this may result in a black mark on one's career. I particularly warn the young people about this.

"Finally, as work progresses, if we do ever reach a point where we become scientifically convinced that an earthquake is imminent, we'll have an obligation to make our findings public, just as Anastasia urged. I've no idea what the repercussions of that might be. As you probably know, not long ago a group of Italian seismologists was sentenced to prison for failing to warn of an earthquake, so reactions to any kind of announcement predicting a future earthquake could be extreme. As a result we have to be very careful on the public relations front. This is what was behind my request for secrecy. The legal and political problems that we may encounter are as unexplored as the scientific ones. There's a line from Dante's *The Divine Comedy* that seems fitting: 'The sea we are entering has never yet been crossed.'

"Other than that," he said with a grin, "it should be fun."

September 10

Corvallis

That evening Carl received e-mails from Anastasia and Kiersten indicating their interest in working on the project. He responded with follow-up queries to José and Mark, who were supportive of their respective charges and who also volunteered to participate as their research advisors. Carl set up organizational meetings at the university for the following morning.

He found Kiersten in her cubbyhole in a corral of gray steel bookcases. She stood to greet him with a handshake and a bright smile. She was Scandi-blond and blue-eyed and willowy in an outdoorsy way. On the wall behind her desk, the only decoration was a poster-size print of two people in a raft going sideways down a monster rapid with two kayakers watching from the pool below.

"Wow, where is that?" Carl asked, gazing at the print.

"Oh, isn't that a great shot? It's from a river trip I was on last summer. That's our gear raft going down the Green Wall of the Illinois River."

Carl leaned closer. "Oh, yes, I see; that's you in the green kayak. But isn't the Illinois a pretty dangerous river? Every year you hear about a few more people drowning in it."

"The main thing is you have to be really careful about the weather. If a big rainstorm comes up when you're in the canyon, you could end up in big doo-doo because it's *really* prone to flash-flooding."

"I see. Hmm. I'd love to do that river myself someday. Besides the river itself, which is quite a challenge, I hear, that gorge cuts a rare section through the Siskiyous that has created a beautiful exposure of the Josephine peridotite. That's an uplifted massif of oceanic mantle that's always fascinated me. If you're into such stuff, of course," he added, sotto voce.

Kiersten, as she introduced herself, was a Minnesotan Swede who had used college as a means of getting out of the upper Midwest and its harsh winters and wound up majoring in physics at Central Washington University. After her sophomore year, she got a summer job there with PANGA, the Pacific Northwest geodetic array people. The experience of running all over the northwest doing maintenance on GPS stations got her hooked on the great outdoors, so she switched to geophysics. Now she was working on a PhD with Mark but hadn't yet settled on a thesis topic.

When he asked her why she wanted to work on his project, she said, "Jason says I'm crazy, but I think this is the most exciting thing I've ever heard of. What a chance!"

Carl recognized the gleam of genuine excitement in her eye. "Who's Jason?"

"Jason is Mark's other student. He sits over there." She indicated a desk piled with computer printout in the corner. "He says earthquake prediction is total rubbish."

"Well, maybe he's right. We're going to find out, though, aren't we?"

Anastasia's office was a windowless sliver on the third floor of the physics building. As she rose to greet him, Carl realized how petite she was. A blond pixie cut set off her slightly broad Slavic facial structure. She was neatly turned out in a snug sweater dress with accessories that projected a shade dressier look than was usual for these parts.

Carl eased himself into her visitor's chair. "So I gather you're from Russia?"

"Yes, from Moscow. I came to America with my parents when I was fourteen. To Brooklyn."

"Ah, Brooklyn. Brighton Beach?"

"No, but not so far away. Sheepshead Bay."

He asked the quintessential New York question. "Where did you go to high school?"

"Brooklyn Tech. Then to City College and after that Columbia for my PhD."

"Wow, a through and through New Yorker, then. Living in Oregon must be a big change for you."

"Yes, is very big change for me. I have six months here. Now I am studying to get my driver's license. Then I will get a car and be like normal person. Ha-ha."

He asked her why she wanted to work on his problem.

"Oh, it is because is real problem. Not like our usual, which is just to play games with differential equations. Usually we are looking only to find some pretty solution for to impress a hundred, let's say, other people in the world who care about such things. But your project is real problem with big importance for people. It is an honor for me to work on such a thing."

Carl had lunch with Mark and José, where they discussed Kiersten's and Anastasia's strengths and weaknesses. Both were concerned about the riskiness of the project for such junior people.

"I told Kiersten that it's a pretty high-risk endeavor for a thesis project," Mark said, "but she's still very keen on it. So I told her to treat it as an adventure. If it doesn't work out, she can just back up and try something else later. She's young enough that blowing off a year is no great setback. She told me that she thought this project was way more important than any career plans she might have, and I had to agree. I just felt obliged, as her advisor, to warn her about such things."

"Anastasia's case is a little more problematic," said José. "As a postdoc she has a few years to make a name for herself if she hopes to get a permanent job. So going off and working on this topic, which isn't even considered to be a proper branch of physics, is a big gamble. But she is very enthusiastic nonetheless. She actually got angry with me for bringing it up. She told me it's the only responsible thing to do. And I agree. I'm going to back her all the way."

"Well," Carl replied, "let's hope that they don't get second thoughts somewhere down the line."

Afterward everyone met in the seminar room.

Carl rose. "First of all I would like to thank all of you for volunteering to join this project. As I said yesterday, there's much work to be done, so we're all going to have a lot on our plates for the coming months. There are two main problems that need to be addressed, one observational and the other theoretical. That naturally splits us into two teams, but I want the whole group to meet together regularly so that everyone stays aware of the full picture.

"The observational problem has to do with the way we think the convergence of the plates stresses them during the interseismic period when the plates are stuck together between earthquakes. There are two possible extreme cases. In the first case, the subduction of the oceanic plate increases both the shear stress at the plate interface and the compressive stress pushing the plates together. In the second case, the subduction increases only the shear stress. These two models have important ramifications regarding SSE behavior. In the first case, the transition region will gradually be driven toward the unstable state. In that case we should observe an evolution in time in which the intervals between SSEs gradually increase, then change to period doubling, followed fairly quickly by the earthquake itself. On the other hand, in the second case, the SSEs will be in periodic steady state. The interval between them will remain constant. In that case period doubling should never occur. If that one proves to be the case, we would be forced to conclude that whatever I observed is not period doubling at all but just some spurious behavior that has nothing to do with any future earthquake.

"In the interpretation I gave yesterday, I implicitly assumed the first case to be true. That assumption was simply based on my conviction that what I was looking at really was period doubling. This verges on circular reasoning, so it needs to be independently confirmed. We can do this by showing that the intervals between SSEs have indeed increased over time. If, on the other hand, we end up finding that the intervals are constant in time, I will offer my mea culpa and we can all quietly fold our tents and steal away to our former lives.

"I have already worked out that this analysis cannot be done with the GPS data alone. The GPS stations are too sparse and have not been running for long enough. So it will have to be done with tremor data. We have about twenty years of seismic data to bring to bear on this problem, but remember that what we are looking for is a second-order effect. It will be a small signal, so I imagine that it'll be no mean trick to tease it out of what is pretty noisy data. This is the problem for Kiersten and Mark.

"The other problem is in regards to my gut feeling that the sighting of a period-doubling event means that the earthquake is imminent. Gut feelings are fine, but they aren't good enough to bet the ranch on. And saying something is imminent is not very useful. It has to be more precise. It has to have a specific time frame attached to it.

"The only way I know how to tackle this is through computer simulations in which we try varying the parameters over what we think are reasonable ranges and see what happens. That's kind of a brute force approach, I know, but with a nonlinear problem like this, I can't think of a more elegant solution, nor can we afford the time to look for one. This is the problem I would like Anastasia and José to take on. It's the part of the problem with which I have the least experience, so I'm not going to try to second-guess Anastasia and José on what might be the best way to handle it.

"That's all for now. I'll leave you to start thinking about it. When I get back home, I'll e-mail you PDFs of all the relevant literature I have that'll help you get started. To begin with I want to have daily team meetings via Skype and will come down weekly, or more often if necessary, for meetings with the whole group. Otherwise, feel free to e-mail at any time, 24-7. I often leave my phone turned off, so that's not a good way to contact me. Have fun."

SEPTEMBER 21

Corvallis

The group was seated around the table in the seminar room.

Carl looked around and said, "Shall we begin, then? Kiersten, can you fill us in on what you've been up to?"

Kiersten opened her notebook and arranged it in front of her. "Yes, well, what Mark and I have been looking at so far is the data handling problem. All the tremor data is archived at PNSN, the Pacific Northwest Seismic Network, in Seattle. We have access to it via their website, but the problem is what to do with it. We're talking about terabytes of data, so there's no question of downloading it to my laptop. Mark suggests we do the computing in the cloud, so I've begun looking into how to do that."

"But hasn't quite a bit of the tremor data already been analyzed for SSEs?" Carl asked.

Mark broke in. "Yes, quite a lot has. A fair bit has been published, in fact. But because our goal is to look at long-term trends, I think that Kiersten should redo the entire data set in a systematic way. Otherwise trying to patch together a hodgepodge of previously analyzed subsets of the data is likely to introduce biases. That could be a real mess to untangle. I think it's better in the long run for her to start over from scratch."

"OK, that makes sense," Carl replied. "Any idea yet about a time frame for getting us some answers?"

"Whoa—way too early to say," Mark said with uplifted arms. "We're in cold start mode. Give us a couple of weeks. We ought to have a rough idea by then."

"Sounds good. Anastasia, what've you been up to?"

Anastasia immediately stood up, thought better of it, and sat down again. "OK," she said. "I started by making a simple one-dimensional model of friction slider and spring system, using the rate-state variable friction law. That part was easy; those equations were already available in the literature. It is just for me to practice on because the results are already known. Is the same as in the phase diagram Carl showed before.

"I made a simple modification to introduce a gradually increasing compression force as Carl suggested. I have some results I can show." She opened her laptop and typed a few lines, then turned it around so the others could see the screen. "This is time series of sliding with gradually increasing compression. It shows first smooth sliding, then oscillations, then the period doubling. So it agrees with what Carl said. So everything checks so far. That means at least I know my program is running OK. In the next stage, I will begin modeling the increase in period of the oscillations as time progresses. This is the problem we need to solve, but nobody has studied it before. Then, when Kiersten gets some results, I can compare them with my theory."

"Bravo!" Carl exclaimed. "Excellent progress!"

In a strained voice, Kiersten asked, "So you are working on the change of SSE period with time? I thought that was supposed to be my problem. Aren't you supposed to be working on the triggering of the earthquake by the period doubling?"

Anastasia replied, sounding a little annoyed, "Of course, but this part is easy to do in the beginning, so I do it first. Later I do the triggering part."

Kiersten looked at Carl. "I don't understand. I thought this was my problem. Kiersten is supposed to be doing something different..."

Anastasia broke in. "What *is* the problem? You are doing data. I am doing theory. When you are finished, you give me your results so I can compare them with my theory. Is simple. No?"

"Maybe for you it's simple, but not for me," Kiersten shot back, raising her voice. "That is my thesis topic you seem to be horning in on."

"Hey, hold it!" Carl broke in. "Everybody's on the same side here. Kiersten, you've got a big job to see if the data show an increase in period or not. Anastasia is just working up the theory that you will eventually test against your observations. There is no reason to compete with each other."

Kiersten and Anastasia exchanged frosty looks, then looked down, gathered up their things, and left the room.

Carl let out a puff and said to Mark and José, "Those two aren't off to the best start. I hope this sorts itself out. We've got a lot riding on them, and the last thing we need is a personality conflict."

"I think they're just under a lot of pressure," José said. "They'll probably settle down after a while. I'll have a chat with Anastasia. She's just being keen, but it comes off as a bit too aggressive."

"I'll talk to Kiersten as well," Mark said. "She sees this as her thesis project, and I think she's looking to mark out her territory. She needs to relax a bit. She's got a case of early-stage jitters."

October 19

Corvallis

It was past midnight when Kiersten walked into her apartment. David was reading in the living room. He put down his book and looked up at her intently, having gathered himself to broach the subject that had been bothering him for weeks.

"You sure are working late these days."

Kiersten returned his gaze, and from the look on his face she realized that her weeks of avoiding the issue had come to a head. What to say? She'd been dreading this moment but somehow hadn't rehearsed it. "Yeah, well, I've got a new thesis project, and I want to make a good start on it."

"You're telling me? I've hardly seen you for the past couple of weeks, and when you're home, you spend most of the time working on your laptop. I don't think we've exchanged a dozen words in the last three days."

Damn. She didn't like where this was going. "Sorry, David, but this is pretty important, and it's kind of got a deadline."

"Deadline? You've only just got started. Take it easy; have a life for goodness sake. You've got a couple of years to do your thesis."

Beginning to feel cornered, she struck back. "I'm sorry, David, but this is too important. You'll just have to bear with it."

He retorted angrily, "How important can it be? Is it more important than our relationship? What the hell is it anyway? What are you working on?"

She gave him a long, steady look, wanting to defuse the situation but not sure how. "I can't tell you that. It's confidential."

He blew up. "Confidential? What? Are you working on something classified? Don't tell me you're working on that DARPA contract of Mark's on nuclear test discrimination? Jesus, honey, I told you before, that's just a front for the DoD's strategy to undermine the Comprehensive Test Ban Treaty. Mark is just being a patsy for those warmongers. What a sellout! Don't tell me you're working on that project, for cryin' out loud!"

Oh, Lordy, she thought, *now he's off on his antiwar kick.* She raised her voice in irritation. "Mark is not a patsy or a sellout! And no, I am not working on that project."

"Well, what is it then?"

"You're being annoying, David. Just mind your own business. You were never interested in my work before, so why should you start now?" She took her laptop, went into the kitchen, and fired it up at the kitchen table.

He sulked for a while in the living room, then followed her into the kitchen and sat down across from her at the table. "You're serious, aren't you? I mean, this must be something really important."

"Yes, David, it's important. It's very important."

"Jeez, how am I supposed to live with you with this between us? It would be like living with a spy, with some terrible secret you're keeping from me. It'll drive me crazy."

"With anyone else I might confide it. But with you, no way! You're a science writer and an activist to boot, and if I told you what I'm working on, the first thing you would want to do is to shout it from the rooftops and tell the whole world about it. And we can't afford to have that happen right now."

"Oh, man! Now I want to know more than ever."

She remained silent and resumed working on her laptop. He got up and stomped back into the living room.

After about an hour, he came back into the kitchen. "Please, Kiersten, you've got to tell me about this. I can't stand this not knowing. I promise I won't tell a soul."

"I don't believe you."

"Honest, I promise."

She looked up and gave a sigh. "All right, David. I can see that you're going to bug me forever about this, so I guess I'd have to tell you about it sooner or later. Sit down and listen." Then she told him.

"Holy moly! You weren't kidding it's important. That's about the biggest thing that could ever happen in this part of the world!" He thought a few moments and said, "I don't understand why you guys want to sit on this. I mean, this will affect millions of people's lives. People need to know about this so they can prepare for it. It's a matter of life and death. They need to be warned about this…like immediately."

"See! I knew you were going to be like that. I already told you, we're not sure about it yet. We need to be a lot surer about it before we can make it public."

"Sure? How sure can you be? I know enough about science to know that nothing is ever absolutely certain. How long is it going to take you to be sure enough? Weeks, months, ten months? By then it's too late. While you guys are trying to nail things down to a gnat's ass, time is being wasted when people could be preparing and lives could be saved. And even if it turns out you're wrong in the end, so what? So you guys are embarrassed. Big deal."

"It's not a question of embarrassment, David; it's a question of credibility. As scientists we can't go around shouting about every half-baked theory that pops into our heads. If we did, after a while the public wouldn't believe anything we say. Sure, there is always uncertainty, but we have to make sure we've got the science right before we start broadcasting it. And we're not there yet. That's what Mark and I have been working so hard on for these past weeks: trying to get the proof."

"That may be the scientist's outlook, but as a journalist, I feel a responsibility to go public on something like this. It is simply too urgent a matter to keep secret. It would be unethical. Think of all the people living along the coast. They're living in mortal danger from a tsunami. Don't they need to be warned? And the sooner the better, I think. It takes time to get ready for something like this."

They went on for most of the night arguing the ethics of the situation. By morning they had not reached any resolution. At nine o'clock David called somebody he knew at the *Oregonian*, and Kiersten pedaled her bicycle off to campus to tell Mark about the impending public exposure of their project.

October 20

Birkett Valley

Carl was getting his computer camera set up for a Skype conference with Kiersten and Mark when Mark called.

"Hi, Carl. We're going to have to scrub the conference this morning. We've got another situation to deal with. Kiersten's boyfriend, David, has been pestering her for days about what she's been working on, and she finally ended up spilling the beans. The problem is that he's a science reporter and is now insisting on writing it up for the *Oregonian.*"

"Oh, shit! No chance of talking him out of it, is there?"

"It doesn't seem like it. But I think you should come down here and talk to them. Maybe you can talk some sense into him."

"OK, I can do that. Where do I meet them?"

"She's here in my office. Let me ask her." There was a pause. "Can you meet her at the Roasting Hut? It's a coffee joint just off Fourth. Do you know it?"

"I can find it. Tell her I'll be there in about an hour."

He hung up and went and told Sally about the situation. "I'll have to go down to see if I can talk him out of it. I shouldn't be more than a few hours. Shall I bring back something for dinner?"

Corvallis

He found a diagonal parking spot in the shade just across from the Roasting Hut. The place had a central barista serving area with booths along the walls. He ordered a two-shot macchiato and selected a small pastry from a tray below the glass counter. He took them to the corner booth and slipped in opposite Kiersten.

"I hope you haven't been waiting too long."

"Oh no, not at all. Thank you so much for coming." She looked a bit shaken, like she had pulled herself together, but just barely.

He took a sip of his coffee. "So what's going on?"

She sighed and toyed with the stirring stick in the frothy drink in front of her. "It has to do with my boyfriend, David. David Kenner. He's a science writer. He writes mainly on environmental issues. He's very dedicated to improving environmental awareness, so I thought that if I told him about what we were working on, he wouldn't be able to keep it to himself. He'd probably want to write about it immediately. So in the beginning, I just didn't tell him what I was working on. Usually that wouldn't be a problem because he normally isn't all that interested in what I'm doing anyway. But I guess he noticed that I'd started putting in really long hours. Even when I was home, I was exchanging e-mails with you or Mark or downloading papers from the web or checking my cloud computing jobs. I guess I was really preoccupied and ignoring him too much. Anyway, it seems that it was bothering him, and he started asking me about what I was working on. I told him something vague about a hot thesis topic. After a while he began going on about how could anything be that important and why don't I have a life and so forth. He kept bugging me like that, and finally I got really pissed off and said, 'What I am working on is really important, so don't bother me about it.' He got in a huff and said, 'Important, or just important to you?' and so on. So to shut him up, I just told him, 'I can't tell you about it. It's confidential, so you'll just have to learn to live with it.'

"Then he really flipped out. 'What! Are you working on some classified DoD project or something?' He even called me a sellout."

"Jeez, sounds like he's a little tightly wired."

"Yeah, I know. I really love it that he has such strong convictions, but sometimes he gets a little too carried away with them.

"Anyway, I finally sat down with him and made him promise that if I told him what I was working on that he'd keep it to himself. He seemed a little leery, but he promised. So I told him everything. I was very clear about why it had to be kept from the public for the time being. I think he was astonished at what I told him, and it seemed to satisfy him. That lasted about five minutes. Then he decided that it was immoral for us to withhold our information from the public. He claimed that it was a life-threatening situation, so we had an obligation to disclose it to the public even if it turned out in the end to be false, yada yada yada. According to him any delay was inexcusable. We spent all last night arguing about it, but I couldn't convince him. The upshot was he plans to write an article for the *Oregonian*. I'm so sorry that all this happened, Carl." She gave him a look that was at once forlorn and relieved.

"Well, Kiersten, I really can't blame you. I'd never ask anyone to jeopardize a personal relationship over something like this. It was bound to get out sooner or later anyway, though I gotta tell ya, later would have been a lot easier to deal with than sooner. So. I'd better have a talk with your David."

"OK, I'll call him." She flipped open her cell phone and speed-dialed a number. "Hi. Yeah, we're finished. You can come over now. OK, see ya."

David arrived in a few minutes. He was tallish and lean, wearing running shoes, long socks, shorts, and a nylon track jacket. He carried a small backpack and was unstrapping a bicycle helmet. Kiersten introduced them and made a quick exit.

David slid out of his backpack and put it on the bench with his bicycle helmet. He leaned slightly forward at the table and fixed his gaze on Carl. A square cyclist mirror protruded from his wire-rimmed glasses.

Carl broached the issue directly. "Kiersten tells me that you're going to write a piece about our project."

"It's already done. I've brought along a copy. Would you like to look at it?"

"Yes, I certainly would."

David dug around in his backpack from which he extricated a thin manila folder that he handed to Carl.

Carl opened the file and began reading. He pulled a pen from his pocket and made some notations as he read. David went to the counter and returned with the same frothy drink in a large plastic cup that Kiersten had been drinking.

The article was faithful enough to what Kiersten must have told him, but it was woefully inadequate when it came to the uncertainties involved. That came as no surprise to Carl. Portraying the nuances of scientific uncertainty is one of the most difficult things in communicating science to a lay audience, and whether from ignorance or a willful knowledge that iffy statements don't make good copy, journalists often get it wrong.

"Did Kiersten tell you why we didn't want the subject of our work made public just yet?"

"Yes. She told me that you guys weren't sure enough about it yet. To me that isn't a good enough reason to sit on a story like this one. People need to know about this, and I feel an obligation to inform them. If it turns out to be wrong, you guys will be embarrassed. So what? Is that a big deal compared with the level of risk society faces from something of this magnitude?"

"It's not a matter of our degree of confidence. Do you realize that what you are reporting on is at present nothing more than a working hypothesis, and a rather sketchy one at that? It has to be tested to see if it even stands up internally, let alone whether it predicts an earthquake or not. There is still a strong possibility that the whole idea could be flat-out wrong. Don't you know that Kiersten, Mark, and I have been working nonstop for the past six weeks trying to answer that question? As long as that doubt exists, we won't feel comfortable about going public. It's not a matter of us worrying about being embarrassed. It's a matter of giving people information that we know may be untrue, information on which people might make decisions that could turn out very costly if that information later proved incorrect. As scientists we have to have higher standards; otherwise why should we expect the public to believe us when we do want to report something to them?"

"Yes, yes. I've heard all this before. Kiersten and I argued it all out last night. In the end I have to follow my own ethical standards as a journalist. I don't want to argue about it anymore.

What I'm willing to do is include a quotation from you stating your reservations about your scientific findings. OK?"

"I suppose that'll have to do." Carl turned the sheet over and wrote a few lines on the back. He stroked out a few words, made some changes, and handed it to David. "Here, use this. "By the way, who is the editor handling this at the *Oregonian*? I'd like to have a word with him."

"It's a her, Joclyn Goodenow, and she's a reporter, not an editor. Feel free to call her."

Carl picked up some salmon at the fish market and headed home. He stopped at the Birkett Valley general store. The screen door banged behind him as he entered the room, an open plank-floored area where two tables faced a counter with several attached stools. This was a sort of café where regulars had coffee and breakfast in the mornings and coffee or beer in the afternoon. Two old men sat at the stools, each with a bottle of beer in front of him, talking with a large stout man in bib overalls behind the counter. This was Josiah P. MacFarland Jr., the proprietor, known to all as Mac save for a few old-timers who still called him Junior in deference to his long-deceased father, who had owned the store before him. They all looked around.

Carl greeted them, "Hello Bob, Fitz." He nodded to the man behind the counter. "Could I have a word, Mac?"

They moved deeper into the store, facing each other across the long merchandise counter.

"I'm afraid I've gotten myself into the news, Mac. You'll see it in tomorrow's *Oregonian.* I don't know how much fuss it'll make, but you never can tell. You might have a few reporters show up tomorrow looking for me. I'd appreciate it if nobody knows where I live."

Mac grinned. "No worry about that, Carl. Strangers that show up around here don't gen'lly get much information 'bout things that ain't none of their bizness. It's an old Birkett Valley tradition. As far as I'm concerned, you're just P.O. Box Fifty-Eight. Eggs and mail, once a week."

"Thanks, Mac; I appreciate it."

Portland

Joclyn Goodenow, the environmental and science reporter for the *Oregonian,* a tiny woman with a short, spiky shock of dirty blond hair who wore oversize horn-rimmed glasses that conspired to give her the appearance of a startled owlet, an impression that would be instantly belied by her deep, plummy, resonant voice, was currently exercising that voice in animated discussion with her features editor, Sid Travic, and managing editor Jill Folger.

"How can you question David's integrity? As you should well remember, we published his series on the Klamath River watershed controversy two years ago, a series that I would like to remind you earned him, and the paper, a Knight-Risser Prize, which, though no Pulitzer, is not something we sniff at hereabouts!"

"I'm not questioning David's integrity, Joclyn," Jill replied. "I'm just saying that it all sounds pretty darn speculative at this stage. That's basically what the head scientist, what's-his-name, Strega, says himself. We don't want to publish something that is not much more that a scare article."

"Yeah," Sid butted in. "The *Mercury* runs one of their earthquake scare stories every couple of years. By now everybody's sick and tired of hearing about Portland collapsing in ruins."

"This is not a scare story!" Joclyn shot back. "This is a science story that also just happens to be pretty scary. There *is* a difference. David's point, and I agree, is that this is an important scientific development with potentially huge consequences for everyone in the Pacific Northwest. We would be negligent to our readership if we quashed it at this point just because it's not a dead cert."

"I follow your point, Joclyn," Jill replied. "But this is damned sure to cause a big uproar. I can imagine certain sectors of the business community getting pretty upset about our running this kind of article. Tourism, for one. How seriously regarded is this guy Strega?"

"I've checked him out with a half a dozen experts. They all vouch for him as a leader in the field. I even ran the article by Nick Singletree, at U of W, my go-to guy on earthquakes. He said it looked like something new. He said Strega had apparently made some startling new observation that had triggered a new theory. He said it sounded fascinating, but he couldn't make out any more from what was in the article. But when I pushed him, he did say that although he personally thought it might be premature to go to press with it at this time, he did think we should take it seriously."

"All right," Jill said. "Against my better judgment, I'm going to bite the bullet this time. We'll run it. Sid, put it on the front page—below the fold." She waved them out of her office.

OCTOBER 21

Birkett Valley

The unseasonable warm spell they had been enjoying had been displaced by a Pacific storm that brought in steady rain. Carl drove down to Mac's store to pick up a copy of the *Oregonian*. There it was below the fold on the front page: "Scientists Predict Massive Cascadia Quake," with a David Kenner byline. It ran on at length on an inside page. Carl quickly scanned the article and grunted with satisfaction when he found that his statement had been printed verbatim.

Mac gave him a thumbs-up. "Great; we got a celebrity in town. Last time we were in the news was when the narcs raided that Mary Jane patch Thorny Johnson was running up Ableman's Canyon. When was that? Twelve, thirteen years ago, as I recall."

By the time he got home and checked his phone messages, he found his inbox full. Several were from local TV and radio stations, a couple from earthquake prediction kooks and self-appointed psychics, one from somebody he'd never heard of in the Reston office of the USGS, and ooh la la, one from someone at the *New York Times*. The pace of phone mail and e-mail traffic kept up all day. Carl turned his phone off and didn't answer any of it.

During dinner he and Sally flipped back and forth between TV channels, catching the reports. All the local stations covered it, and Fox, CNN, and CBS had segments on their national news broadcasts. With great amusement they watched an interview the local TV channel aired of Mac in front of the Birkett Valley store. Mac was putting on his hillbilly act and obviously enjoying himself hugely. He got in his "eggs and mail, once a week" line. The TV interviewer kept referring to Carl as "the reclusive scientist."

Carl remarked, "So it looks like David hit the jackpot. It must have been a slow news day."

"Good for him, Carl, but how are you going to deal with all this media attention?"

"With silence, for the time being. I've said my bit, which David, good to his word, reported in his article. That will have to hold them until we have something more concrete to report. In the meantime I'm hoping that this will blow over and they will leave us alone to do our work."

"I hope they do too, Carl, but I've a feeling that you're not being very realistic about the news media. I still can't believe that you gave that quote to that reporter, David what's his name."

"What do you mean?"

"It's so goddamned arrogant, in the first place. I mean, just listen to it: 'This prediction is based on theory that has not been fully verified and is therefore premature. Work on testing the theory is underway. The results will be reported in a timely manner.' End of quote."

"What's wrong with that? It's an accurate statement. It says exactly what I wanted to say."

"It's the tone, honey, the tone. It's so stuffy and klutzy. You're talking down to the public. And that 'reported in a timely manner' bit will be red meat to the news media." Sally's bell-like laugh rang out. "Carl, I'm afraid you're going to need a media consultant if you want to get through this business with your sanity intact."

Portland

Margie Yamaguchi had barely entered the Department of Geology and Mineral Industry offices in the state office building on Oregon Street when her colleague Mel Kesterke called out from his cubicle, "Hey, Margie, did you see this morning's *Oregonian?*" as he waved the newspaper.

"No, what is it?" She scanned the headline. "Oh, my!" She read further. "Oh my God! Can I take this, Mel? Thanks."

She hurried to her own cubicle. She had just sat down when the phone started ringing. It was Hamid Salani from the Oregon Office of Emergency Management in Salem, wanting to know what she knew about all this.

"I've just read the article myself, Hamid. Let me try to get some more info, and I'll get back to you."

As her computer booted, she read the article over more carefully, making a few notes. Her e-mail inbox contained an earthquake news notification from Science News Reports. It was a copy of the same *Oregonian* article. There was also a message from Ron Stickles, her opposite number in the Washington State geologist office in Olympia. He had gotten the same notification and also wanted to know if she had any more information.

She Googled Carl Strega. The web larder was pretty bare. There was no Facebook account, no LinkedIn site, and no other social media activity. *This guy must be some kind of troglodyte*, she thought. She scrolled down and found an old faculty profile, an even older award citation from the American Geophysical Union, and links to several technical publications on seismological topics. The faculty profile told her that he was a professor of geophysics, specializing in earthquake physics, and that he was married with two children. That was five years out of date. The *Oregonian* article had told her that he was now retired, living in

Oregon, and working with a small research group at the local university.

Her search on David Kenner proved more fruitful. He was a Californian with a bachelor's degree in environmental sciences from the University of California, Santa Cruz and a master's in environmental science journalism from Columbia. He was now a Corvallis-based freelance science writer who had written widely on environmental issues, including a prize-winning series on water and land use in the Klamath River catchment of southern Oregon and Northern California. According to her parsing of the *Oregonian* article, the earthquake prediction piece was based entirely on a confidential source within the Strega research group. No trail there.

She called Sue Garland at the USGS office in Seattle, who picked up immediately.

"Hi, Sue. It's Margie Yamaguchi from DOGAMI."

"Oh, hi, Margie! I bet I know what you're calling about. Oh, yeah, we sure heard about it, all right. The phones in our outreach office have been ringing nonstop all morning. We, in the meanwhile, have been struggling to get a handle on this thing so we can provide something edifying for our bosses at USGS headquarters back east in Reston.

"According to our earthquake people at Menlo Park and Professor Singletree here at U of Washington, all of whom who know Strega, either personally or by reputation, he is a brilliant if somewhat unconventional expert on earthquake physics. They say that what they can glean from what is written in the *Oregonian* is that he seems to have discovered something new but that there simply isn't enough said there for them to evaluate it one way or the other."

"That's a big help. So what are we supposed to do, then?"

"Right. Good question. So what Singletree says is that we should follow what Strega is quoted as saying in the article, which is basically, hey, we are not quite sure about this yet. When we are, we'll let you know. So we should wait."

"Oh great, wait. But wait for how long? This supposed earthquake is scheduled to happen next August. Even if we started now, we wouldn't have nearly enough time to make even the most basic preparations for something as big as this."

"I know, I know. What can I tell you? I think I'd rather not know anything than have a little teaser like this thrown at me."

Margie called Hamid at Emergency Management and related to him what she had learned. They agreed to hold a meeting of their joint emergency planning committee to discuss the matter and decide what actions, if any, to recommend to their various stakeholder groups.

Seaside

Rick Ostreim got the news over KXL just as he was finishing breakfast on the deck behind his house perched on a bluff overlooking the Pacific. He looked up at his wife just after the earthquake prediction item ended and the news switched to the Trailblazers' latest debacle.

"Holy shit! Can this be for real?" he blurted, half to himself, as he put down his coffee cup and rose from the table. "Katie, honey, can you take Hugo to the vet? I can't do it. I've got to get down to the office pronto. I'll call you at work when I find out what's going on with this." He gave his startled wife a quick kiss, grabbed his bag, and headed out the door.

He picked up a copy of the *Oregonian* at the strip mall convenience store at the end of his road and turned right onto Highway 101, heading south. He parked at his assigned spot in front of the Seaside City Hall. As he entered the foyer, Lucinda, the receptionist, rose and said, "Rick, did you hear—"

"Yes, I heard it on the radio, Lucinda. Give me a minute to read this article; then get me the mayor."

"The mayor's already on the line."

"OK, well, tell him I'll call him back in five minutes." He scooted down the hall to the city manager's office, entered, closed the door, sat down at his desk, and started reading. He read it over three times, got the gist, let it sink in a bit, and began translating it into possible policy options. Then he called the mayor.

"Hi, Mike. Yes, I've read the article. Yes, I know. Yes, I do imagine you're getting calls. From the sound of it, we are too. Yes, we'll certainly have to tell people something. I'm going to set up a meeting of the Emergency Planning Committee. Can you make it here at 11? OK, we'll try for that then. See you there." He pushed another button on his phone.

"Lucinda, can you ask Jean to set up a meeting of the Emergency Planning Committee for eleven? She has the list, doesn't she? Tell her no excuses: everybody has to be there. Thanks."

He sat and thought for a while. Then he called Margie Yamaguchi. She told him what she had told Hamid Salani. They discussed the possible implications, and then he rang off, "OK, Margie; thanks. Let's keep in touch."

He next called Will Stanaway. He and Will had gone to Seaside High together and then on to Oregon State. Will had been on the police force at Seaside before he had landed his current job as city manager of Cannon Beach, the next beach town to the south. They had a longstanding and close working relationship.

"Hello, William. I imagine you've been having a busy day. Ha-ha, don't tell me the genteel residents of Cannon Beach are all up in arms about this. Ha-ha, I'll bet they are. Here we only get the motel owners threatening such things. Listen, Will, Margie Yamaguchi told me you've already talked to her, so you know as much as I do at the moment. What I wanted to touch base with you on is about how you guys are thinking about responding to this business."

"Well, Rick, I obviously haven't had much time to think about it, but my gut reaction is do the precautionary thing and treat this seriously, even though it seems pretty far-fetched at the moment. I think we have to play it on the safe side, even if it's only for ass-covering purposes."

"I agree."

"So I'm calling a town meeting for Thursday. I am going to propose that we go ahead post haste with the seismic retrofit of the Ecola Creek Bridge. If that bridge doesn't survive the earthquake, then all our tsunami evacuation routes for the north end of town become unusable. It's something that we've already agreed to and voted on, and we have the credit lines set up to cover it. It's just a matter of doing it this winter instead of putting it off till sometime next year. It'll cost a little more doing it in the winter, but so what."

"Good idea. And if I may point out, you'd better get right on it because if this prediction becomes credible, there won't be any credit forthcoming for any coastal community, least of all for infrastructure projects."

"Oh, shit; I hadn't thought of that! Thanks for that one. That should win over the more conservative old bastards on our town council. They'll cheer up over the idea of screwing the banks."

"Cheers. Have a nice day." He hung up.

The Emergency Planning Committee met in the mayor's conference room. Besides Rick and the mayor, Mike Tilson, the committee consisted of the chiefs of the police and fire departments, Robert Newhouse and Andy McHenry; Tommy Torgerson, the chief of coastal security, who was the head lifeguard and who coordinated search and rescue missions with the Coast Guard; and Ralph Wycliff, a consulting engineer who had to come down from Astoria for the meeting. The mayor, who was formally the chair of the committee, greeted everyone and thanked them for coming, then turned the meeting over to Rick.

"I assume by now that everyone has read the report in this morning's *Oregonian* or some version of it." He then gave them a rundown of what Margie had told him.

"So it is still quite speculative that this earthquake might occur next year. Even if the prediction proves to be true, it says only that there will be an earthquake next summer of about magnitude 8 somewhere along the Cascadia Subduction Zone. Margie Yamaguchi from DOGAMI tells me that a magnitude 8 would affect about 200 kilometers, or 120 miles, of coastline. So there are a lot of places between Cape Flattery and Cape Mendocino to stick a magnitude 8 and not affect us much here in Seaside. Nevertheless, as I am sure you are all aware, if such an earthquake occurred right offshore, it would have dire effects. We're not particularly worried about the earthquake itself but the tsunami that would follow it about twenty minutes later. The coastal engineers estimate tsunami heights ranging from thirty to fifty feet for those kinds of earthquakes. I don't need to tell you that highest elevation in Seaside is less than ten feet. You get the drift. So how should we react to this, gentlemen?"

The mayor jumped up. "Yeah, yeah, we've heard all that tsunami stuff before. But this isn't much more than a rumor, is it? It's just some crazy scientists spouting off with their latest half-assed theories. They even say as much in the article. So what are we supposed to tell people? This is going to be ruinous for our tourism business, which I don't have to tell you is our only business. My phone has been ringing all morning from motel and business owners screaming at me to do something. George Westerly from the Chamber of Commerce is livid, to say the least. He's threatening to sue somebody over this."

"OK, Mike, I understand the pressure you're getting, but let's be calm about this. You're right; the scientists say they're not at all sure that this will even happen. So I think we should tell people that at the moment there's nothing to worry about and that they should go about their business as usual. We can prepare a notice from the mayor to that effect to run in the next edition of the *Seaside Signal*.

"As far as our tourist business goes, the season is already over for this year, and it is a long time till the next season, so we have plenty of time to worry about that later, if need be. I think it more likely that this is a tempest in a teapot and it'll all blow over in due time. So we should treat it that way.

"However, I think there are some precautionary steps we should take. These can be done in a quiet way that won't needlessly alarm people. As you all know, we've set up a system, following state guidelines, of tsunami evacuation routes to get people safely out of the expected tsunami inundation zone, which is pretty much all of Seaside, and up into the hills east of town. These have been signposted and well advertised so that everybody in town knows what to do in the case of a tsunami alert. But a big question that remains is what to do with the people once they get to the evacuation assembly areas.

According to the DOGAMI reports I get from Margie Yamaguchi, Highway 101 and all the east-west coastal access highways are expected to be knocked out by landslides and bridge failures in the event of an earthquake, so we have to expect that tsunami survivors will be cut off from rescue for at least a week following the disaster. We've set up a system in which we've contracted with homeowners in the evacuation areas to store drums of food, water, and other survival gear. This is partly city financed but mainly voluntary, where we encourage families to purchase and stock the drums for their own use. But in actuality because there hasn't been any sense of urgency, little has been done, and those preparations are more on paper than in reality.

"Cannon Beach is way ahead of us on this. They've begun erecting storage sheds in their evacuation assembly areas and stocking them with food, water, tents, and other survival gear. I propose we follow their lead. Just before this meeting, I identified several tracts of city-owned land in those areas that could be used for this purpose. There are enough funds in our emergency kitty to start on this. With a little digging around in our budgets, we can probably find enough to finish this job without involving the city council, which avoids making it into one of our usual public dogfights and getting the whole town into an uproar. So I propose a motion in which you authorize me to go ahead with this plan.

"Can I see a show of hands on this? All agreed. Thank you, gentlemen. The meeting is adjourned." Rick returned to his office to call his wife.

Salem

J. Gordon Parkington was not having a nice day. He paced his spacious office in the suite the Oregon Tourism Industry Association occupied on Chemeketa Street, a few blocks from the Capitol Mall. He had just fielded an angry call from George Westerly, president of the Seaside Chamber of Commerce, who had demanded, like all his other callers that morning, that he do something about that damned earthquake scare article that had appeared in the morning's *Oregonian*.

He buzzed his secretary. "Lili, call Hank Wilcoxen, and tell him to get over here ASAP. We've got an emergency. Yes, right away."

OTIA was a major client of Hank Wilcoxen's public relations firm, so when he got the call, he dropped everything and rushed over. When Lili ushered him into the inner office, he took one look at Parkington's flushed face and said, "I guess this is about this earthquake flap, eh, Gordon?"

Parkington glared at him. "Yes, I would damn well guess so. Jesus F. Christ, Hank, this could be a disaster for us! An earthquake scare is bad enough, but with all the news coverage we've been having about the tsunami in Japan and what was the one before, in Thailand, people are scared shitless. Nobody is going to visit a beach resort on the coast if they think there is going to be a tsunami, for Christ's sake."

"It was in Sumatra, Gordon."

"What?"

"The other earthquake. It was in Sumatra, not Thailand."

"Fuck Sumatra. In Thailand the fucking tsunami killed tourists, didn't it? Swedes. People relate to Swedes."

"Simmer down, Gordon. This is not worth blowing a gasket over. This is simply a matter of public perception. It can be handled like any other PR problem."

"It's not just public perception. This morning I got a call from Ed Steiner, from Pacific Resorts. They're planning a major golf development in Gearhart, complete with a Scottish-style seaside links course like the one at Bandon. Do you know what that would mean? That would put Oregon in the major leagues of the golf circuit. This morning he heard from their backers. They're thinking of pulling the plug on their financing because of the so-called tsunami risk."

"So what? It's still just this one article in the *Oregonian.* The important thing is to nip it in the bud before it gets ingrained in the public imagination. We'll discredit the article and, for good measure, the people associated with it. You'll see; this'll all be forgotten in a few months."

"How are you going to do that?"

"Don't you worry about it. The web is far mightier than the pen, my friend. Traditional media like the *Oregonian* can't compete with the web in shaping popular opinion. This will be child's play compared with some other things that have been dealt with that way, like all the brouhaha over climate change." He smiled broadly. "And I know just the man for the job."

When Wilcoxen got back to his office, he buzzed his secretary. "Get me Herman Stackhouse on the line."

October 22

Birkett Valley

The next morning Carl left to go down to the university to meet with the troops. As he was locking the gate at the end of his drive, he was startled by an unexpected presence. An overfed little man in a yellow slicker and rain hat was across the road, leaning against a red Jeep Cherokee and snapping away with a big digital SLR camera.

"Hey, what do you think you're doing?" Carl shouted, advancing on the little man.

"Hold still, Professor Strega. Hold it right there. You're a public figure now, so learn to pose for your public."

"Who the hell are you? And how did you find out where I live?"

"You may think you've got a nifty hideout here, Professor, but I've got news for you: the county tax man knows where everybody lives. And allow me to introduce myself: Herman Stackhouse, freelance journalist." He proffered a card with an exaggerated flourish. "I think you will be becoming quite familiar with the name in the not too distant future."

Carl shoved the card in his jacket pocket. "I don't see why I should. Now, would you mind moving your car? It's in the way."

Stackhouse got into his Jeep and pulled it around. He lowered the passenger-side window, leaned over, and said with a smirk, "Kenner may think he's got the inside track with his girlfriend working for you, but I've got my own ways of finding out what your lot is up to." He spun his wheels in the gravel and shot off down the road.

As he turned to get into his car, Carl thought, *What the hell was that all about?*

◆　◆　◆

All were present and attentive when Carl strode into the seminar room and faced the group.

"As I'm sure you're all aware, the cat is now fully out of the bag on our little project." Anastasia was frantically waving her hand. "Yes, Anastasia?"

"What I want to know is who told this reporter all about what we are doing?"

Carl could see, out of the corner of his eye, Kiersten shrinking down in her chair. "That's no longer of any importance, Anastasia. It was bound to get out sooner or later. Unfortunately it was a little sooner than I'd expected. The important thing is that this now puts us under even more time pressure than before. Aside from a lot of calls from the press, not to mention a lot of crank calls from various nutcases, I've been contacted by quite a few of our scientific colleagues wanting to know what we're up to. They have a legitimate right to know. All of this leads me to conclude that we need to set a firm deadline for when we disclose our first findings. The annual meeting of the American Geophysical Union will be held in San Francisco the second week of December. I talked to one of the AGU program chairmen this morning, and he agreed to give us a time slot in one of the sessions so we could present our results. Although the abstracts deadline for the meeting is long past, under the circumstances he was willing to make an exception. This gives us about six weeks to get ready. So what I want to do today is to review our status and try to see what we can hope to accomplish in that time frame."

Mark raised his hand. "The article mentioned that a group here at the university is working on this problem. I've already had couple of calls from reporters asking about it. What should we be telling them?"

"Yes, well, it shouldn't take too long for the press to ferret out who's involved, so I expect all of you will be approached eventually. I made a statement about our position that was quoted in the article." He smiled wryly. "My wife thinks that my phrasing was a bit clunky. Be that as it may, I think that what I said was defendable. This is a touchy topic, and we have to be careful to neither overstate nor understate our case. I have decided to not say anything more to the press at this time and have not been answering any of their inquiries. As for you guys, I would like to ask that you not make any public comments. You can refer all questions to me, which I'll duly note and then ignore. I think it's important for us to speak with one voice. We'll hold a press conference at the AGU after our presentation. Let's hold off until then.

"Now, let's get to the science. Anastasia, can you start us off?"

Anastasia rose. "OK, I have been up to now mainly coding. I have implemented the rate-state variable friction law for the constitutive equations. I make the general case so we can use either Dieterich or Ruina versions. Up to now I have just gotten the discrete version running. The continuum version I am now working on. It is just at the stage of debugging. It should run by end of next week, maybe sooner. So then we can start making the simulations. Only 2D, of course. The 3D I have not even been thinking yet. So for this AGU deadline, I think maybe we can make the 2D simulations."

José broke in. "I've been looking at the computer requirements for the simulation matrix that we'll need to do. For the 2D case, it's not too bad. They can be run on PCs, as Anastasia has been doing. We have six PCs running Linux in our computer lab that can be used for this job. I think if everything goes well, we can cover the parameter space we need to explore in this time framework. But for the 3D simulations, it's another matter. For that we'll need a multiprocessor array machine. The fluid dynamics group has one with 200 nodes. I've been talking with them about our using it. So far no decision has been made. It depends a lot on how much time we'll need, and I haven't come up with a good estimate yet."

"OK," Carl said. "At least we'll have the 2D results in time for AGU."

"But," Anastasia said, "there is problem. We don't know how reliable is the 2D case for the real one, the 3D. It might be like the bowling ball problem."

"The what?"

"Is example. The 2D version of bowling ball is cylinder with holes in the end. In the reality it doesn't roll too good." Everyone chuckled.

"OK, I get you. But we'll just have to take it one step at a time. Kiersten, what do you have for us?"

Kiersten gave a rundown on the approach they were taking on the data handling problems they had encountered. "But I think we have that under control now. We'll begin making the real calculations next week. I think we should have some answers by the AGU deadline."

"OK. Good work, everyone. It looks like we're making nice progress. I'll leave you to get back to it. Oh, one more thing. I've shut my phone down for the duration. You can't believe the amount of calls I've been getting since yesterday. On the way here I stopped at a phone store and bought one of those unregistered prepaid phones. When I was trying to explain to the kid at the counter what I wanted, I think I described it as an anonymous phone or something like that. He stared at me for a moment and then said, 'Oh, you mean you want a burner?' and laughed his head off. I had to Google the word later to get the big joke. Anyway, I've written the number on the board. Make a note of it before I erase it. This is for project use only. Whatever you do, don't give this number out to anyone."

On the way out, he took Kiersten aside. "This morning I had a run-in with an obnoxious fellow who said he was a journalist. He gave his name as Herman Stackhouse. Can you ask David if he knows anything about this guy?"

◆　◆　◆

Carl got his first call on the new phone that evening.

"Hello, professor; this is David Kenner. Kiersten gave me your message. She said you had a run-in with Herman Stackhouse today."

Carl related the encounter.

"This is very bad news. Stackhouse isn't so much a journalist as a hired gun for various far-right organizations. He's been playing a major role in the global climate change denial movement. It looks like he's taking on your case now. He's already posted a blog on it. I e-mailed you the link. Have a look."

Carl went to his computer and clicked on the link. After a minute he went back to the phone. "This is disgusting! What he's saying is outrageous."

"Yep, that's Herman. Character assassination is his prime MO. I'm afraid that this is just the opening salvo of a campaign. Unfortunately, Stackhouse has a wide following in this state and plenty of connections nationally. You'd better be prepared for a lot more of this. I suggest you pick up a copy of *The Hockey Stick and the Climate Wars* by Michael E. Mann. Mann is a climate scientist who's been a major target of the climate change deniers. You'll get an idea from his book of some of the dirty tricks those people can get up to.

"You'll get some support in the press from me," David continued. "I'd like to follow this story as it develops. I wonder if you'd permit me to sit in on your group meetings as an observer."

"Hmm. Well, I can't see the harm in it. However, we're planning to present our findings at the AGU meeting in San Francisco in early December and to give a press conference afterward. So if I give you this access, I think it's only fair to ask you to embargo any writing about our new results until that time."

"That's fair enough. I agree. I'd also like to interview you for background material. Could we do that at your next group meeting?"

Carl agreed, then rang off, printed out a copy of Stackhouse's blog, and took it into the living room, where Sally was working on the proofs of her latest novel, which were spread out over the dining table.

"Listen to this blog from that guy Stackhouse. 'Scientists attack Oregon tourism economy with earthquake scare.'

"It goes on, 'Once again, the same left-leaning scientists that brought us the global climate change fraud are mounting an attack on the free enterprise system with a bogus earthquake prediction that threatens to ruin the Oregon tourism industry and destroy property values statewide.' Blah, blah, blah, more of the same rubbish. Then get this: 'Strega, the leader of the group, lives behind a locked gate in a mountain hideaway in Birkett Valley, a notorious hangout of former hippies turned pot growers and drug dealers. The natives, ever hostile to strangers, refused to reveal his whereabouts, but this reporter tracked him down to his gated compound (see photo).'" He showed Sally the photo of himself looking threateningly at the camera.

"Then there is this. 'Strega is a former university professor who took early retirement under mysterious circumstances.' What the hell is that?"

"It's called insinuation, darling. On the web people can write anything they want, and equally the readers may make anything out of it that they want. If you know the code, everything is perfectly clear. It's a kind of unwritten agreement between like-minded people."

When Carl checked his voicemail on his iPhone that evening, he found his first anonymous hate mail. Carl downloaded everything onto his computer.

October 28

Corvallis

Anastasia was presenting her latest modeling results with a slide showing a 2D model of oscillatory stable sliding in which the compressive stress was increased in increments after each slow slip event.

"So as you can see," she explained, "the interval between the slow slip events gradually increases. This is qualitatively the behavior that Carl proposed. We need to explore parameter space to see how robust is this result, but I need to get some results from Kiersten's work on the data to see which way to go with that. So maybe Kiersten can tell me when I can have them?"

Kiersten flushed and responded with an irritated tone, "Well, I'm sorry, but I have a really big data set to work with, and it's not so easy as that. We're making progress, but it'll take some time. When I'm ready I'll present my results to the group. You'll just have to wait like everybody else."

"Well, what am I supposed to do in the meantime?" snapped Anastasia, glancing at Carl for support.

Carl inwardly flinched at the tension that had suddenly filled the room.

"There's no point in trying to rush Kiersten, Anastasia. She has a monumental data analysis problem on her hands, and she doesn't need any more pressure than she already has. Anastasia, you and José and I should get together later and work out a set of likely parameter values for you guys to explore. You can run your model systematically through that parameter space. Then you'll have a complete solution space solved to compare with Kiersten's results when they are ready."

With that, the meeting adjourned.

◆　◆　◆

That evening at dinner, David asked, "Is something bothering you? You seem really snappish tonight."

Kiersten gave him a sharp look. "It's Anastasia. She's really pissing me off. She is so pushy, always bragging about her results. Plus, she is horning in on my project. I thought she was supposed to work on the nucleation problem, but she's modeling the period-increasing effect that

I'm working on. That's supposed to be my fucking thesis project!"

"Why don't you talk to Mark about it?"

"I have, but Mark is so easygoing. He says it's fine that she does the modeling part—that she needs to do that just to set up the nucleation problem. He says not to worry; we can collaborate on that part. I'll still have a fine thesis problem. That's not the way I feel about it.

"Today she had the gall to suggest that I was holding everything up. That's fine for her to say; all she has to do is run some models. I've got four terabytes of data to get into shape. She seems to think that's an easy thing to do.

"Besides, she's always kissing up to Carl. Like she is some hot shit or something. Even her voice gets on my nerves. She has this shrill whiny Russian accent that sets my teeth on edge."

David reached over and took her hand. "Sounds like you need to calm down a little bit. Just ignore Anastasia if she's acting like that. She probably has her own demons. Get on with your own work, and let Carl and Mark deal with the other stuff. Carl's the group leader—it's up to him to make sure that the team runs smoothly, and he strikes me as a straight-up kind of guy. And I'm sure Mark has your best interests at heart."

October 29

Los Angeles

In the sumptuous office of Harold C. Lautenbach, chairman of Pacific Resorts, Ed Steiner was listening to his boss warming up to the issue that was on his mind.

"I don't have to remind you, Ed, the Gearhart Dunes Golf Complex is the biggest expansion project we've done in quite a few years. It's the biggest new golfing venue to be started up from scratch on the West Coast in more than twenty years. It promises to remake the whole golfing circuit. I've got almost a billion in private equity lined up behind this deal, and suddenly this earthquake and tsunami rumor pops up and threatens to queer the whole thing."

Ed squirmed in his seat and offered this bit of consolation: "I don't think it's such a big deal, Harold. It's just a few scientists mouthing off. They're always talking up there about the 'big one' coming, just like they do here in California. These earthquake scares never amount to a hill of beans. People forget about 'em after a while."

"Well, I don't give a damn about what happens 'after a while.' The timing of this couldn't be worse. My backers are getting squirrely. I want this rumor squelched, but good. That should be your job."

"Sure, Harold. I already had a chat with Gordon Parkington, the head of the Oregon Tourism Industry Association. He got Herman Stackhouse on the case. He has already started a blog campaign against it—I sent you the links."

"That's fine as far as it goes. Stackhouse will get the Tea Party wackos all up in arms about it, but that doesn't go far enough. I want some real business-oriented muscle coming down on this, in the mainstream media and behind the scenes. I mean in the governor's office. And what about that university where those scientists are working—can't some pressure be put on there?"

"Sure, let me look into those avenues. I'm sure I can find a few pressure points. I'll make some calls."

"You do that. But keep our name out of it. Pitch it so it's hurting the little guy: property values and jobs and so forth. You know the drill."

◆　◆　◆

Back in his office, Ed called Warren Jacobson, president of the Oregon Association of Realtors, followed by a call to Bill Lacis, a member of the editorial board of the *Oregonian.* With the latter he made the point that the *Oregonian* ought to display more balance when it came to the earthquake scare they had fomented by publishing Kenner's article. They could start with an op-ed piece that pointed out the sort of economic havoc that might result from that sort of rumor. He suggested Jacobson for the job.

He leaned back in his chair and thought for a while, then riffled through his Rolodex. He picked up his phone and called Arnold Buchanan on his private line.

"Hello, Arnold; this is Ed Steiner at Pacific Resorts. Yes, it has been a while. Listen, Arnold, I hate to bother you, but we're getting a bit concerned about this earthquake scare that we've been reading about in the *Oregonian.* Yes, I agree, it probably is a lot of baloney, but the timing is bad. It's making our backers for the Gearhart Dunes project a little nervous."

"I'm sorry to hear that, Ed, but I don't see what I can do about it."

"The thing is, Arnold, this earthquake report seems to have come out of your old alma mater, which, as I seem to recall, you're on the board of directors of, am I right? So I thought maybe you could look into whether the university really wants to be behind something like this."

"Oh, I see your point. But I'm a just a trustee of the University Foundation. We're just concerned with fundraising for the university. We don't have any authority to say what kind of research they do there."

"I realize that, Arnold. But this line of research is highly detrimental to business interests in Oregon. A lot of people are not going to look kindly at the university's sponsorship of this kind of research. I can certainly say that this is true as far as Pacific Resorts is concerned, and it won't be long before this gets around in the business community. That might affect your ability to raise funds for the university. So it seems to me that it might be of some interest to your Foundation."

"I got you. OK, I'll look into it. I'll have to get the low-down on what's behind all this and talk to a few other people, both on our board and the Board of Higher Education. It may take a little time. I can't go to the university president half-cocked on something like this."

"Thanks, Arnold. And give my regards to Meg."

Ed hung up, leaned back in his chair, and with a beatific smile contemplated his upcoming luncheon engagement.

NOVEMBER 2

Portland

Joclyn Goodenow found herself once again in the office of Jill Folger, where she had been peremptorily summoned. As soon as she was seated, the managing editor looked up from a pile of the daily output of the *Oregonian* news staff and greeted her curtly. "Good morning, Joclyn. The flak has already started to fly about Kenner's earthquake prediction article."

She pushed a blue-penciled sheet across her desk, which Joclyn began reading. It was an op-ed article signed by Warren Jacobson, who was identified as the president of the Oregon Realtor's Association. His expressed concern was about the effects of the 'earthquake scare' on homeowners' property values. He particularly emphasized the plight of homeowners within the designated tsunami inundation zones of coastal communities. As long as there was a perceived threat from a tsunami in the near future, he claimed, their homes had essentially no resale value. This would have a disastrous effect on the personal equity wealth of hardworking citizens. He also pointed out the depressing effect that such rumors would have on the tourism and construction industries and the extensive job losses that might result. His theme was the irresponsibility and lack of transparency of scientists who publicly proclaimed dire warnings of natural catastrophes without considering the damaging effects on peoples' lives and livelihoods. He also objected to the publishing of such unfounded rumors in the *Oregonian*. The tenor of the argument borrowed heavily from Stackhouse's web screed but was couched in more temperate terms. He hinted at the possible liability of the involved scientists to lawsuits from angry homeowners.

Joclyn passed the sheet back to Jill. "I can appreciate the concern of the business community over possible losses that might arise over David's report," she said. "But it's unfair to blame the scientists of irresponsibility. The Strega quote in the article made it quite clear that the scientists were unhappy about their work being publicized at this stage. That was our decision, based on our perception of what the public needed to know."

"And now we're facing a consequence of that decision," Jill replied. "It's just what I'd been worried about. Jacobson does have a point that we may be culpable of stirring up false fears among the public."

"Under the assumption, that he is implicitly making, that it is indeed a false alarm. But we don't know if it's a false alarm, do we? That's not for him or for us to decide. It's a scientific issue."

"Be that as it may, we're going to run this tomorrow. I just thought I would give you fair notice."

"I see. I don't suppose this came in over the transom, did it?"

"No, it came from Bill Lacis. And he's the one who decides what goes in the editorial pages."

"I think we should run something alongside it for balance. Suppose I get something from the people at the state Office of Emergency Management on their response to the earthquake warning. Would you run that?"

"I'll certainly be happy to have a look at it. If it looks good, I'll push for it. That's the most I can do."

◆　◆　◆

The following day the Jacobson op-ed ran in the *Oregonian*. Just below it ran an op-ed from Hamid Salani and Margie Yamaguchi of the Office of Emergency Management. They outlined the ongoing preparedness measures their office was taking to mitigate the effects of future earthquakes and tsunamis in Oregon. They emphasized that the prediction publicized by the *Oregonian* was little more than speculation at the present time and that the public should not presently be taking any precautions other than those listed in their office's website as everyday disaster preparedness. Their office would be continuing to closely monitor the situation as it developed and would notify the public if the situation changed.

The paper also ran a series of letters to the editor. Several of these were clearly from the Stackhouse camp. Others were from people demanding more specific information about the dangers they faced, both from the earthquake, and among coastal residents, from the greatly feared tsunami that might result.

In the meantime discussions of the prediction were spreading rapidly on the Internet, both in the blogosphere and via social media. They ranged from people talking on forums about precautions that families could make against earthquakes and tsunamis to more specific conversations among residents of potentially affected areas to arguments about the pros and cons of the prediction itself. Many of the latter were political in nature. A particular theme of critics was that the prediction was a publicity stunt cooked up by scientists as a ploy to get more research funding from the federal government. These discussions quickly morphed from regional to national and began to attract the attention of the mainstream news media.

Carl sifted through his growing file of phone mail and e-mail messages that had accumulated unanswered since the appearance of the original *Oregonian* article. Among the strident noise of the cranks and the urgent entreaties from the news media, he found several messages that needed his attention. The first call he made was to Mercedes Davidson, head of PANGA, the Pacific Northwest Geodetic Array, run out of Central Washington University.

"Hello, Mercedes; this is Carl Strega. Sorry to take so long to get back to you; things have been a bit hectic here. Yes. Yes, you're right. The data we used I did indeed get from your website, and I agree we do owe it to your community to provide access to our analysis of it. Yes. I agree. What I'm going to do is e-mail you a figure of a screenshot showing our analysis of the GPS data on the latest SSE. I'll include a caption describing the figure. Yes, of course you have permission to post this on your website."

"Oh, by the way, you should be delighted to know that one of your former students, Kiersten Lundqvist, is playing a major role on our project. Yes, we think she is terrific, too. Thanks, Mercedes. Bye."

He then called Nick Singletree at the University of Washington and Tom Mitkins at the USGS in Seattle. He explained to both of them the gist of their findings and clarified a few points that seemed cryptic to them about

David's article. He then told them about the forthcoming PANGA posting and that he would be presenting a full accounting at the San Francisco American Geophysical Union meeting.

NOVEMBER 4

Corvallis

Kiersten was in a triumphant mood. After weeks of struggling to get her data sets in the right shape and format for processing, with many frustrating missteps along the way, she had finally gotten good results from her overnight runs on the cloud. She thought, in fact, that they were beautiful. She was impatiently waiting for Mark to get back from his class so that she could show them to him.

Just then Anastasia burst into her office and with her piercing voice exclaimed, "Hello, Keerstoon; how are you doing?"

Kiersten winced. "Oh, fine, Anastasia. What's up with you?"

"I am doing very fine, now getting very nice modeling results. And you? Are you getting results yet?"

"Yes. As a matter of fact, I got some just this morning. They look pretty nice."

"Can I see results pleez?"

"What? No. I just got them. I haven't even showed them to Mark yet. I'm not going to hand them over to you just like that. You can see them at group."

"But I must see results. To compare with my models."

"Sorry, but I can't show them now."

"Why not? We are on same team, no? I need some data to compare with my models. Otherwise I am like blind person."

"Look, who do you think you are, anyway? Barging into my office and demanding to see my results! You can damn well wait till group meeting to see them, just like everybody else. Then you can present your results, and I'll present mine. I'm not giving you my results so that you can present them along with yours and take credit for everything."

"Is too late to find out at group meeting. If I cannot check with your data, I do not know to use what for parameters. My models maybe give so different result from yours. Then I look like idiot, no? Then I have to do all over again. Is stupid waste of time."

"That's your problem. Look, why don't you go back and play your computer games. I've got work to do."

"Computer games! Your stupid data is worth nothing without my theory. Why you acting this way? I am not wanting to steal your data, just to compare with my models. This is so stupid!" She stomped out of the office in a huff.

Kiersten turned back to her work, muttering under her breath, "Stuck-up bitch!"

Anastasia immediately went back to the physics building and stormed into José's office. "José, I want to quit this project!"

José looked up in surprise. "What? What's going on?"

"It is that stupid girl, Keerstoon. She won't show me her results. I have to see her data to compare with my models. Without it I don't know if my parameters are correct."

"Wait a minute. Why doesn't she want to show you her results?"

"She is crazy, that one. She thinks I am stealing them! We are working on same project, no? How I am stealing? I only need to have her data to check my theory."

"There must be some misunderstanding. I'll have a word with Mark about it and try to see what's going on with Kiersten."

"Anyway, I don't like this project. I make a big risk to work on this. Is not even my field. How can I make my name in physics when I work on some stupid geophysics problem? Now I have to be dealing with this jealous girl. And there are too many people on this project. Carl will take all credit, and I will become fourth or fifth author. Is not good for me, I think."

José phoned Mark, who had just finished talking with Kiersten, who was likewise upset and angry.

After discussing the situation, Mark said, "The girls have been under a lot of pressure. I guess we shouldn't be surprised that there was some kind of blowup. Kiersten is just being very protective of what she now considers her thesis project. She seems to think that Anastasia is trying to poach on it. Yes. I can see Anastasia's problem. The problem with us getting involved is that Kiersten will expect me to be her advocate, and I imagine Anastasia will expect the same from you. Let's get Carl down as an arbitrator. Maybe he can calm things down."

Carl met Mark and José in Mark's office. They explained the situation to him. It was a priority dispute, a kind of academic mini–turf war. Kiersten, as Mark explained, was becoming possessive about what she now considered her thesis project and was nervous about this physics postdoc horning in on it and taking more credit for the work. José said that on Anastasia's part, she had a similar sensitivity. As a beginning postdoc, her career was on the line, and she was worried now about wasting her time on some project on which she might end up as a fourth or fifth author and not get enough recognition.

Carl sighed. "Oh, boy. What a mess, but I guess we could see the symptoms developing. I'll go have a talk with them."

Anastasia and Kiersten were waiting in the seminar room, sitting on opposite sides of the table with sullen looks, avoiding each other's gaze.

Carl sat down at the head of the table. "OK, what's the story?"

Anastasia said, "She won't share her work. Is saying her work is more important. What is this? She is working on data only. I am doing theory. What is data without theory? Is nothing. Am I right?"

Kiersten angrily broke in. "She is trying to take charge of this whole project. She thinks she's a big shot because she is the big important physicist doing the theory and I am just the little geophysics student to give her some data to look at. Hah, what does she know? Theory is just bullshit without data to show what is really happening."

Carl interrupted them sharply. "OK, calm down! This is all crap." He made a mollifying gesture and said, in more measured tones, "Look, both of you have been given what I consider to be absolutely crucial pieces of the larger puzzle that we're all working on. Your tasks are equally important, one not more than the other. This project is bigger than any issues of personal professional ambition. It's too important for us to get all twisted up on issues of ego or priority. There'll be plenty of room for glory for everybody involved, or ignominy, for that matter, depending on how things turn out. I told you at the outset about the risks of getting involved in this endeavor. And this business about the relative worth of theory versus observation is bunk. The two are complementary: they are the yin and yang that make the argument whole.

"Now, about credit. At San Francisco I'll give the paper for all of us. You two will be second and third authors, followed by José and Mark. I'll let you flip a coin over which spot you'll each have. In addition I'm going to try to wangle permission for each of you to give a poster presentation at the AGU in which you can present your own work as first author. We'll worry about publications much later, after this whole thing is over. Let's get the work done first, OK?"

He saw, with relief, their eyes clear and lighten up. He left, knowing that he had averted what could have become a crippling disaster for the project.

That evening Carl did a little web browsing. He noticed that the bulletin board at Cascadiatectonics.org was already hosting a very lively discussion of the PANGA posting of his figure. He chuckled at some of the speculations.

November 5

Salem

The office of Herman Stackhouse could be reached from the street by a doorway between a pharmacy and a pet supply store. The doorway opened into a small vestibule that led to a flight of stairs. Herman was not listed on the wall directory, but his office could be found two flights up, third door on the left. His room was identified only by a number, 32, affixed at chest level beside the door. Upon entering the office, a visitor's attention would immediately be taken by a huge mahogany desk that dominated the room and clashed with its drab surroundings. The floor was covered by gray industrial carpet and the walls painted in the grayish green shade that is usually found in government offices that are far from public view. To the right of the desk was a large steel cabinet that contained an extensive collection of photographic, video, and surveillance equipment. There was an alcove behind the cabinet containing a small divan and a flat-screen TV. In front of the desk were two straight-backed chairs for visitors, although Herman never invited clients here and seldom had other visitors. Behind the desk was a high-backed black leather swivel armchair of magisterial proportions. There Herman sat hunched, eyes fixed on the computer screen propped up before him on the desk.

Herman was doing an assessment of the performance of this latest campaign, which he had begun calling "Quake-gate." Since he had begun the series of blogs on this new topic, his daily hit rate had risen 27 percent. He smiled at this result and nodded to himself. Anytime he exposed some new shenanigans from the liberal conspiracy, he would get a surge like this. It proved that he was hitting the right nerves with his web following. His blogs were also getting linked to all the important conservative websites, so he knew that he was building it into a national issue.

He leaned back and thought, with satisfaction, "Bee-yoo-tee-ful. Everything is a-OK for the next level." He looked at his watch and said to himself, "Speaking of which, time to move."

Herman pulled his Cherokee up behind the blue van of Kenny, his video guy, that was parked in the small lot in front of the main entrance to the state capitol. It was well before 9:00 a.m., so few people were around yet, and they wouldn't expect to be bothered by the capitol police. Kenny had already set up his video camera, and his crew of actor-activists was parading around with signs with slogans like QUAKE SCARES KILL JOBS! and IN GOD WE TRUST, NOT SCIENTISTS. Kenny finished taping the "demonstration" in about ten minutes. Herman helped him get his equipment back into the van before they caused any real disturbance. The "activists" all went their own ways, happily pocketing a day's wages for thirty minutes of work.

Herman received the ninety-second video clip from Kenny two hours later. Kenny had overdubbed a reportorial monologue (himself), added some traffic and crowd noise, and even Photoshopped a crowd on the capitol steps into the background. *Perfecto*, thought Herman. He posted it on his blog and on YouTube. Then he sent it attached to an e-mail to someone he knew at Fox News.

That evening Fox News ran a short item using a clip from Kenny's video, billing it a grassroots protest against the controversial Cascadia earthquake prediction. Herman watched it in his alcove with considerable satisfaction. Then he called Hank Wilcoxen.

NOVEMBER 10

Washington D.C.

Catherine Bisquette, the Director of the US Geological Survey, was ushered into the office of the secretary of the interior, Malcolm Bretheridge, by an aide who quickly departed, closing the door behind her.

Bretheridge rose to greet her. "Thanks so much for coming in, Catherine. Would you like tea or coffee?"

When she demurred and had settled into a chair by his desk, he continued. "Sorry to take you from your busy day, Catherine, but this earthquake rumor on the West Coast is beginning to stir up a lot of flak. I'd like to know what your people are doing about it."

"There's not much we can do at the moment, Malcolm. Most of what we know comes from an article printed in the *Oregonian*, a Portland daily. It said that Carl Strega, who is a well-known earthquake scientist, and a small research group at the local university are developing a prediction of a large earthquake in the Pacific Northwest. The article was pretty skimpy on the details, and so far our people in Seattle and Menlo Park haven't been able to find out much more."

"Well, they're going to have to do better than that. There are a lot of business interests who are pretty unhappy with this development. Nobody can plan anything with something like that hanging over their head. I'm feeling a lot of political pressure to get this issue resolved. We have to get in front of this situation, Catherine, and I'm relying on you to do that for us."

"I understand, sir. We've got the best people in the business in Menlo Park. I'll put the spurs to them and see what they can come up with. In the meantime I'll ask my assistant to activate a standing committee we have on the books. We use it to evaluate earthquake predictions in just this kind of situation."

"That sounds fine, Catherine." He stood to signal the end of the interview. As he ushered her out, he said, "And please keep me informed. This is just the sort of thing people are always wanting to ask me about."

Menlo Park

At the Western Regional Headquarters of the US Geological Survey in Menlo Park, California, Mitch Appleby walked into a small conference room where there waited a half dozen scientists of various earth-quake-related specialties.

"Afternoon, everybody. As I mentioned in my e-mail, the director has asked me to get some people together to try to figure out what Carl Strega and company are up to with their Cascadia earthquake prediction.

"I sent you all copies of the *Oregonian* article, which is the source of all the flap. It's pretty vague I realize. I've tried reading between the lines but haven't been able to find any secret code there." He clicked a control stick, and a projector came on, projecting an image on a screen at the end of the room. "The only thing else we have to go on is this image from Strega that was posted on the PANGA website. Its rather cryptic caption says that it's a screenshot of the analysis he did of the most recent SSE in Cascadia.

"I realize that nobody here is an expert on the SSE business in Cascadia, so I've asked Tom Mitkins from the Seattle office to join us by speakerphone." He tapped on the Polycom teleconferencing module on the table and leaned over. "Are you there Tom? Can you hear us OK?"

A disembodied voice with a British accent responded, "I can hear you fine. But please don't tap on the bloody mike. It makes a hell of a racket."

"Oh, sorry. Tom, what do you know about this business that Strega is up to?"

"Not much, I'm afraid. I had a phone call from Carl a few days ago. He apologized about the newspaper report.

He said they weren't really ready for prime time yet, but there was a leak to an overzealous reporter. They have some major uncertainties still and are in the midst of running tests, so he wasn't ready to discuss their findings yet. I tried to pin him down, but he clammed up. He did say that they plan to present what they have at the AGU. That's only about a month away, so I suppose we wait till then."

"Yeah, well, our director seems to think that we're not doing our jobs unless we can come up with something sooner than that. That's the purpose of this meeting. The one thing we have to go on is this figure he posted on the PANGA website. What do you think of it, Tom?"

"Well, at first blush the displacement plots look pretty much like what we're used to seeing for SSEs. But he's also plotted their derivatives, which are the velocity plots shown just below the displacement plots. They show a change in the shape, from single peaked to double peaked, as the SSE progresses. We're not used to looking at the data that way, so I went back and did that analysis on a number of SSEs from earlier years, and they don't show that change. So I'm guessing that it's this change of shape that's at the root of what he's driving at."

Mitch looked around the table. "Any ideas about what that might mean?"

Steve Feingold, sitting in the corner, raised a finger. "The newspaper article said they were predicting that the earthquake would occur at the next SSE, which is expected to be next August. So it must be that this change in shape of the SSE is somehow telling him that things are ready to go kablooey. But more than that, I haven't a clue."

Duncan Jones, their leading theorist, rose and eased his portly frame around the chairs, gazing at the screen as he approached it. "Those lower figures are spectra," he muttered. "They show it changes from a single to a double peak." He made his way around the table in front and peered closely at the screen. "It's hard to make out the scale, but it looks like one peak is at half the frequency of the other." He looked around, puzzled, and then his face lit up. "I got it! Half the frequency is double the period. It's period doubling. I've heard that term before. It's something to do with chaos theory." He glanced around and saw that Monika Velez had her laptop open. "Monika, Google period doubling."

Monika typed in a few words and did some clicking. "You're right," she said. "It is from chaos theory. It says here that period doubling marks a bifurcation between regular periodic motion to irregular, chaotic motion. The example they show, though, doesn't look anything like what we're looking at."

Everyone gathered around her laptop. Duncan leaned over her shoulder. "Do a deeper search," he said. "Put in period doubling *and* friction *and* earthquakes."

She ran the new search. "Oh, wow, there's a whole literature on this stuff." She clicked on an item and started scanning it. "So it looks like in theory the friction laws somehow contain period doubling, and it seems to be just at the boundary between stable and unstable behavior."

"That's it! That must be what he's getting at," Duncan declared excitedly. "The appearance of period doubling must be telling him that the instability is imminent. Mitch, gimme a bit; I'll track this down. I'm going back to my office to download some of this stuff and do some reading." He rushed out of the room.

"Let me know what you figure out, Duncan," Mitch shouted to his disappearing figure. He turned to the others. "OK, that's it. I think that's as far as we can take it today. I'll write a little memo for Catherine about this, though I'm not sure what good it'll do her. Thanks, everybody."

November 28

Corvallis

The group was having its last full meeting prior to getting ready for the AGU meeting. Kiersten was wrapping up her presentation. "This slide summarizes our results. The mean period of SSE events, as determined from tremor episodes over the last twenty years, is 429 days. However, you can see a steady phase shift in the data stack that indicates a gradual increase of the interevent period that amounts to four days over those twenty years. So we have a positive confirmation of Carl's conjecture. Furthermore, the magnitude of the change, as you will hear from Anastasia's talk, is consistent with theoretical expectations."

The excitement in the seminar room was palpable. Anastasia rose to speak. "OK, so we have done 2D simulations with our model. We assumed, for the friction between plates, the rate-state friction model with two state variables. Then, as Carl suggested, we looked at a model where each slip event adds a small increment of compressive stress to the plate interface. This slide is example. You see the increase of period of the SSEs. So it seems that Carl's intuition is good. The next slide shows the rate of period increase for a wide range of possible parameters. It has some interesting behaviors, but the main point is they agree with Kiersten's result within a factor of two, as you can see. Actually, we got these results more than a week ago. When Kiersten kindly showed us her results yesterday, we were so excited. The agreement is amazing for us. OK, maybe we should just say they are consistent." There was a murmur of amusement from the group.

"In the next stage, we zoomed in to look at period-doubling regime. We found, like Carl guessed, that it very quickly goes unstable, after only two or three episodes. In this slide I show the instability. The SSE starts as usual, accelerates, then slows down, but then the second acceleration grows exponentially without limit. We think this is the nucleation of the instability. If we put in the parameters to get true time, we find that the nucleation lasts one or two days. As you can see, it should be clearly observable with GPS.

"We did statistics of many runs covering the parameter space and found that it goes unstable in the second cycle about eighty percent of the time, in the third or later cycle about twenty percent. This is only 2D case, so we should be cautious. But is saying that the possibility of the earthquake next year is about eighty percent."

Carl rose. "That's fantastic, you guys. Those are really great results. They bring us to a new level. I think we'll have a really good story to present at AGU with this, and something more concrete to tell the media about just what we can and cannot predict. But before we finish, I want to share something else with you. When Anastasia sent me that figure of the instability growth curve a few days ago, it struck a bell. The slide I just put up is a map of the Nankai Trough, which marks the location of the subduction of the Philippine Sea Plate beneath the Eurasian Plate in southwest Japan. It runs offshore Japan from Suruga Bay, southwest of Tokyo, west-southwest to the Bungo Channel between Shikoku and Kyushu. It's the site of many great earthquakes, the penultimate ones being the two magnitude 8.4 Ansei earthquakes of 1856, the first of which ruptured the eastern half of the plate boundary, followed thirty-one hours later by the second, which proceeded on to rupture the western half. In the early part of the modern era of Japan, the Japanese government, following a disastrous earthquake in 1891, enacted a scientific program with the optimistic goal of eventually learning how to predict earthquakes. One of its provisions was to carry out precise geodetic surveys at regular intervals to monitor crustal deformation in tectonically active areas. So it transpired that in December 1944, in spite of it being in the middle of the war, a surveying crew was dutifully at work leveling on Cape Omaezaki, which is the point of land just there at the end of Suruga Bay. On December fifth and sixth, they had to keep redoing their leveling lines because they kept getting large discrepancies in their results. On the morning of December seventh, the ground was tilting so rapidly that they couldn't keep the bubble centered in the spirit level. An hour later the magnitude 8.1 Tonankai earthquake occurred just offshore. It was followed two years later by the magnitude 8.2 Nankaido earthquake that ruptured the remaining sector just to the west. Forty years later the Japanese seismologist Kiyoo Mogi reexamined the original field books and reconstructed the tilting that was occurring during those days. I show his result in the next slide and compare it there with the nucleation phase that Anastasia has just obtained with her model. The resemblance is remarkable; both have the same exponential increase with time up to the earthquake. I think the conclusions are obvious: in 1944 those surveyors serendipitously observed the nucleation of a great subduction zone earthquake. Their observation required a lot of luck—they had to be surveying at just the right place at just the right time. Their observation has never been repeated since, but in this age of continuous GPS networks monitoring subduction zones, we should expect to see it again. And, I would imagine, pretty soon."

"OK, that wraps it up. Please send me all your materials. I'll be spending next week putting together the AGU talk and a press kit for the media. Oh, and by the way, Kiersten and Anastasia, I've gotten the OK from AGU for you guys to give poster presentations on your work. So get them ready to bring to the meeting."

As everyone was gathering their things together to leave, David, who was sitting in the back of the room, signaled to Carl. Carl walked back and sat down opposite him.

"What's up?"

"This stuff is getting really exciting. I'm beginning to understand the process you guys go through to reach your conclusions. I have to admit I didn't get it earlier. I mean, I didn't understand the rigor involved. My background is in ecology, which is really soft science compared to what you guys are doing. I'm getting an article ready to release after the AGU meeting, and I'm really stoked about it." He gave Carl a rueful look. "By the way, have you seen the latest Stackhouse blog?"

"Well, no, I haven't been keeping up."

David slid a sheet of paper across the table to him. "You'd better have a look at this then."

The headline read, "Quakegate Scientist in Sexual Harassment Scandal." Carl quickly scanned through the text.

"Hmm. So I see. He's gotten onto the Janice Hooper affair and with his usual slather of innuendo made it into something that bears little resemblance to reality. What a load of crap." In disgust he tossed the paper back across the table.

"On face value it paints a pretty damaging picture, Carl. He claims that you were accused of sexually harassing a female graduate student and that this led to your forced retirement. This is a direct attack on your credibility, so we can't just let it pass. Do you mind telling me about what happened?"

"Oh, sure. Janice was a grad student in my department. She failed her orals—actually she kind of broke down in the middle of them. It was a pretty sad scene. In retrospect, though, she decided that her performance had suffered because of gender pressure—her committee was all male, and she had felt gender bias against her. Maybe that's true; I really don't have any idea about what caused her emotional meltdown, which was certainly real enough. But I didn't feel that there was anything out of the ordinary in terms of the line or tenor of the questioning she was facing, and certainly not from my side. I actually have a very good record in mentoring female students. But the upshot was she decided to sue the university for gender bias and got herself a hotshot lawyer who talked her into putting down every possible grievance she could think of. They ended up with a seventy-five-page-long lawsuit that, among other things, accused at least a dozen members of the department of allegedly sexually discriminating against her one way or the other. I was one of those mentioned."

"Tell me about your part."

"Not much to tell, really. The year before her orals, she gave a seminar presentation at which I made some critical comments from the audience. That's nothing out of the ordinary. I consider criticizing student presentations part of my teaching obligation. Anyway, it had nothing whatsoever to do with her gender. It had to do with the science she was presenting. Unfortunately she didn't take it as the constructive criticism intended. She seemed to take it as a personal affront and never came around to talk to me about it afterward, as I had suggested. But whatever she thought about it, the charge was of gender bias, not sexual harassment. I would say there is a pretty big difference between the two, to put it mildly."

"What was the final outcome?"

"I believe there was a settlement with the university, but the details were never disclosed, nor was I particularly interested in finding out what they were. I don't know what happened with Janice later on."

"Did this business have anything with you taking early retirement?'

"Nothing, aside from the fact that the whole affair soured departmental politics to an annoying extent. Pro-Janice and Anti-Janice camps arose, neither of which I wanted to have anything to do with. Anyway, I didn't retire until three years after it was all over. There was no direct connection."

"OK, that sounds fine. The thing is, I've been looking for a chance to fight back against Herman's campaign against you guys. I've been wanting to write an op-ed piece for the

Oregonian, and this looks like it might provide the hook I need. How can I document this?

"Well, Janice filed suit in the state of Massachusetts, so it must be a matter of public record. And there were a couple of articles about it in the *Boston Globe* at the time. Will that suffice?"

"Good. Great. That should do it."

"Explain this to me, David. I just don't get what's with this guy Stackhouse. I mean, if the beef really is about tourists getting scared away by us, you would think that it would have been a better strategy to just let things slide. All this would have been pretty much forgotten by now. Instead he persists on keeping it in the news, what with his bogus demonstration in Salem and all. If his backers really are the tourism people, you would think that this wouldn't be in their best interests."

"That's not how it works, Carl. They're happy about keeping it in the news as long as they're the ones shaping it. Their strategy is to steer the discussion along on their terms. That's why I want to do an op-ed piece, to put Herman on the defensive for once. That'll have to do until after AGU when the whole science story can come out.

"Besides that, once somebody like Herman gets onto something like this, he makes it his own crusade. For one thing it boosts his blog hits and therefore his advertising revenue. Plus it also makes him into a hero to his right-wing followers and gives him more national attention among those circles. There is a lot more going on here than just your earthquake prediction issue. This is a small part of a much larger attack from the right on the credibility of science. It all started years ago with the tobacco companies supporting phony science to try to discredit the fact that smoking cigarettes can kill you. It spread into the larger culture wars with the so-called debate about evolution versus creationism and more recently the campaign, supported by big oil and other conservative interests, to deny global climate change and the need to convert to renewable energy resources. The mistake you scientists make is in thinking that you're providing unbiased scientific evidence and are therefore neutral, but to them you aren't neutral at all; you're the enemy. Their greatest fear is of a world organized according to science-informed public policies. Their strongest weapon against that is to discredit science in the eye of the public through disinformation campaigns. The news media doesn't help by treating each side equally in the name of 'fairness.' So Carl, I am afraid that you've wandered unwittingly into this battlefield and have become a pawn in a larger struggle."

"Well, what a lot of hookum! No amount of propaganda on their part is going to change the scientific facts. Nothing that they can say is going to slow down plate tectonics."

"Of course you're right about the physical reality, Carl, but these people are concerned with the political reality, which is an entirely different matter," David said with a grimace. "You'll win the argument in the end, but by then it may be too late. In the meantime they'll have had their way, which is really all they care about. Science is all about long-term consequences, while mammonism, and its hand-maiden, the venality of politicians, is all about short-term gains.

"To change to a more pleasant subject, while I've got you here, could we have that interview on the background?"

"Sure; now is as good as any other time."

"Thank you." David got out a small tape recorder. "I hope you don't mind if I record this."

"No, not at all."

"So shall we begin? Since I became interested in this topic, I've read everything I could get on you and your work. I'm afraid I haven't read your scientific papers, though. They're a bit too technical for me. I'm curious that you never refer to yourself as a seismologist. So what are you? I mean, aren't seismologists the ones who study earthquakes?"

"Well, yes, historically that is true. But early on seismologists specialized in the study of seismic wave propagation in the earth. Their great program has been to determine the structure of the earth's interior by that means. For a long time, most seismologists regarded earthquakes as a side-line; they were only thought of as the sources of the seismic waves and secondarily as hazards to be reported to the public. It's been only in the last few decades that many of them have turned their efforts toward the 'source problem,' as they call it, and toward investigating the inner workings of earthquakes. I have to say they've done a marvelous job of this. Nowadays they produce beautifully detailed descriptions of the interior structure of earthquakes. But, elegant as their methods are for producing such pictures, they are still only descriptions. People like me, who study mechanics, and in particular rock mechanics, are more interested in the primal mechanisms behind earthquakes."

"I see. I wonder if you could you tell me how you, personally, became interested in earthquakes?"

"Well, I suppose you might say it started with an childhood epiphany. When I was nine, my father had some business in San Diego and took the family along to make a vacation out of it. One day while my father was off on his business, the rest of us were visiting the San Diego Zoo. Suddenly there began an intense shaking. You could hardly stand up. The shaking was accompanied by all kinds of strange roaring and clanging sounds. People were stumbling and falling down and screaming. Stuff was flying out of a vendor's kiosk in front of me. Then the motion changed to a side-to-side swaying, which much later I realized must have been the surface waves. Tall palm trees swayed back and forth at impossible angles. It felt like I was riding in a boat at sea. I remember all of this vividly as though it were a crazy montage of film clips in slow motion. Then the motion stopped as suddenly as it had begun. During this whole episode, which lasted maybe ten seconds, I had stood transfixed, raptly soaking in what seemed at the time to be an out-of-world experience. In the sudden quiet after the motion ceased, I heard a disembodied voice coming to me as if I were waking from a dream—it was my mother calling to me. I turned and saw her crouched on the ground, clutching my screaming sisters. I walked up to her and said, dizzy with awe, 'Wow, what was that?' She looked terrified. 'It was an earthquake,' she said. 'Get over here right now! We've got to get back to the hotel and wait for your father.' 'But what's an earthquake?' I asked. 'Ask your father when we see him,' she said.

"Back at the hotel, everybody was very excitedly talking about the earthquake, so I knew it hadn't just happened at the zoo; it had shaken the whole city! Later, when my father arrived, as soon as he entered the room he started hugging my mother and looking around anxiously at us kids, saying, 'Oh, I'm so glad to see you. Are you OK? Is everybody OK? Wow, what an earthquake! You must have been scared to death...' His anxiety made me even more impressed about this thing called an earthquake.

"I immediately began pestering him to tell me what earthquakes were. After hemming and hawing for a while, he finally sat me down at the little kitchenette table in that hotel room and in the tone of voice he used to explain serious things to me, said, 'There are big caves under the ground. And sometimes big rocks fall in the caves and shake the ground and that makes an earthquake.'

"I remember thinking a big disappointed *Huh?* Later that night there were reports about the earthquake on TV. They showed a map of the earthquake epicenter. It had occurred way out in the desert, a zillion miles it seemed from where we were. They showed big cracks that had gone across a highway and houses that were wrecked in some little desert town. Then I realized that the explanation that my father had given couldn't possibly be true. There couldn't be caves big enough or rocks big enough to shake us that hard so far away from where it had happened. *What a stupid explanation!* I remember thinking. That really shocked me. This was obviously a momentous thing that had occurred, yet my father didn't have the foggiest idea what it was. Either my father was a moron, which I certainly didn't want to believe, or this was a big mystery."

"That's a fascinating story. Isn't that what the ancient Greeks thought about earthquakes? Aristotle, maybe?"

"Epicurus, actually. That was his explanation of earthquakes as related by Lucretius in *De Rerum Natura*."

"Your father must have had a classical education, then."

He laughed. "Hardly. He was an engineer. I've no idea where he picked up that notion. Later when I asked my teachers in school the same question, I got similarly nonsensical answers. This experience stuck in my mind and gradually grew till it eventually led me to choose the study of earthquakes for my life's work.

"Don't get me wrong; I'm not belittling Epicurus—far from it. His was the earliest attempt we know of to explain earthquakes as natural phenomena. Before him it was always the doings of angry gods. We didn't get a better explanation until late in the nineteenth century, when practitioners of the young science of geology began visiting the sites of major earthquakes and, seeing freshly formed fault scarps, connected earthquakes to the sudden slip on faults."

"Let's move on to your current research. I've only heard about it from what Kiersten has told me, much of which, I have to confess, I didn't fully understand. I wonder if you could describe it in layman's terms."

"OK, let me try by describing things with what we call a toy model. This isn't a model of the real system but is a very simple model that illustrates the characteristics of the real system. Suppose you take a string and pin its ends to the wall some distance apart. Let there be some slack in the string so that it droops in the middle. Now imagine a little ball that resides on the string. No matter where we start the ball, it'll roll down the string and settle in the bottom of the droop. We call the droop a basin of attraction: it defines a position of stable equilibrium at its bottom. All things within that basin are attracted to its bottom. Now imagine taking a slippery rod and lifting the string from a point between the two pins but closer to the left pin. Now two droops will appear in the string, the left one being higher than the right one. So now we have a system with two basins of attraction and two corresponding stable equilibrium positions, one higher than the other.

"Friction often can be described as this kind of system: the upper equilibrium point is what is called static friction, and the lower equilibrium point, the dynamic or sliding friction. If the system jumps from the static friction to the lower dynamic friction, we'll get a stress drop and sudden slip. That jump will occur with a bang. That's called stick-slip friction. I'm sure you've encountered this. If you're trying to push a heavy object, you might have noticed that it often proceeds in jerks, accompanied by screeching or squawking noises. That jerky motion is stick-slip. Stick-slip is usually annoying and troublesome. We oil the wheel to get rid of the squeak. But sometimes it's desirable. A violin string vibrates to make its tone because it's being constantly plucked by stick-slip friction between it and the drawn bow. In that case we want to enhance the stick-slip, so we resin the bow to increase the stick.

"The same stick-slip friction is the basic mechanism of earthquakes. As the tectonic plates move in response to the underlying convective flow of the earth's mantle, they stick together at their boundaries until the static friction is reached. Then sliding at the boundary begins, at first slowly and almost imperceptibly. Then, after a small amount of slip, the frictional resistance to slip drops suddenly to the lower dynamic level, which results in an instability, and a large slip then occurs very suddenly. That is the earth-quake. That rapid slip produces sound waves that radiate outward in the rock. Those seismic waves cause the shaking and damage in the earthquake. They're the equivalent of the screeching noises that you experience in moving some heavy object. In the case we're discussing, however, we aren't talking about the sticking part of the plate boundary but the region just below it, where the behavior is a little more interesting. To return to our string model, if we always start the ball on the left-hand side, it will always go to the upper equilibrium point. It would be energetically favorable to go to the lower one, but it can't get there because there's a hill in between, where the rod is, which we call an energy barrier. If we gradually move the rod upward, the basin of attraction on the left will become higher and shallower. Eventually it will become shallow and flat-bottomed enough that any slight perturbation, say from a puff of air, will start the ball rolling so that instead of staying stationary at the bottom of the well it will tend to oscillate back and forth. These oscillations are what we are observing as slow slip events. Are you with me so far?"

"Absolutely. I'm just drawing pictures of your string in my notebook."

"Good you have one. I usually end up scribbling on napkins. Let's see, where was I? Oh, yes. The rod in the toy model represents, in the real world, the compression between the plates. Each SSE cycle increases the compression a small amount, which is the equivalent of raising the rod. So now imagine lifting the rod a bit more so that the left-hand basin becomes even shallower and flatter. You'll reach a point where the fluctuations of the ball will take it to the top of the hill between the basins of attraction, which coming from the left isn't much of a hill any longer. It then will teeter there for a moment and then roll back into the left-hand basin. In the real system, that teetering is what we observed as the period-doubling motion that we first saw during the SSE last year. It means that the system is just at the brink of the instability. It is almost ready to topple and fall into the deep right-hand basin. Once the ball rolls past the top of the hill, which we think will happen on the next SSE or two, there's no turning back. The ball is now in the lower basin of attraction and will begin to accelerate down the right hand slope. This is what we call the nucleation phase. According to the simulations of Anastasia and José, which you saw just now at the group meeting, when this occurs, we should be able to observe it with GPS, and it should last no more than one or two days. Once the ball reaches a steep enough point on the right-hand slope, it'll plummet to the bottom like a stone, pun intended. That's the earthquake."

"Then it *is* like a rock falling in a cave!"

Carl laughed. "Yes, it is, now that you mention it. But it's an energy cave, not a physical one.

"To continue with the cave analogy, as you put it, now imagine it in three dimensions. The string is now a sheet, and the droops in the string now become depressions in the sheet—energy wells, we call them. Once some spot falls into the deeper depression, it can no longer support the stress it has been holding. That stress then gets transferred to the rim of the concavity, where it drives the adjacent points over their energy barriers so they also plunge into the energy well, and so on. In this way the instability propagates outward, just like the ripples in a pond spread out from the point of impact of a dropped pebble. This happens at the speed of information flow—the speed of sound in rock, which is about three kilometers per second, or about 2,000 miles per hour. The rupture doesn't stop until it reaches some impediment, like a high-strength barrier, which may lie somewhere along the plate interface, or until it reaches the end of the plate boundary. All the sound waves rattling around during this process are the seismic waves that we experience as an earthquake. And that's it in a nutshell."

"Wow, that is amazingly clear. Thank you so much for explaining it to me that way. But to get back to your model for how the earthquake initiates, how do you know that it's the correct model?"

"We don't really know if it is the correct model. It's a working hypothesis. It's based on a model that has been tested with laboratory friction experiments. We know that it explains a lot of earthquake behavior, but it's never been previously used for the purpose that we're applying it to now. So we keep testing it against the observations we have as we go along. If it passes those tests, as it has so far, we keep it as our working hypothesis. If it should fail one of our tests, we have to rethink things and try something else. The ultimate test is if the earthquake it predicts happens or not."

"Gosh, it seems like you're taking an enormous chance."

"Well, you know, as Pasteur famously said, 'Chance favors the prepared mind.' One gets a sort of intuition based on a lot of experience, a feeling of how things should work. It just feels like everything fits."

◆   ◆   ◆

David's op-ed appeared in the *Oregonian* the following Monday. It was a general critique of the series of blogs posted by Herman Stackhouse attacking the earthquake prediction scientists. He countered the claim of the lack of transparency of the scientists involved by pointing out that he himself had first publicized their work, against the wishes of the chief scientist, who had felt that the work was not yet ready for public disclosure, with his conviction as a journalist that it was in the public interest that the work be divulged, even if it was still in a speculative stage. The scientists, he pointed out, would be providing a full airing of the project's findings at the AGU meeting in a few weeks' time. He also exposed the misinformation in Stackhouse's blog regarding Carl's role in the university sexual discrimination case. He had also tried to connect Herman through his known association with Hank Wilcoxen to financial backing by the Oregon Tourism Industry Association and the Oregon Realtors' Association, but that section had been excised by the editors on the grounds that he had no smoking gun to prove his allegations. In this form of combat, the rules of engagement are asymmetric, to the advantage of the Herman Stackhouses of the world.

December 11

San Francisco

The group had taken the early morning flight down from Portland and was in a state of high anticipation as they descended the escalator into the subterranean halls of the Moscone Center in San Francisco. At the bottom they stepped into the wide busy passageway that connects the cavernous exhibition halls to the left with the warren of lecture rooms, great and small, to the right. For this week each December, the Moscone Center is the great global hub of geophysical activity. The Fall Meeting of the American Geophysical Union is the largest such event in the world, where some twenty thousand earth scientists meet annually to discuss the latest scientific findings on everything from the physics and chemistry of the sun and planets to the ecosystems of tiny organisms living at abyssal depths in the earth's oceans.

The broad corridor bustled with activity. Groups of scientists wandered by, each enclosed in their own orbit of animated conversation and oblivious to their surroundings. Here and there, in eddies along the walls, clumps of senior scientists in small cabals discussed funding programs and scientific politics while their eyes maintained a flickering interest in the passing crowd. Through this streamed schools of neophytes: postdocs and grad students clutching laptops and iPads while scurrying from one meeting room to another in a vain effort to catch all of the show, while keeping a weather eye open for potential jobs.

The group split up. Kiersten and Anastasia, toting their poster tubes, left for the exhibition hall to hang their posters. José went off to attend a session on nonlinear geophysics that he had been delighted to discover in the program was of particular interest to him, and Mark went off to rendezvous with a couple of his seismological pals. Carl, happy to be left on his own, wandered down the hallway toward the area where the various scientific publishing houses had set up their stalls.

As he progressed through the crowd, he was greeted every few feet by old colleagues. Carl hadn't attended an AGU meeting for quite a few years, so many of them expressed surprise and delight to see him again. Many of them also commented on his earthquake forecast. They had all heard about it one way or another from the media or from the scuttlebutt it had generated in scientific circles. It also seemed to be widespread knowledge that, even though it was not listed in the meeting program, he was going to give a presentation about it at 11:30 a.m. News travels fast at meetings like this. More than a few of the people he ran into in the hall tried to winkle some information out of him about what it was all about, but Carl kept putting them off in a good-natured way, telling them, "Just come along and listen to our paper."

He reached a stagnation point where the flow of people from the corridor met the stationary crowd milling about in the entrance to the exhibition halls. Carl paused to take his bearings. Off to his left, he caught a fragment in the familiar penetrating tones of a well-known blowhard: "Looks like Strega has finally gone off his rocker..." Carl instinctively began moving the other way.

Once he had left the general hubbub and entered the backwaters of the bookstall quarter, Carl was able to regain a measure of calm. He had a mild case of agoraphobia, and being exposed to the constant necessity of responding to rapid-fire communication with so many people got on his nerves. First there was the greeting, with variations. Then came the necessity to listen to what project the other person was working on and then to reciprocate. Then maybe some quick gossip followed by an exit line and then on to the next person in the crowd. He imagined that speed-dating must be something like this.

Among the books he ran into one of his oldest friends dating back to his postdoc days, Mitch Appleby. Mitch had gone to the USGS in Menlo Park right out of graduate school, where he had since been enjoying a long and successful career in seismology without the pressure of the constant grant-getting that is the bane of academic science. He had been one of the happy few to buy a small house in Palo Alto before the dot-commers came along and put the price of local real estate out of the reach of mere mortals. Mitch steered him off to a distant area, where, much to Carl's surprise, there was a small espresso bar.

"Yeah, how 'bout that?" Mitch said. "After so many years of people bitching about the lukewarm slop they used to trot out in those old five-gallon convention urns, the AGU finally convinced the Moscone Center to get with the modern age and provide us with some decent coffee."

After they took their coffees to a table, Mitch settled back and said, "So Carl, I gather that you're up to your usual mischief."

"Oh, come on, Mitch. I wasn't looking for trouble. I just fell into this business."

"Oh, I believe you, Carl, but you have to admit that you have a habit of getting into, shall I say, controversial situations." He chuckled. "But hey, that's what I like about you. With old Carl there's never a dull moment. This time, though, you've really stepped in it. There are murmurings coming out of Reston about a NEPEC hearing on this Cascadia deal."

"NEPEC? Oh, the old National Earthquake Prediction Evaluation Council. Is that old relic still in business?"

"Bureaucratic entities may fade away, old friend, but they never die. Sure it's still around. They just haven't had a real live prediction controversy to chew on since 1990 when that charlatan Iben Browning claimed to have predicted an earthquake in New Madrid, Missouri. That turned out to be a real media circus."

"Well, so be it, then. I'll be happy to give this thing a full public hearing."

"I'm sure you would be, Carl, but you have to realize that the chances of the NEPEC approving your prediction are next to nil. That's not their function. They're basically in place to shield the director from crackpot predictions that have gained too much traction with the public. It's a formalized disavowal mechanism."

"That's their lookout. It'd be tragic if they disapproved us out of hand, but the onus would be on them. If they pick it wrong, the losers will be the people. As far as the scientific question goes, what they think doesn't really matter anyway. The earth will be the final arbiter."

"Well, let's hope you lose that bet."

"Yeah, I hope so too. But what the fuck; I'm not in charge. I'm just the messenger here."

Carl got to his assigned meeting room with fifteen minutes to spare. It was just as well, because the hall was already filled to the gunnels. It was one of the larger rooms, seating maybe 500 or more in row after row of folding chairs. It was standing room only, with people packed along the tall moveable walls decorated with their convention center pattern of repetitious motifs. More people were continually cramming in through the doorways at the rear. The word had gotten out about this talk, and the room was bristling with excited chatter.

Carl downloaded his talk from his memory stick onto the laptop on the table in the speakers' area, found a seat next to the session chairman in the front row, and sat down to wait for the last scheduled speaker to finish. When his time came, he rose and quickly and from long practice slid into his delivery. The session organizers had very generously given him the last thirty minutes of the session instead of the usual ten-minute allotment. Carl, completely engrossed in the logical flow of his argument and cued by his slides, was oblivious of time yet stopped to the minute of his allotted time. After inviting the audience to visit Kiersten's and Anastasia's posters, he thanked them and asked for questions.

After a moment of stunned silence, hands began popping up. The chairman picked a tall bald man out of the front of the audience whom Carl did not recognize.

"You are proposing to predict a great earthquake, sir, which is an event of enormous impact but very low probability. Nassim Taleb called such things black swans. He showed that it is impossible to predict such events. How do you reply to that?"

Carl cogitated. The question was a bit off-the-wall, but he caught the reference. "Taleb was thinking as a stock trader. He was talking about the impossibility of probabilistically predicting something like a sudden large movement in the stock market. Although, as I recall, he didn't offer a formal proof in his book, he's most likely right about that. But here we're not making a probabilistic prediction. We're making a deterministic one. We have identified a physical precursor to the event. So we are, to use his metaphor, the possessors of inside information. As is well-known, insider trading enjoys a much reduced risk of failure." The audience responded with a ripple of appreciation for this riposte.

The next questioner was Antonio Barlotti, a well-respected Italian seismologist. "I'll grant you that with your method you may be able to predict the time of nucleation. But that doesn't allow you to predict the size of the earthquake that ensues. To do that would require prior knowledge of the initial conditions: the state of stress all over the fault. And that you cannot know."

This was a question Carl had been hoping for. There hadn't been time to explore this aspect in his talk, but now he had been given the opportunity. He replied, "You're thinking in the conventional way that nucleation occurs at a point within the seismogenic zone. In that case you would be correct. However, we're talking about the nucleation occurring in the transition region below the seismogenic region. Our calculations indicate that a slow slip event in the transition region must occur over a length of about 100 kilometers before nucleation occurs and runs rapidly over that length. So our nucleation is a line source, not a point. This line of nucleation occurs at the base of the seismogenic zone where the stresses are highest, so there is nothing to stop the earthquake rupture from propagating upward, through lower-strength regions, to the surface. So that means our minimum earthquake size will have a length of 100 kilometers and its width will be the full width of the seismogenic zone, which is between sixty and seventy-five kilometers, depending on where along the Cascadia Subduction Zone it starts from. That yields a minimum earthquake magnitude of between 7.8 and 8.0. Beyond that point, your assumptions become correct, and we cannot predict how much larger than that it might become. That does depends on the initial conditions, which, as you say, we don't know."

Carl answered an additional flurry of questions, and although several were skeptical to plainly antagonistic in tone, none exposed the scientific equivalent of a smoking gun that might invalidate their conclusions.

The session chairman finally rose and cut off the discussion, citing time limitations. There was a buzz of excitement in the air as the members of the audience began breaking for the exits.

Carl, accompanied by his group, walked into the AGU press room thirty minutes later. He was at first taken aback: there were twenty or thirty people sitting there in the folding chairs provided. There was even a TV crew. He hadn't expected such a crowd. He strode to the podium and introduced himself and the members of his team. He looked around at the audience. He didn't recognize anyone except David, who was sitting in the middle of the second row in conversation with a tiny owlish woman. Then he spotted Herman Stackhouse lurking in a rear corner.

"Thank you for your interest in our work. In my talk this morning, I gave the scientific case for our statements concerning a coming Cascadia earthquake. In your press kit, you'll find an extended abstract of our presentation, as well as copies of all the figures used in the talk. I invite you to study that material at your leisure.

"For now I'm sure you are most interested in exactly what we do and what we do not predict about earthquakes in Cascadia. First of all let me clarify a few terms. Earthquake prediction is usually defined as the accurate and precise prediction of the time, place, and size of a coming earthquake. As I will explain to you, what we can say does not exactly fit the bill on any of those criteria. What we can say has a certain degree of imprecision to it: it has what I like to call a well-defined vagueness. You may think that this sounds like an oxymoron, but bear with me while I explain it. Because of this vagueness, I prefer to say that what we are providing is a foreshadowing rather than a prediction.

He turned to the whiteboard, selected a marker, and wrote: One of the next few slow slip events in Cascadia will trigger a large earthquake. "This is what we claim. Let me now parse this statement for you.

"First let's consider timing. The slow slip events, or SSEs, as we call them, produce two to three centimeters of slip in a narrow strip just below the base of the seismogenic zone and propagate north or south along the strike of the zone at about ten kilometers per day. They occur in Cascadia every fourteen months, and each lasts for about three weeks. The next one is expected to begin in the second week of August next year. Our simulations currently indicate that the probability of the earthquake occurring during the next SSE is about eighty percent, with about a twenty percent probability that it will occur during either the second or third SSE, that is, two or three years later. So, simply stated, we claim that there is an eighty-percent chance of a large earthquake occurring in the last three weeks of August next year. We plan to perform more sophisticated simulations to help narrow that down, but the numbers will probably not change hugely from those given.

"Next, what do we mean by a large earthquake? I am using the term large earthquake in a technical sense to mean an earthquake that ruptures through the entire seismogenic zone from bottom to top. For Cascadia this means an earthquake of a minimum size of magnitude 7.8 to 8.0. Note that an increase of magnitude unit of 0.2 indicates a doubling of the earthquake size in terms of energy release. So our estimate of the minimum earthquake size has an uncertainty of about a factor of two. However, I emphasize that this is a minimum estimate. That is the starting size. Once such an earthquake initiates, we have no way of predicting how far it will propagate farther along the plate boundary to the north and south.

"The final issue has to do with location. At the present time, we do not know where the next SSE will initiate, so we cannot say where along the Cascadia Subduction Zone the events I have just indicated will occur. It could be anywhere between central Vancouver Island and Cape Mendocino, California, a distance of 1,100 kilometers. We will, of course, be able to narrow that down once the next SSE begins next August, so we will be able to give a more precise short-term prediction at that time. In the meantime one of the goals of our research is to try to discover some systematic pattern of SSE occurrence based on the record we have of their occurrences over the past twenty years. If we are successful in that endeavor, we would be able to specify the location of the earthquake before the SSE begins in August. In that event we will, of course, make an announcement of it.

"So ladies and gentlemen, there you have it. I am happy to take your questions now."

Hands were raised in the audience. Carl selected a woman in the first row, who stood and asked if the earthquake they were predicting would be the "big one" that everyone had heard about.

"The question is, if I may paraphrase, what is the likelihood that the earthquake will be the 'big one,' that is, the magnitude 9 that has been long talked about? A magnitude 9 would be an earthquake that ruptures the entire plate boundary. That is the maximum earthquake that could occur in Cascadia, but as I have said, we have no way, or at least I know of no way at present, of predicting how far the earthquake, once initiated, will propagate and hence how large it could become beyond the minimum size I have specified. The people who study the history of past Cascadia megaquakes from the geologic record of prehistoric tsunamis say that over the Holocene, that is, the last 10,000 years, there have been many total Cascadia margin events, the last one being in 1700. They have also found evidence for a large number of smaller events in the geologic record. Those are events that ruptured only portions of the plate boundary and would have commensurately smaller magnitudes. Unless a great deal of new evidence becomes available between now and then, there is no way of betting on the size of the next one beyond the minimum size that we have specified."

The second question came from a man in the rear. "What's the use of making a prediction like this that is so vague?"

Carl replied, "The question is, considering how vague our predictions are, what use are they for preparing for such a disaster? I too wish we could be more precise, but we have to work with the cards nature has dealt us. We realize we've put the emergency preparedness professionals in a quandary with such a range of possibilities to deal with. As to what they should do about all this, I am certainly not the one to tell them how to do their jobs. We can also ask the question, as some have: is such incomplete information worse than no information at all? That one I leave to the philosophers. As scientists I believe we have an obligation to make these findings public. After that it's out of our hands. I should also like to remind everyone of the recent case of a group of Italian seismologists who were convicted and sentenced to prison terms for having failed to warn the local populace of an impending earthquake. This precedent forces our hands—we feel compelled to publicly reveal our findings even though they have a degree of uncertainty at the present time."

A woman in the second row asked, "How well established is this theory you are using to make your prediction? We have been told for years that earthquake prediction is impossible, and now you seem to have come up with a new theory that claims the opposite."

Carl smiled. "That's a very good question. The concepts we use in our model are based on a friction theory of earthquake that is fairly new but is now mainstream science.

Those concepts are combined with results from the branch of physics known as nonlinear dynamics, which is sometimes popularly called chaos theory. This branch of theory is often thought of as new physics, as opposed to classical physics, but it's been around for thirty or forty years, so it now has well-established roots. However, our particular formulation of it, and our application of it to earthquake physics, is novel. Our colleagues have heard about it today for the first time. I'm sure you can find many experts at this meeting who were in the audience this morning and who will be willing to give you their first impressions, but it'll take a little while even for experts to digest what we've said and come to more considered opinions. As far as testing our theory is concerned, ladies and gentlemen, this earthquake forecast *is* the test."

After the Q-and-A crowd dispersed, Carl was approached by a blond man with tinted glasses wearing a brown corduroy jacket.

"Hello, I'm Alan Askew, with USGS headquarters, Reston. Nice talk, and, may I say, you handled the press quite well."

Speak of the devil, Carl thought as he thanked him for the complement.

"I've been unsuccessfully trying to get a hold of you by phone and e-mail ever since this thing broke. You're a hard guy to get in touch with."

"Oh, sorry about that. I've had so many calls from cranks and the media that I had to shut down my phone and my regular e-mail account. We've been very busy, and I just haven't have time to deal with any of that."

"I understand. Listen, as one of my duties I serve as executive secretary of NEPEC, the National Earthquake Prediction Evaluation Council. The director has asked me to follow developments of your Cascadia prediction and to prepare for a possible council hearing on the matter."

"Oh, yes, I've been expecting to hear from you people about that."

"It's been our practice to not initiate such proceedings until we've received a request from the appropriate authorities, which in this case would be the governors of the affected states. I would imagine that in your case such a request will be forthcoming shortly. I just wanted to meet you personally to give you prior warning so that you can be prepared for such a development."

"Oh, thanks for the heads-up. I'd like to ask you, though, to give us a couple of months to prepare. We're still in the middle of our research, and we need some more time to better establish our case."

"I'll do what I can, but time is limited, and the political pressures are growing on the secretary and the director to get out to the public a clear consensus statement on this issue."

Carl gave him his new phone and e-mail information, and they parted.

The group gathered for lunch at an Italian restaurant off Union Square. It was a giddy affair, everyone still on an adrenaline high from the excitement of the morning. The girls were particularly ecstatic, and a bit frazzled. Their poster presentations had been mobbed, and they had been besieged by reporters plying them with leading questions.

After the meal Carl stood and said, "All right, that worked out fine. I want to thank everybody for a great job. Now, let's get back to the airport. We've got work to do."

December 15

Birkett Valley

The AGU talk received full national media coverage in the following days. The *New York Times,* in addition to a news piece, ran a lengthy article in the *Science Times* section that attempted to describe the science behind the prediction, using graphics derived from the figures Carl had handed out at the press conference. It also contained a number of reactions elicited from leading seismologists, which ranged from cautious to outright skeptical. A *News and Views* article summarizing the theory also appeared in the international science journal *Nature* by the Cambridge seismologist Emily Shifton. She pointed out that the situation was remarkable and highly unusual in that a new scientific theory with major immediate social consequences was now being tested and debated in real time and in full public view.

PBS Newshour ran a lengthy segment, using some similar graphics, as well as video clips from Carl's AGU news conference. It turned out that the TV crew at the AGU meeting had been from KQED, their San Francisco affiliate. They had as their expert commentator Jack Albertine, head of SCEC, the Southern California Earthquake Center, who gave, in Carl's opinion, a very balanced and statesmanlike commentary.

The *Wall Street Journal* featured an article that summarized the various estimations that had been made by engineering groups about the possible financial losses that would result from a magnitude 8.5 to 9.0 earthquake in Cascadia. It quoted figures of 80 to 90 billion dollars worth of direct financial loss, much of it uninsured, and made the point, emphasized by its headline, that this would equal or exceed losses from the hurricanes Katrina in New Orleans or Sandy in New York and New Jersey. It also pointed out that those estimates did not include losses from the subsequent tsunami, which, in the case of the 2011 Tohoku earthquake in Japan, had far exceeded the damage from the earthquake itself. Although in the Cascadia case there were no nuclear power plants, so a Fukushima-type disaster would be averted if a tsunami occurred on the Oregon coast, all the coastal cities and towns would be inundated, producing many casualties and perhaps as many as 50,000 homeless refugees. A tsunami on the Washington coast would be far less destructive, because, except for several sizeable seaside resorts on Willapa Bay and Grays Harbor in the south, the Washington coast is very lightly inhabited, being within several Indian Reservations with no significant coastal communities or resorts.

It was front-page news in Washington and Oregon. The *Oregonian* ran a front-page news article by Joclyn Goodenow and inside a news analysis article by David Kenner that focused on the science and the people behind it. An unsigned editorial written by Bill Lacis focused on the untested nature of the theory behind the prediction. It warned of the potential economic losses that might result from the cloud of uncertainty and doom that this prediction would cast over the entire Pacific Northwest even though, if in the small chance that the prediction were to become true, a magnitude 7.8 or 8 earthquake would affect only a small part of that region. There was also an article in the business section that reported that since the prediction first became publicized there had been a large increase of applications for flood insurance from homeowners within the tsunami inundation areas of coastal communities. It ran, "Insurance companies have been routinely refusing to accept those applications. Harold Ficht, a spokesman from the Oregon Department of Consumer and Business Services, which oversees such matters, stated that under the National Flood Insurance Program homeowners within designated high-risk flooding zones are required to have flood insurance. However, the tsunami inundation zones defined by

DOGAMI cover much more extensive areas than the high-risk flooding zones identified by FEMA, which are areas that are subject to frequent flooding from conventional sources, not including tsunamis. Many homeowners in those broader areas do not have flood insurance, and it is those people who have been recently seeking flood insurance. In a strict interpretation of the NFIP, which does not include tsunami hazards, insurance companies are not required to issue policies for homeowners in the tsunami inundation zones beyond those areas that are already considered high-risk flooding zones. A spokesman for the insurance industry did not return calls regarding this issue."

Margie Yamaguchi and Hamid Salani wrote an op-ed piece in which they described the fragility and lack of resilience of critical infrastructures like power and communications of the city of Portland in the event of a major Cascadia earthquake. Carl continued to be media shy, so Mark became the de facto spokesman for the group, regularly appearing on local TV and radio news and talk shows over the next few days.

Fox News followed the Herman Stackhouse line, which by then was being repeated and amplified on all the conservative outlets. Conservative talk radio shows had been ranting about it for weeks. The Northwest Institute of Advanced Science, a bizarre quack science outfit based at a farm outside of Grants Pass, had posted a pseudoscientific anti-earthquake prediction diatribe on their website.

The message to denigrate and ridicule the prediction was consistently adhered to throughout all the Fox broadcasts, from regular news shows, one of which showed a video clip of a Fox reporter pursuing a flustered and annoyed secretary of the interior just as he was leaving a golf course, to the O'Reilly Factor and the usual Fox gang of snarky sofabound commentators. Jon Stewart mocked them on *The Daily Show*, featuring a doctored film clip of a toga-clad Bill O'Reilly playing the fiddle with background footage of the Japanese tsunami sweeping away a village.

Salem

Chip Salzman, special assistant to Governor Bruce McGinty, sat at his desk fiddling with his pen set as he listened impatiently to a long disquisition by Margie Yamaguchi on the fragility and lack of resilience to earthquake damage of the power, communications, fuel, and transportation lifelines of Portland and adjoining Multnomah County. Her boss, Hamid Salani, sat nervously fidgeting in the other chair facing his desk.

Margie continued, "We had a meeting of our earthquake preparedness committee in early November, not long after the story broke in the *Oregonian*. We focused on the resilience of the systems. It's not very encouraging. The Bonneville Power Authority people estimate their recovery time for restoring power would be from seven to twenty-one days, and that is a best-case scenario. A big problem, even for backup power, is that all the fuel depots for northern Oregon and southern Washington are on landfill sites on the banks of the lower Willamette that are likely to be destroyed by soil liquefaction during the earthquake. We discussed prepositioning backup generators and fuel depots. The people from Bonneville Power and the other utilities are unwilling to make that kind of investment unless there is some sort of emergency declaration from the governor backed up by state and FEMA financial support. What we need is—"

With perfect timing, Chip interjected, "That is not likely to happen. Look, I don't need to remind you that next year is an election year. If the governor pulls out all the stops like you guys want, it'll mean that he's officially endorsing this earthquake prediction, which would be political suicide. He already has the real estate and tourism interests down his throat on this issue. The Tea Party people are also making big noises about it, egged on by that jackass Herman Stackhouse. They would have a field day over it. They've already announced the formation of a new super PAC named—get this—SavingOregonsCoast.org, with a large donation from Harold Lautenbach, head of Pacific Resorts. On the other hand, if the governor does nothing and this earthquake actually happens on his watch, his political career would be down the toilet. The last thing the governor needs is a potential disaster issue like this in an election year. It would completely cloud over everything he's been trying to accomplish for this state. It could become the one big issue in the elections. Help me out here, people."

Hamid cleared his throat. "I have a suggestion. A few days ago I had a call from a man named Alan Askew. He's from the US Geological Survey Headquarters in Reston, Virginia. He told me they have a standing committee called the National Earthquake Prediction Evaluation Council. It was set up particularly to deal with this kind of situation. What they do is hold hearings on the proposed prediction, with expert testimony both for and against. It is presided over by the council, which is composed of a panel of leading scientists, who in the end make a recommendation to the director of the Geological Survey to either approve or disapprove the prediction."

"That sounds like that might be just the ticket," Chip broke in. "How do we get this rolling?"

"The USGS will act upon a request to the director, Catherine Bisquette, from the appropriate authorities, which should be the governors of the affected states, Oregon, Washington, and California."

"OK, I think we can arrange that. How soon can they hold these hearings?"

"He said they would have to give the various parties time to adequately prepare. He thought two months would be about right. That would make it in early February."

"Fine. That's great. That will turn it into a federal matter. That should defang the issue and take the governor off the

148

hook. Whichever way it turns out, the Tea Party people can bitch at the feds, not the governor. I think that's our solution, people."

As he ushered them out the door, Chip said, "Thanks for all your help. And keep up the good work on your emergency preparations. The governor appreciates what a good job you folks are doing."

As they walked down the capitol steps, Margie drily remarked to Hamid, "So much for getting help from the governor."

Corvallis

Virgil P. Henderson, president of the university, sat in a wingback chair in an alcove of his spacious office. Opposite him in the sofa was Arnold Buchanan, chairman of the Board of Trustees of the University Foundation. Virgil's aide had just placed a coffee service on the table between them and retired from the room.

Virgil poured, then took his cup, and settled back in his chair. "So what's on your mind, Arnold? You sounded a bit anxious over the phone."

"It's this earthquake prediction business, Virgil. Several of the trustees are pretty upset about it. It's put an economic damper on a lot of business in this state. There's an old saw that business never likes uncertainty, and you can't get much worse in the uncertainty department than having the threat of an earthquake disaster hanging over your head."

"I can certainly appreciate that, Arnold."

"A lot of important people think that it's all a load of hogwash. What alarms us on the Foundation board, though, is that it has the name of the university associated with it. That gives it a certain amount of credibility. It also tarnishes the good name of the university in the eyes of many of our long-term supporters. I'm thinking about possible future donors here. This couldn't happen at a worse time; we're right in the middle of a major endowment drive. Several of our most generous givers have even threatened to change their allegiance to our sister institution down in Eugene. I might add that a couple of members of the State Board of Higher Education have also mentioned to me their concerns about this issue."

"I see." Henderson leaned forward and put his cup back on the table. "Well, you've certainly gotten my attention. What do you propose I should do about all this?"

"We've had some people look into it. It seems like it's kind of a renegade operation. This fellow Strega, who's the leader, has some sort of oddball position with the university, visiting adjunct professor, whatever that means. The others seem to be junior faculty and students who he recruited and who seem to be working on his project on a volunteer basis. There is evidently no university-administered research grant supporting this work. So it looks like this is not an officially approved university project, yet it seems to be using university facilities, computers, meeting rooms, as well as the university's name. That doesn't seem right to me. Can't the university just disassociate itself with them and order them to cease and desist or kick them off campus?"

"I see your point, Arnold, but it's not as easy as you might think. I have to be careful about matters like this: there are issues of academic freedom and so forth that must be considered. The title Strega holds is a courtesy position. It carries no salary or contract. It merely gives him certain privileges, such as use of the libraries. Some people with those positions also have research grants from external funding agencies that are administered by the university. I don't know about Strega's case. In any event, those positions have no term. They're at the pleasure of the dean, so they can be easily terminated. As far as what other measures can be taken, I'll have to consult with my advisors, legal and academic. I'll keep you informed."

December 19

Corvallis

Mark phoned in the morning and gave Carl the bad news: the university had kicked them off campus.

Carl said, "I'm sorry to hear about that. I'm also really sorry to have put you guys in such a spot."

"Don't worry about us," Mark replied. "Right now we have to figure out what to do. We need to get together and talk about how to proceed. We can't meet on campus any more. I've been talking with Manny, the owner of the Roasting Hut. He has a private meeting room there that he says we can use, so I set up a meeting for this afternoon at one. OK by you?"

Just as Carl hung up, he got a call from Mac telling him that he had a registered letter at the post office. On the way down to Corvallis, he stopped by to pick it up. Mac walked down along the counter, entered the post office cage through a side door, and handed Carl the letter in question through the wicket in front. Carl signed for it, opened it, and scanned through it.

He grunted, "Well, Mac, it seems like I've just been fired by the university."

Mac snickered. "I guess you must have pissed off some important folks with all that foofaraw about earthquakes you been spoutin' about, eh?"

"Maybe so," Carl said, adding dryly, "I wonder how that could have happened?"

In the Roasting Hut, Carl was greeted by a tall, wiry mustachioed man with a hawk nose and eyes to match. "Sir, are you Professor Strega?" When Carl nodded he went on. "Allow me to introduce myself; I am Manuk Bedrossian. They call me Manny. I am the owner of this modest place. I will take you to your friends; they are in the back." He led Carl down the passage in the rear that led to the toilets. He opened a door to the right that revealed a room where the team was already assembled around a large table.

"Pliz," said Manny, ushering him in. "They told me what is going with you and the university. It is my privilege and honor to offer you this place for private discussions." He bowed and left, closing the door behind him.

Carl gave Mark a quizzical look.

"That's Manny." Mark explained, "He's an ethnic Armenian Christian from Tehran. He and his kinfolk had a tough time

153

of it after the mullahs took over in the Islamic Revolution. He managed to get out of Iran with his family intact, but he has bitter memories of it. I think because of that, when he built this place he included this room as a private meeting place for, as he says, people who do not agree with the authorities."

"In Corvallis?"

"Well, I know Corvallis is not exactly a hotspot of radicalism, but various activist groups do use this space. He told me there is even an agnostic AA group that meets here twice a week. When I told him we'd been banned by the university, he was thrilled to have us meet here."

"Agnostic AA? Sounds pretty subversive," Carl remarked drily. "Speaking of which," he said as he sat down, "I just got my letter of dismissal from the dean. I no longer have any official connection with the university nor am I allowed on university property without express permission. How do you like them apples?"

Just then he noticed a newcomer in the corner. "Oh, Shuichi, glad to see you're back from Japan. This is Shuichi Kato, everybody, a colleague of mine from Applied Math. So Shuichi, you've been on leave for a couple of months, so you've missed all the excitement."

"Oh, not at all. I've been reading all about it in the Tokyo newspapers. You guys have been making big news in Japan."

"Is that right? Well, welcome back. You're just in time to find out about our run-in with the campus hierarchy.

So, Mark and José, fill us in about your encounter with the dean."

José gave a disgusted frown. "The first thing this morning, Mark and I were summoned to the Dean's office. The Dean said there were concerns about our participation in the earthquake prediction project. He pointed out that our talks at AGU using university bylines violated regulations concerning the presentation of university-sponsored research without prior approval. When I told him I'd never heard of such a regulation, he showed us some boilerplate documents that listed numerous regulations, and there it was: prior approval is needed for the submission of university-sponsored research for publication or presentation at public meetings."

"He said we had embarrassed the university by connecting it with the earthquake prediction controversy. He then went on to say that we're no longer allowed to pursue our project using university facilities. He was careful to say that we were free to continue our work as a matter of private research but that we couldn't associate the university's name with it. He also said they don't want any students involved in it."

Kiersten blanched at that.

"What do you think brought all this on?"

"I don't think it came from Dean Agusta," Mark said. "He seemed a tad bit apologetic about the whole thing. And this regulation, which I've never heard of before, seems like the sort of pretext some lawyer would come up with. I think the whole thing was handed down to the dean from higher up. Probably from Henderson, our mealymouthed president. Henderson is, when it comes right down to it, a political appointee. Probably somebody on the State Board of Higher Education came down on him about it and he caved. It sounds just like him. He is such a fucking toady."

"So, what to do?"

"Well," Mark said, "we just continue, of course." Everyone agreed with this essential point. They began discussing logistical issues.

Mark continued, "We'll have to be a little careful about not being too obvious about what we're up to. We can meet here. This is fine place; there's even a blackboard," he said, indicating a self-standing unit in the corner. "As far as Kiersten goes, I see no problem with her continuing her work. She has everything on her laptop and in the cloud, and we still have access to all the data from the PNSN and PANGA."

"Anastasia and I will continue the modeling work at night in my computer lab," added José. "If the authorities want to make a beef about that, I'll threaten to take it to the University Senate or to court. I don't think they'll want to make it into a public dispute. The big problem is that our use of the fluid dynamics multiprocessor unit is now out for sure. That is definitely a university facility."

"That presents a big problem. We were counting on that for the next push into 3D modeling."

"What I'm going to do is put out a plea for computer use on a couple of physics web bulletin boards and see if anything turns up that way."

"OK, let's hope that works. Now, let's move on to new work that needs doing. Shuichi, are you interested in joining our little band of outlaws?"

"Certainly. I would be honored to join you."

"Great! Let me explain to everybody. Shuichi is an expert in pattern recognition. Before all this started, Shuichi and I had been collaborating on a project to try to understand the pattern behind the SSE occurrences. It's now become vitally important to solve this problem so that we can narrow down where the next one will happen, which will give us an important refinement of our prediction. So I propose that Kiersten and Mark start working with Shuichi and me on this problem. It turns out that I have a small NSF grant through the university to work on that project. Now that I've been eighty-sixed by the university, I'm going to contact my project manager at NSF and have that grant transferred to Shuichi. Kiersten can then be put on that grant, which will make her legit as far as the university is concerned. José, we can put Anastasia on that grant, too. No sense in you paying her off your grant when she's working on this project. How does that sound?"

There were general murmurs of approval. "OK, fine. That should cover it. Why don't those of you working on the pattern recognition problem stick around, and we'll discuss the nuts and bolts of it."

Just then Kiersten's officemate, Jason, who had been quietly sitting in on the last few meetings, raised his hand.

"Hello, I'm Jason; remember me? A bunch of the grad students have gotten pretty upset about how you people have been treated by the administration. We've been talking about it to some people on the staff of the student newspaper. We think that the actions of the administration are not only a violation of academic freedom but also a deliberate attempt to squelch the university's responsibility to inform the public about a serious danger to society. So we're preparing an article along with an editorial to appear in tomorrow's edition. We're hoping students will get stoked up enough to organize a protest about it." He brought out a camera. "Can I please take a picture of you guys for the article?"

JANUARY 4

Cannon Beach

A winter storm out of the Gulf of Alaska had passed on to the southeast and changed five days of heavy rain into a clearing sky. The morning fog had lifted, the beach was in full sunlight, and the temperature had risen above fifty degrees, promising one of those brilliant winter days known only to full-time residents and the occasional off-season visitor to Cannon Beach. Down on the beach, a few people strolled with their dogs, and in the flats out by Haystack Rock, several clamdiggers dug for their suppers in the muddy sands exposed by the low tide.

Two men sat drinking coffee at a table on the seafront deck of The Breakers Motel. The elder of the two, Mervyn Tomlinson, the motel proprietor, was holding forth in an animated fashion with the much younger man, William

Dekker, an investor who was building a restaurant in the building next to the motel.

"You bet I'm putting up the tsunami evacuation notices in my guest rooms," Mervyn said. "Just because in the last town council meeting they voted down Stanaway's proposal to make it mandatory doesn't make it right. The other motel owners were saying that it'll scare off the tourists, and anyway it isn't practical to have to look after the tourists. The way they look at it is we're only gonna have twenty minutes to get to high ground once the earthquake hits, so it's every man jack for himself. Everybody in town knows the evacuation routes down pat, but there won't be enough time to try to organize a bunch of panicked tourists and herd them to safety. I say that's not right. My father built this motel in 1955, two years before this town was incorporated. Sixty percent of our guests are long-time repeat customers. Some families have been renting our kitchenette units for two weeks every summer for twenty years or more. Raised their families here on the beach. Jim Bloedsoe, who runs the restaurant at *The Vagabond*, was one of those kids. What I'm trying to say is our guests are like family to me. I'll be damned if I'm not going to do everything possible to make them safe if a tsunami comes. And I don't buy the crap that putting the signs in the rooms will scare off the tourists, neither. Hell, we all have to put up fire evacuation signs, and that don't scare nobody off."

"But Mervyn, do you really believe this earthquake scare business? Everybody is saying that it is all some cockamamie theory dreamed up by some loony scientists."

"Who says that? The Tea Party people and that rabble-rouser Stackhouse is all. Hell, they would say anything that serves the big business interests. I'd rather listen to what the scientists say and not take any chances.

"Most of the other business owners in Cannon Beach are Johnny-come-latelies. They've all shown up in the last twenty years or so since the town started to get artsy-craftsy. Now they think they know what's best for the place. But I'm old school—born and raised on the coast. You only really know a place if you've grown up there. I'm old enough to remember the Good Friday tsunami of 1964. That was caused by an earthquake way up in Alaska, so we got some warning of it aforehand. Somebody, Coast Guard, I think, phoned my dad to warn him that a tidal wave was comin'. That's what we called them in those days, tidal waves. So he came and got all us kids out of bed and hustled us, along with the few guests we had at the time, up to the second-story deck. None of us knew what to expect, not even my dad. I remember it was a full moon that night. After a bit we saw the ocean draw back, way back, a mile or more past Haystack Rock. I can remember it as if it happened yesterday. It was so weird, seeing all that sea bottom out there that we'd never seen before, exposed like dry land in the moonlight. Then way off in the distance we could see what looked like a black wall coming. We could see it because the moonlight reflected off the waves breaking on it. It rushed toward us like a superfast high tide. It ran clear up over the beach and broke over this seawall you see right in front of us. I'll never forget it.

"There wasn't much damage in town, just a bit of flooding, but it rushed up Ecola Creek more than a mile and took out the highway bridge. Why, pieces of that bridge were washed 300 yards up the creek. A whole bunch of houses on the north side of the creek were wrecked, taken right off their foundations, moved up the creek, and smashed into kindling. It took out a campground where Les Shirley Park is now. Washed some trailers right up the creek. It almost got the school, too, where I was in the second grade at the time."

"But that was nothing compared to what they say will happen from an earthquake right offshore here. Have you seen the video animation that DOGAMI put out? I'll loan the CD to you. It shows a computer model of what the tsunami here would be like. It'll go right over the top of town in three or four waves. Who knows what would be left after that happens?"

The old man chuckled. "I used to say that the sixty-four tsunami was the best thing to happen to Cannon Beach. See, Highway 101 used to go right through the center of town. After the tsunami took out the bridge and washed out the highway in a couple of places, they decided to rebuild it a half mile inland on higher ground. That's why Cannon Beach is such a nice quiet little place. If the highway still ran through town, instead of the art galleries and high-end restaurants we have now, we'd have a row of gas stations, chain hotels, and fast food joints like every other burg along the coast.

"But now that I've got this new tsunami on my mind, I'm thinking differently. To tell the truth, it's got me plenty worried."

Takonda Cove

Just south of Takonda Head, there is a narrow, unmarked dirt road leading off Highway 101. After a short distance, it ends in a thick forest of Port Orford cedar at a locked gate marked with a no trespassing sign. Michael Stumpf entered the combination, unlocked the gate, and drove his car through, locking the gate behind him. He drove another 400 yards through the forest until the road ended in a small grassy clearing. From there he took a well-used path for another few hundred yards, finally coming out into sunlight on a flat overlooking a beautiful cove. A group of wave-sculpted rocks lay just offshore, upon which a small raft of Steller's sea lions lazed noisily. Below a low sea cliff, a white sand beach curved along the shore. Near the rear of the raised Holocene shoreline terrace was an ancient cabin of hand-hewn logs in a clearing among a grove of windswept shore pines. Smoke rose from the chimney of a massive stone fireplace that formed most of the cabin wall facing him.

Takonda Cove is not marked on any map. The few who venture off the Oregon Coast Trail to take the side trail to Takonda Head would be able to get a glimpse of it from the end of that trail and might wonder how to get to it. A screen of trees would hide the cabin from their view.

As he walked up the steps to the front porch of the cabin, Michael made sure he made a lot of noise, shouting, "Grandpa, it's me. Michael." He rapped heavily on the door several times and then entered. The cabin was snug and tidy. To his left was a huge old cast-iron wood-burning stove beneath a large window that looked out over the cove. Nailed to the wall next to it were shelves made from old wooden fruit crates, still showing their colorful but now faded labels, stocked with provisions. In front of the stove sat a table and two chairs and beyond that a bed in a heavy hand-carved wooden frame. An old man with a flowing beard sat in a large rocking chair beside the fire. He was clothed in gray woolen long johns over which he wore a tattered red plaid Mackinaw jacket. His feet, swathed in heavy woolen socks, were propped on a small footstool that sat upon an oval hooked rug across the plank floor in front of the hearth.

Michael pulled a chair from the other corner and sat down on the opposite side of the fire.

"Grandpa, how are you?" he said in a loud voice. The old man was a bit hard of hearing.

"I'm fine just as always," the old man replied after a moment. "What brings you out here, bub?"

"Just thought I'd stop by and see how you were doing is all."

"You're not going to start telling me about this tidal wave nonsense, are you?"

"Well, actually. As a matter of fact, er, Nancy and—"

"Well, don't bother. That ranger, Rickshaw or whatever is name is, came by a week or so ago. Tried to tell me I oughta get out. Told me a big tidal wave was gonna come and wash away my cabin any day now. I told him I'd like to see the wave that could do that. Told him if it washed away my cabin I'd just as soon go with it. Nothing's gonna get me outta this cabin as long as I'm still breathing."

"Actually, Grandpa, that's probably a good idea, what the ranger said. Nancy and I, we were thinking, maybe you should come and live with us in Eugene for a few months. Just till this tsunami scare is over."

"Listen here, bub, I was born in this here cabin, and I'm ninety-three years old, if'n I ain't lost count. When I settled with the State twenty years ago, I sold them my eight miles of coast, what my daddy left to me, for their goddamn precious state park. Part of the deal was that I could live in this cabin for the rest of my life. And that's what I mean to do. This tidal wave baloney is just another trick to get old man Stumpf out of here so they can take the land. I know those rangers. They're just dying to take this cove as part of their park. They want to let a lot of skinny-dippers and abalone hunters in here to make a mess of the place. Hell, boy, this is the only place on the coast where you can still pull abalone off the rocks at low tide. You know why? Because I'm not lettin' those fools in, that's why. And I'm not gonna let 'em open it up while I'm still alive. That's my final word, so don't you and Nancy worry about it no more."

"But Grandpa…"

"Don't but me, boy. I've been living on this coast all my life, and I plan to die by it. If this big wave comes, I'll be happy to see it. And if it takes me, I'll be happy to go out that way."

Corvallis

Carl was addressing the group in Manny's back room. "Jason tells me that it looks like Henderson was saved by winter break. All the kids went away for the holidays, and the issue is all but forgotten. Too bad—I would have liked to see Henderson squirm a bit for his cowardly intrigues, but student demonstrations wouldn't really have helped us out. But thanks, Jason, just the same. I loved the editorial in student paper. They didn't pull any punches."

"I've got some good news," José interjected. "I got an e-mail this morning offering us time on a multinode parallel processing computer."

"Far out! That is fantastic news, José. Who's our angel?"

"You'd never guess: the SETI Institute."

"Setty, setie, oh SETI; do you mean the search for extra-terrestrial intelligence people?"

"The very ones. Someone put it up to their board, and they decided that who else but them should support people doing politically unpopular high-risk research. They offered us a full two weeks on their biggest machine, together with programming support from their tech staff."

"That is really great news. When do you start?"

"Anastasia is leaving tomorrow for the SETI headquarters in Mountain View, California. Please congratulate her! She just got her driver's license, so for her first driving experience, she's going to pick up a rental car at the San Francisco airport and drive it down the Peninsula to Mountain View." There were cheers. "I have a few teaching obligations to take care of first. After that I'll have my schedule cleared so I can go down on the weekend and stay till the job is done."

Carl rose. "Well, that's a big relief. I have an announcement of my own to make. I've been officially notified by the USGS that NEPEC will hold hearings on our prediction. According to the USGS guy, Alan Askew, the hearing was requested by the governors of Oregon, Washington, and California. How do you like that? They've scheduled the hearings for February fourteenth in Seattle. Valentine's Day—what a date! I haven't yet found out how these things work, but they've requested that we provide them a report that describes the basis for our prediction. They want it by the end of the month, so that doesn't give us much time."

An undercurrent of murmuring ran through the group. "So some writing assignments are in order. I'll handle the body of the report in which the theory is presented and also the summing up. Kiersten, could you please write up your section, and Anastasia, if you have any spare time down in Mountain View, please write up the 2D modeling and, hopefully, any 3D results you will get while you're at SETI.

"Over the holidays Kiersten combined her tremor data set with the GPS data set that Shuichi and I had already assembled. That just about doubles the number of SSEs we have in our database, so Shuichi and I have some confidence that we'll be able to make more sense of it than we were able to earlier. Kiersten and Shuichi are about ready to start running it through his library of pattern recognition algorithms. We're hopeful, but it's still early days. Let's meet in two weeks with a rough draft, and hopefully by then Anastasia and José have some 3D modeling results to show us."

When the meeting adjourned, José told Carl he needed to speak to him privately about a personal matter. They went into the outer room, took coffees, and settled in at one of the rear booths.

"I didn't tell you before," José began, "but a few days ago, my department chairman called me in for a little chat, as he called it. He'd been surprised to see me in that photo of us in the student newspaper. So he called the dean and discussed the situation with him. The main point is that he basically told me that he thought that it wouldn't be good for my career advancement to be associated with this project. He offered his opinion that I'd be wise to discontinue my involvement. I took it as a kind of threat."

"Oh, that's rotten," Carl said with a shake of his head. "So what are you going to do?"

"Of course I am going to continue, but I have to tell you something. For many years my father was a professor at the Institute of Physics in Sao Paulo. When the military regime came to power in 1964, he was no longer allowed to pursue the work he loved. He was forced to work on some military project. He never told me what it was, but I knew that he hated it. He believed it was a waste of time, and worse, it violated his sense of humanity. He lost twenty years of his research life because of that. When the military regime finally ended, he couldn't get back into his former work—he had been too long away from it; the field had moved on, and so had he. He remained very bitter about this till the end of his life. That's the main reason I came to this country. I never wanted this to happen to me, and so I'll never accept such an order from any authority like I just got from my chairman."

"I certainly understand your feelings, and I also think your chairman was completely out of line to make such a demand. But what are you going to do about your visit to SETI?"

"I've been telling people in my department that I am going to Stanford to work with some colleagues there. It's actually true that I have a project with some people down there, and I do plan to spend a couple of days with them once we get the programs compiled and Anastasia is running models at SETI. I'm not worried too much about that. I just felt I had to tell you what's going on with me."

"I thank you for that, José. And let's hope that everything works out and you don't have any problems about this. But what about Anastasia? Is she going to be in hot water, too?"

"No, Anastasia is in the clear. When you switched her to Shuichi's grant, she became part of Applied Math, so as far as my chairman is concerned, she no longer exists."

JANUARY 18

Newport

Angelo Bregas was in an ebullient mood as he and Nestor strolled down the gangway leading to the fishing fleet docks in Yaquina Bay. He was about to take delivery of a saltwater fishing boat. It was an Egg Harbor 43, over thirty years old but in top condition, perfect for the charter fishing business he had been dreaming for years of starting up. He had been born with fishing in his veins, as his papa used to say, proud that his son would continue in the long tradition of Portuguese-American fisherman along this coast. He'd caught his first record-breaking steelhead at age eleven on the upper Chetco and had worked as a Rogue River salmon guide ever since starting out in the trade during his high school summers.

Ever since he and Manuela, his high school sweetheart, had married and started raising a family, they'd been scrimping to save up to buy this boat so he could get into the potentially more prosperous and stable business of salt-water charter fishing. His hometown, Gold Beach, wasn't well established as a charter fishing destination, but he believed he could build it up. There were plenty of salmon to be hooked in the seas off the mouth of the Rogue, and many from his long list of clients had expressed enthusiasm for the prospect of trying those waters. Although river fishermen were generally of a different breed than their saltwater variety, Angelo was confident that there would be plenty of demand for a charter boat service out of Gold Beach.

As they rounded the broad bow of a big tuna troller, they caught sight of the eponymous mop of George 'Red' Finnegan just as he spotted them.

"Hello, fellers; come along on board. Glad to see ya. I was beginning to worry you weren't gonna show. Got cold feet or somethin'."

"No worry, Red. We just got slowed down by some construction on 101 down around Coos Bay. This here is my crewman, Nestor. He'll help me sail *The Sea Dancer* back to Gold Beach."

"Glad ta meetcha, Nestor. Listen, boys, how's about a beer to celebrate?"

He descended to the small cabin, returned with a six-pack and handed them around. "Here's to ya. And here's to many a profitable year ahead for you and *The Sea Dancer*."

They took their beers into the snug cabin, where they settled around the built-in mess table to do the paperwork required to transfer ownership of the boat.

When Angelo handed over the certified check to close the deal, he inquired, "What're your plans now that you've sold your boat, Red?"

"Oh, I'm gettin' out of the charter business. After twenty years of it, I'm fed up with it. Not the fishing, mind you; it's the clients I'm sick and tired of dealing with. You'll see—some of 'em can be a royal pain in the ass. A lot of 'em are more interested in drinking than fishing, so even when they hook a good-sized one, half the time they're too pissed to be able to handle it. They end up losing the fish, getting sore, and then, when you're back on the dock, arguing about the fee. You bet I'm happy to be shed of all that. It's commercial fishing for me now. As soon as you made your deposit, I put a down payment of my own on a salmon troller up in Sitka. It's a fifty-six-foot double-ender. I'll be able to stay out a week with it. Just as soon as I cash your check, I'm off to Sitka to pick her up. The old man who owns her is retiring, and I got a real sweet deal on her."

They shook hands on their deal. Red turned the starter key, and the twin Detroit diesels sprang to life with a muted baritone.

"Let's cast off, and I'll help you get her out of the harbor. Get you familiar with the controls."

As they passed the quay at the harbor mouth, Red leaped ashore with practiced agility. He gave a friendly wave to Angelo and Nestor and watched until the boat, which had for many years been his dearest possession and partner, passed under the Yaquina Bay Bridge and headed out the harbor mouth for the open sea.

Corvallis

Anastasia had pulled down the projection screen at one end of the room and at the other end of the table attached her laptop to a small projector.

"OK, first I show the 2D results. You already saw these before; is just for you to remember. I show the last stages only. Here you see the SSE propagating along. Then it becomes the period-doubling phase, with the second horn appearing, and then finally it makes the nucleation stage at the end. OK. Now I show a video animation of the same thing in 3D version. This first one is at constant speed." She put up the next figure, which was a black video screen with a run arrow, and clicked on it.

They saw, depicted in color contour plots, the development of the slow slip event as it propagated from left to right on the screen. Then suddenly a bulbous growth appeared in the center, zipped off in both directions, and then seemed to explode off the top of the screen.

There was an uproar from the audience. "Whoa! Wow! What was that? Show it again!"

She ran it again. They still couldn't follow it.

"OK, this time I slow down the last part." This video showed the SSE inching along almost imperceptibly, time-step by time-step. Then, like a desert plant blooming in time-lapse photography, the slip grew like a petal from the center of the image and spread rapidly out to the left and the right. Then it suddenly flashed from right to left, and the entire upper screen exploded in slip colors. She ran it again. "So what you see is that the second horn of the SSE in this stage becomes, so to speak, one and the same as the nucleation. It starts somewhere in the middle and propagates bilaterally at about ten times the usual SSE speed. When it reaches the critical nucleation length, it propagates dynamically back at the shear wave velocity. That last flash is the earthquake. That part we cannot resolve with our present method."

There were cheers and applause from the small audience. Anastasia beamed.

"Spectacular!" Carl called out. "Fantastic results! We could never have guessed that it works that way. But it *is* beautiful. Having seen it, I can now see that this has to be the way it works. Yes! What are your time and length scales, Anastasia?"

"It is dimensionless scale. But if we put in, shall we say, reasonable values for parameters, we get for the nucleation propagation speed about 100, 200 kilometers per day. For the nucleation length, we get 100 or 200 kilometers. So the length of the nucleation stage is one or two days."

"So that means," said Carl, "that when we see the onset of nucleation, we'll know the earthquake will follow in one or two days. That'll allow us to make a short-term prediction. Good work, you guys."

◆　◆　◆

As the meeting broke up, David, who had been sitting in the back taking notes, waved to Carl as he rose to leave the room. "Can I have a minute, please?"

Carl took a seat opposite him. "Sure, what's on your mind?"

"You guys are naturally enough focusing all your attention to predicting this earthquake, but I wonder if you would comment on the broader implications of your work."

"I don't think I quite follow you."

"I mean, what happens after? What happens after this August, when the earthquake does or doesn't happen?"

"Well, if it doesn't happen, we have to wait for another two SSE cycles to see if it happens during one of them. There's that possibility. If that fails we're back to square one. We either figure out what went wrong with our theory or we chuck it altogether. End of story."

"And if it succeeds?"

"Oh, well, then we would have hit the jackpot. If it succeeds it means we've verified a method to predict earthquakes. It can then be used to predict future earthquakes elsewhere."

"Oh, so you mean you think the method is general? I mean, it's not specific to this particular circumstance?"

"I don't see anything specific about it. All subduction zones that have been monitored by GPS have so far exhibited SSEs, so I should think that they all behave pretty much the same way as Cascadia. So to predict large earthquakes on them would require monitoring with a network of GPS receivers in order to detect the onset of period doubling. And this should work not only with subduction zones, but in other settings as well. SSEs have been observed beneath the San Andreas Fault, too, so it looks like crustal faults behave in much the same way."

"Wow! You mean all major earthquakes could be predictable?"

"I wouldn't say that, exactly. On major plate boundary faults like the San Andreas, and on some subduction zones, perhaps yes. They can be recognized as major threats. and the expense of monitoring them can be justified. But that leaves plenty of small minor, slow-moving faults, which are often not recognized as being threats but are still capable of producing catastrophic earthquakes. Maybe you remember the earthquakes that devastated Christchurch, New Zealand, in 2010 and 2011? Those occurred on slow-moving faults that were hidden beneath the sediments of the Canterbury Plain and had not been previously recognized by geologists. Those earthquakes weren't that big, 7.1 and 6.3, but they occurred very near and just beneath the city, and so they were very damaging. We wouldn't be able to apply our method to those kinds of earthquakes."

"But just the same, to be able to predict even some earthquake is an enormous development—revolutionary, even. So there's an awful lot riding on this 'experiment,' as you call it."

"There certainly is, David. There most certainly is."

"Won't you be thrilled if it actually works out?"

"I will be astonished, but at the same time, not surprised."

FEBRUARY 14

Seattle

The NEPEC hearing was being held in a small lecture theater on the University of Washington campus. Carl's group arrived early, and having successfully worked their way through the ruck of demonstrators picketing the entrance to the hall, encamped near the end of the front row of seats. Carl went along to greet the NEPEC council members, who occupied the center seats. Most of the members of the council were well-known to him. Seven of them were prominent academics, the other five equally prominent USGS scientists. They were accompanied by Alan Askew and two other USGS staffers, who were handling matters such as the video recording of the proceedings. He also introduced himself to the other scheduled speakers.

The audience began trickling in. Gradually the flow of arrivals increased, and the small hall began to fill. The seats near the front and center seemed to be largely occupied by the press. Carl recognized several faces from the AGU press conference. There were also several Japanese among the passel of reporters. Carl recalled Shuichi's remark that their doings had been making big news in Japan. In contrast to America, where massively destructive earthquakes and tsunamis are considered by most of the public as things that happen only in distant primitive lands to be secretly enjoyed as vicarious terrors on the evening TV news, in Japan earthquakes are thought of as an existential threat and are treated by the press with appropriate gravity.

Carl also noticed David and the owl lady sitting together among the press corps. Herman seemed to be absent. Carl supposed that he must be allergic to science.

Margie Yamaguchi and her friend Jackie Ahrens of the Portland Bureau of Emergency Management filed in and found seats near the front next to their Washington colleagues Ron Stickles and Sue Garland. Jackie was telling them about her efforts to get Portlanders to assign a closet at home for emergency earthquake supplies.

"It's a standard thing in Japan. Every Japanese household has a store of emergency water, food, medicine, and things like lanterns for use in case of earthquakes. We've had this in our brochures for ages, but now I'm making a push for people to really do it. I managed to convince

Fred Meyer Stores to create special 'earthquake supplies' sections in their supermarkets, and Coleman is actually going to advertise an 'earthquake special' on their propane lanterns."

"Super," Sue replied. "I hope it works. "We should do the same thing in Seattle. People tend to be so complacent about such things. I should talk. I've been meaning for ages to set up an emergency supply at home and have never gotten around to it."

Tom Mitkins and Nick Singletree slid into the row behind them. Tom was head of the USGS Pacific Northwest Earthquake Team in Seattle, and Nick ran the Seismological Laboratory at the University of Washington, so they were both keenly interested in the day's proceedings. They had each brought fresh notebooks and cracked them open for the occasion.

The audience buzz died off when the NEPEC chairman, Professor Maarten van Duijn, from Harvard, climbed the steps to the podium and rapped on the mike a few times.

"Welcome, everyone. Welcome to this special session of the National Earthquake Prediction Evaluation Council. My name is Maarten van Duijn, and I am the chairman of the council. Let me first give you some background about the council and its work. The council was formed as part of the Earthquake Hazards Reduction Act of 1977. Its purpose is to provide advice and recommendations to the director of the Geological Survey on earthquake predictions and related matters pursuant to the director's delegated responsibility under the Stafford Act to issue timely warnings of potential geological disasters.

"Today we are meeting to evaluate the prediction issued by Professor Strega and his research group of a large earthquake specified to occur in the Cascadia Subduction Zone in August of this year. These hearings are being held at the request of the governors of Oregon, Washington, and California. I am pleased to welcome their representatives to this meeting." He gestured to a small group of men and women in suits at the left front of the auditorium.

"The agenda for today's meeting is up on the screen. We begin with a presentation by Professor Strega of his group's findings and their argument for the basis on which they are making the proposed prediction. That will be followed by testimony from a number of experts, who will offer differing perspectives on the strengths and weaknesses of the Strega prediction. At the end of the public hearings, Professor Strega, as agreed in negotiations with myself, will be offered a period of time to reply and rebut any criticisms that may have arisen in the previous discussions regarding his group's prediction. Following the public part of these hearings, the council will meet in private session to deliberate on the recommendations it will make to the director.

"I need to mention a few guidelines. Questions may be directed to the speakers only by members of the council. There will be no questions taken from the audience. No photographs or other recordings may be made during the presentations. The proceedings are being recorded by video, and the complete videotapes will be available to members of the press and to the public in a timely manner. And of course, everyone, please turn off your cell phones and other electronic devices. Now I am pleased to introduce Professor Strega."

Carl went to the lectern and thanked the council for allowing this opportunity to present the findings of his group. His presentation followed the structure of his AGU talk, but because in this instance he had a full hour allotted, he went into more depth on the background of the theory on which their predictions were made and also on the philosophy and spirit underlying their thinking. He pitched it both at a level technical enough to satisfy the several members of the council who were experts on such matters but also on a level that could be followed by the more general audience, which included the other council members. He began by discussing the rate and state variable friction laws that are the backbone of modern earthquake physics. These laws were first discovered by laboratory experiments on rock friction. When applied to earthquakes, these laws explain not only the occurrence of earthquakes per se but also the whole gamut of earthquake phenomena. They explain why earthquakes occur in sequences in which foreshocks are an incidental phenomenon but aftershocks have a well-defined statistical structure. They explain the now well-known fact that earthquakes can trigger one another at a distance and with delay times much longer than the transmission times of seismic waves. He pointed out that they explain why some subduction zones produce great earthquakes while others slide along quietly. Then, while showing the slides of the slow slip events in Cascadia, he explained how the friction laws predict this phenomenon and how such behavior could be interpreted through them.

He described how he had serendipitously discovered the period doubling, and he described his first inklings, following from his initial interpretation of it in light of the friction laws, of the dire consequences of that observation. The subsequent testing of that hypothesis, with Kiersten's work showing that the period of the SSE cycle was increasing with time, validated the theory he was using. At this point he made a small digression, anticipating one of the later speakers, in pointing out that there were several versions of the friction laws current but that the form they were using was the only one that was consistent with the observations they were dealing with.

The next question, he continued, was how imminent the earthquake was. He explained that with nonlinear systems one could not solve such a problem analytically: one could only run computer simulations to test various possibilities. He described the 2D modeling and the results that the probability was about 80 percent that the earthquake would occur during the next SSE event, which would be in the coming August. Then he revealed the 3D modeling results that Anastasia had obtained at SETI. He showed them in the same sequence as Anastasia had, first in constant time steps, then in slow motion for the final nucleation phase. He noticed out of the corner of his eye that most of the council expressed a startled reaction similar to what the group had felt when they saw them for the first time.

He summarized, "So to us the observations predict certain things. The size of the event will be at a minimum magnitude of 7.8 to 8.0. It might be larger, but the final size of the earthquake is undeterminable by our methods. We know it will be somewhere in the Cascadia Subduction Zone, but we will not know its location more precisely until the next SSE begins, which will give an alert window of a week or two. We are presently trying to decipher the pattern of SSE occurrences from the past record. If we are successful with this, then a medium-term alert with a more specific location can be given at that time. The nucleation phase, as shown in our modeling, should be easily detectable by the continuous GPS measurements that are being made at many sites in the Pacific Northwest. That will provide a short-term warning with a lead time of one or two days and an even more precise indication of the location of the earthquake. So we believe that the scenario we have developed provides a workable road map for emergency precautions that could result in a significant reduction of potential losses of life and property should the earthquake and subsequent tsunami occur as expected."

He thanked the council and the audience and asked for questions.

Daniel Rubenstone, a council member from USGS Menlo Park, asked a question regarding the computational methods used in the 3D modeling. Carl deferred the question to Anastasia, who rose and answered it in such technical detail that probably no one but herself, José, and Rubenstone fully understood what she was talking about. There were no more questions, and Carl returned to his seat. He was disturbed by the lack of questions. He had expected to take a real grilling from the council. Were they so convinced by his presentation or, as he suspected with dismay, simply not taking it seriously?

Hugh Duckworth was the next speaker. He began by describing the Holocene history of great earthquakes on the Cascadia plate margin as determined by the study of paleo-tsunami deposits. Two methodologies were used. Along the coast certain bays and estuaries were faithful recorders of earthquakes and tsunamis. The earthquake itself would cause a sudden drop of the land level of several meters that would result in drowned coastal lowland forests and marshlands. Those strata were overlain by poorly sorted gravels and other debris that were washed in by the subsequent tsunami. In the walls of deep-sea canyons leading to the oceanic trench, turbidite deposits recorded undersea landslides triggered by the earthquake shaking. Both types of events could be dated with radiocarbon age dating and other methods. These characteristic sedimentary sequences could then be correlated at various sites up and down the coast to give an estimate of the date and length of each earthquake rupture. He showed a space-time plot of the prehistoric earthquake tsunamis through the Holocene, the most recent 10,000 years of Earth history. The most common type was the magnitude 9 earthquakes that rupture the entire plate boundary between Vancouver Island and Cape Mendocino, California. There had been nineteen of those in the past 10,000 years, the most recent being the earthquake and tsunami of 1700.

"This is the origin of the 530-year recurrence time that is frequently quoted in the media." He warned that this number was misleading. "The sequence is quite aperiodic. There have been periods of several thousand years when the recurrence time has been only about 230 years, separated by quiescent periods of up to a thousand years." He put up a map showing the rupture zones of other great earthquakes that had occurred along the Cascadia plate boundary. "In addition, there have been other great earthquakes, as shown in this slide, which rupture only a portion of the plate boundary. Four of those ruptured from Willapa Bay, in southern Washington, south to Cape Mendocino. Those would have been about magnitude 8.8. Another ten events, of about magnitude 8.6, ruptured south from near Lincoln

City, Oregon, and another ten, estimated at about magnitude 8.4, were confined to the region south of Coos Bay."

He then directed himself to the topic at hand. "The spacing between our observation points is 50 to 150 kilometers, which we believe gives us a complete record of earthquakes down to magnitude 8.0 and perhaps as low as 7.8. We've never observed an earthquake that small. It seems to us, therefore, that the minimum-size earthquake specified by the Strega group greatly underestimates the size of any earthquake that is likely to occur. If we take this a bit further and suppose that the length of the Cascadia earthquakes are controlled by some sort of physical barriers on the plate interface, then we might conclude that the rupture segmentation shown by the prehistoric record is a permanent feature. That would allow us to guess the size of the earthquake from the place where it initiated. If it nucleated north of Willapa Bay, it could only be the full size magnitude 9. If it started between Willapa Bay and Lincoln City, it could be either a magnitude 9 or an 8.8 type, and so forth." He put up a diagram showing the various possibilities. This was all new to Carl, who feverishly took notes, cursing himself for not having spoken to Hugh before the hearing.

The next speaker was Dick Johnson from the University of California, Irvine. He was someone who fancied himself the scourge of earthquake prediction. For many years he had been analyzing seismicity catalogs with various statistical tests that invariably found that earthquakes were random events and hence unpredictable. He liked to trot out, erroneously in Carl's opinion, the fashionable theory of self-organized criticality to dress up his rather pedestrian results. As he droned on in his characteristically pompous style to fill his allotted hour, Carl, none too surreptitiously, dozed off.

The group took lunch in a nearby student cafeteria. They noticed various other people there from the hearings, so they took a table in a far corner. They were talking about Duckworth's segmentation idea, which had been the surprise of the morning.

Carl leaned over and said, "Did you know about this, Mark?"

"No, the first I've heard about it was this morning. It's so like Hugh to keep something like this under his hat. I imagine that he's been thinking about it for quite a while. He's a very cautious guy. He hates talking about what if scenarios. This is probably the first time he had the right opportunity to bring it up."

The speaker after lunch was Michael Edgerton from Chicago. He gave a long, somewhat pedantic disquisition on the various forms of the rate and state variable friction laws and their behavior in terms of simulating slow slip events. While he didn't directly criticize the particular form that Carl was using or its application, he made it clear that he, the dean of earthquake mechanics theory, was having none of it.

The last scheduled speaker was Luc Beaudreau, a young Frenchman from École Normale Supérieure, Paris. He was the wild card on the program. Carl didn't know him, and when he had e-mailed him prior to the meeting in an attempt to find out what he would be speaking about, he had gotten no reply. That had set off warning bells.

Beaudreau had developed a computer model of earthquakes that he had applied to the Cascadia Subduction Zone by trying to fit it to Duckworth's earthquake history. It soon became clear that he had developed this model specifically with the goal of refuting the Strega prediction. The point, which he aggressively made, was that there had not been enough time since 1700 for the stresses to have built up enough so that an earthquake was possible. Carl was not impressed. The kind of model he was using had enough free parameters that it could be used to fit just about anything and to predict just about anything as well. It was an example of the old maxim about computer models, GIGO: garbage in, garbage out. Nonetheless, his testimony was quite damaging, and Carl knew that he couldn't combat it by merely scoffing at it.

After a five-minute recess, Carl went to the podium for his rebuttal.

"It's been a long session, ladies and gentlemen. Let me try to sum up. Professor Johnson mentioned self-organized criticality. If this theory applies to earthquakes, it is a global theory. It says that for a large enough region, say the entire earth, there is always some spot that is at the critical point and ready to have an earthquake. But as the former Speaker of the House, Tip O'Neill, used to say about politics, earthquake prediction is always local." That got a few isolated chuckles from the audience.

"Locally, earthquakes on a given fault obey a cycle in which the stress is relaxed during an earthquake, followed by a period of quiescence while the stress builds up enough for the next earthquake to occur. Dr. Beaudreau brought up this point, and I'll return to it later. Earthquakes are not statistical points in a catalog but physical phenomena. The prediction we have made is not based on a statistical calculation of probabilities but on a deterministic theory. We have made a case that the phenomenon that we have observed is precursory—that it foreshadows a coming earthquake. The predictions that we made in terms of the location, size, and time of the coming earthquake are, by the very nature of the physical process, presently vague, but vague in a well-defined way. We have shown how those predictions will be progressively improved as the time before the predicted event shortens. Professor Duckworth has described a method by which we will be able to predict the size of that earthquake with much more precision than I indicated in my earlier talk. Furthermore, he showed why our minimum estimate of the earthquake size probably underestimates the expected size, which should be at least magnitude 8.4 and possibly much larger.

"We agree with Professor Edgerton that there are several versions of the rate-state variable friction laws and that these give different predictions of the behavior of slow slip events and their connection with the earthquake cycle. However, as I was at some pains to point out in my talk, the particular version we use was selected on the basis of the observations we have of Cascadia and was validated by further testing.

"Now let me address the model of Beaudreau. It is based on a failure criterion in which the earthquake occurs when the stress on the locked part of the subduction interface reaches a critical value. That is the crux of his argument against our theory. The model he uses is called the time-predictable model, and it has had a poor track record when applied to places where we have a long earthquake history. The main problem with it is that for an earthquake to initiate, it is only necessary for the stress to be at the critical level at a single place, the nucleation point. After the earthquake initiates, the stress concentration associated with the tip of the rupture front is sufficient to cause the earthquake to propagate into regions where the stress is lower. Given that the stress distribution on the interface is likely to be very heterogeneous, it's no wonder that the time-predictable model doesn't work very well. The important point here, though, is that Beaudreau misunderstands our model at a very basic level. What we are saying, contrary to conventional thinking, is that the earthquake doesn't initiate when a critical point is reached within the locked zone, but instead when the transitional zone, the region of slow slip events, goes unstable. The physics of the two are entirely different. In our scheme the locked zone does not have to be critically loaded for the earthquake to occur. In fact, we would argue that this is probably the main reason why earthquake recurrence models, such as the time-predictable model used by Dr. Beaudreau, work so poorly."

He pushed a key on the laptop on the table in front of him, and a slide appeared on the screen. "I have one last slide. This shows the record of tsunamis in Grays Harbor, Washington, over the last 4,000 years. The most recent was the event of 1700. That was preceded by 700 years of quiescence, which was immediately preceded by three great tsunami events separated by intervals of 200 to 300 years. Preceding that cluster of activity was another long quiet period, this time of 900 years, which again was preceded by a cluster of three events in relatively close juxtaposition in time. Unfortunately, neither the model of Beaudreau nor our model can explain this clustering of the earthquakes. Therefore, we have no way of knowing, from first principles, whether the 1700 earthquake is the first in a cluster of earthquakes with intervals of 300 years or so—which would mean the second is just in the offing—or whether, for some unknown reason, it is an isolated earthquake, a singleton.

What our argument has been, coming from an entirely different direction, is that it appears that the first of these possibilities is the correct one.

"Let me now address a few final comments to the council. As I understand it, your mandate is to find upon the scientific merits of this earthquake prediction as it has been presented to you. An important point in your deliberations will be that we are using, in this prediction, a novel and untested theory. In fact, whether the earthquake occurs as specified or not *is* the test of the theory. If the consequences were not of such a catastrophic nature to society, we would simply let this natural experiment take its course and see how the theory fared. But we don't have that luxury, which is why we find ourselves in this room today, debating this issue in a public forum.

"Finally, in considering the value of an earthquake prediction it is hard not to think in terms of a cost-benefit analysis. The cost of a prediction, regardless of whether it should prove to be true or false, has, in this case, been much ballyhooed in some segments of the news media and blogosphere. The possible benefits of such a prediction, should it prove to be true, have not been similarly discussed. Such benefits are difficult to estimate, and in any case their value is probably self-evident to most people. I'll not attempt to go into this here. My point to the council is that such issues are not within your purview. It's your job to make recommendations based only on the scientific merits. Costs and benefits and scientific credibility are entirely separate issues. Such social costs and benefits are not the concern of the council but of the director of the Geological Survey and the people whom she chooses to consult. Thank you for your patience, ladies and gentlemen."

Carl stepped down from the podium, and the chairman, Maarten van Duijn, took his place.

"The public segment of these hearings is now concluded. I would like to thank all the speakers for their participation in what has been a fruitful discussion. The council will now meet in private session to discuss the issues with the goal of coming to a consensus recommendation. We will meet back here at six o'clock, when we will announce our findings. The meeting is adjourned until then."

◆　◆　◆

The audience quieted as the council members emerged from behind the stage and took their places at a table that had been placed at the center of the proscenium. The chairman rose and proceeded to read from a written statement.

"The council has met and thoroughly considered all the points made during today's hearings. The council members also benefited from written reports that had been earlier submitted by all the participants and which have been carefully studied. We have also given due consideration to other communications that have been addressed to the council during our period of preparation for these hearings. These have been from members of the scientific community expressing their opinions on the scientific merits of the proposed prediction, as well as from other parties who have expressed their concerns regarding possible impacts of the outcome of our deliberations.

"We wish to express our appreciation of the seriousness of the hypothesis brought before us by the Strega group. We find the theory that they have presented to be intriguing and worthy of our utmost attention. It represents thinking that is well outside the mainstream of current understanding in the field of earthquake mechanics. In this sense it is salutary work. As a foundation for public policy, however, we find it less than compelling. We are applying a standard here that is higher than what would be used, say, in considering whether a paper is suitable for publication in a scientific journal. We are considering whether or not to recommend to the director of the Geological Survey to approve this prediction as a matter of official US government policy and to advise the public accordingly. The consensus opinion of the council is that the Strega prediction does not meet this standard. Therefore we are recommending that the director disapprove this proposed prediction."

Carl let out a burst of air from between pursed lips. He and the rest of his group silently filed out of the room with the rest of the audience. In the foyer they were met by a small mob of reporters. Foremost among them were a Japanese man wielding a large shoulder-mounted Sony video camera paired with another proffering a fuzzy microphone at Carl.

"We are NHK Japanese TV," the microphone poker said. "The Japanese people have been urgently following these developments for many months. Please, Professor Strega, will you give our Japanese viewers your reaction to today's decision?"

Carl looked into the camera, shrugged, and said, "*Shoganai.*" Then he joined the others and left the auditorium.

Birkett Valley

Carl took the evening flight to Eugene and was home by 11:00 p.m. He sat down in the living room with Sally and over a bottle of wine related to her the day's events.

He gave her a disgusted, forlorn look. "I feel like chucking it all. I never should have started this whole business in the first place."

"It's a little late in the day for that, Carl."

"I know, I know. I've been thinking about it the whole way back on the plane. I mean, what was I thinking? How could I have had such conceit, such hubris, to think that I, and only I, knew what the earth is going to do at some point in the future? Those people on the NEPEC panel are no idiots. They know that we scientists don't really know jack about earthquakes. Shit, it seems like every big new earthquake that comes along shows some new wrinkle that screws up a few of our old pet preconceptions. Then we revise our theories accordingly and say, 'Oh, now we understand,' only to have to change them again the next time. So who am I to now stand up and say, 'Aha, this time I *really do* know what's going to happen'? When I think about it that way, my arguments seem pretty pathetic. Mother Nature is a wily old bird; she makes fools of people like me all the time."

"Stop with the self-pity, Carl. You had to say what you believed. Look at those Italian scientists—they ended up in prison for failing to warn the people about that earthquake."

"Oh, yeah, the L'Aquila Seven. That was a pretty sorry affair."

"Why so? Their mistake was to tell the people there was nothing to worry about. That was the very crime that Voltaire decried, regarding the Lisbon disaster of 1755, 'Deluded philosophers who cry, "All is well," hasten, contemplate these frightful ruins.' That disaster was also an earthquake and tsunami, wasn't it?"

"It was indeed. You never fail to surprise me with the things you come up with, Sally. I guess it's that classical education of yours. I used to think that it was a waste of time reading all those old books, but the longer I live with you, the more I think that I've missed out on something important.

"But you mistake me about L'Aquila. I think the people there had a real beef with the authorities. The L'Aquila story serves as an object lesson in how not to go about such things. L'Aquila is the capital of the Abruzzo, the highest and most tectonically active part of the Apennines. It sits astride a series of active faults and had been destroyed by earthquakes in the fifteenth and eighteen centuries. So it was about due. The local people were quite aware of the earthquake hazard and of the danger of being caught within a building during an earthquake. The old town is full of medieval stone buildings that are susceptible to collapse when subjected to seismic shaking. The local custom was that whenever earthquakes were felt, the people would spend the night camped out in the piazzas of the city to avoid being trapped in collapsing buildings.

"In the spring of 2009, a swarm of small earthquake had been shaking L'Aquila for several months, and the local populace was in a state of near panic. To make matters worse, a local amateur had been professing to predict earthquakes based on radon emissions from wells.

"In response to the growing uproar, the authorities decided to convene a meeting of a commission of experts, the Italian equivalent of NEPEC, in L'Aquila, a meeting that would have fateful consequences. Several scientists on the panel later admitted that their assumed role was to discredit the self-proclaimed predictor and calm down the local populace. They failed to discuss the enhanced risk indicated by the swarm, the hazard imposed by the fragility of the buildings, or any actions that should be undertaken. That was one problem. But the main problem occurred at a press conference, broadcast on Italian television, which was held just after the meeting by two members of the commission along with local officials. There, in front of the cameras, one member of the commission—who was not a seismologist, by the way—assured the people that the situation was normal and posed no danger. Then, to gild the lily, he made the patently false statement that the small earthquakes serve as a safety valve to release the energy and reduce the danger of a big one. He then flippantly suggested that people should relax and enjoy a nice glass of the local wine.

"Six days later, at eleven o'clock in the evening, a magnitude 3.9 rattled the city and startled the already terrified residents. Many of them debated leaving their homes for the piazzas but decided against it based on the assurances of the scientific panel. At three o'clock the next morning, a magnitude 6.3 destroyed the center of the city, killing 300 people. Only the old people, who follow the traditions religiously, stayed outside that night and were spared."

"So what are you whining about, Carl? That goes to show that even if your prediction ends up being wrong, you're doing the right thing."

"You're right, Sally, as usual. It's such a fucked-up situation, though. I'll be damned if I'm right and damned if I'm wrong. But, so it goes. Damn the snarkedos; full speed ahead!"

FEBRUARY 19

Birkett Valley

The NEPEC decision was widely covered by the local and national media. *The Oregonian* featured it in a front-page article in which they quoted a statement issued by Governor McGinty: "Now that we are out from under this cloud of gloom and doom, business can go back to normal in the state of Oregon. We are prepared to welcome visitors who should have no concern for their welfare while enjoying the many attractions of our fair state." He also went on to say that he had full confidence in the preparedness measures taken by the Oregon Department of Emergency Management for any real natural disasters that might occur.

The Oregonian also ran an editorial by Bill Lacis. In it he congratulated the USGS and NEPEC on their responsible actions in ending the controversy over the so-called

Cascadia earthquake prediction. He castigated Carl Strega and his group (the latter whom he referred to as "well-meaning dupes") for creating unwarranted panic among the citizenry and potentially great losses to businesses statewide. Among other things, he called their actions "scientific speculations run wild."

Joclyn Goodenow, who was the only reporter from the *Oregonian* to have attended the NEPEC hearings, had another take on the matter, which she confined to posting on her blog. Under the heading "The Cascadia Earthquakes: Which Experts to Believe?" she wrote, "The hearings in Seattle yesterday by the National Earthquake Prediction Evaluation Council on the Cascadia earthquake prediction had all the trappings of a star chamber. This panel of experts, selected by the USGS, was convened to judge upon the scientific findings of a small group of scientists, led by Carl Strega, that had led them to predict that a large earthquake might occur off the coast of the Pacific Northwest next August. However, there was little in the way of real probing into the veracity of the science behind that claim.

"The hearings began with testimony by Strega that laid out his group's findings and the basis behind their prediction. This was followed by presentations by a number of other experts. Those witnesses for the most part skirted around the actual issue of the prediction. Only one of those, Luc Beaudreau, from Paris, offered a direct challenge to the theory behind the prediction. In a rebuttal Strega seemed to easily parry Beaudreau's attack. During the proceedings there was a complete absence of cross-examination by council members of Strega or any of the other speakers.

"In his summary statement, Strega warned the council that their mandate was limited to finding upon the scientific merits of the case, and they should not to be concerned with the broader social implications of predicting an earthquake. A check on the NEPEC web page confirms this statement. However, in his statement justifying the council's rejection of the Strega prediction, Council Chairman Maarten van Duijn of Harvard said that while the Strega theory may meet the standards of publication in a scientific journal, it did not meet the higher standards for setting public policy. This clearly exceeds the remit of the council in just the way that Strega had warned. The standard for publication in a scientific journal is the way science is judged. Any higher standard must involve other issues of a nonscientific nature.

"I am not a seismologist and therefore not capable of judging the scientific merits of this case. However, as an interested onlooker, I believe that in yesterday's hearings I witnessed the scientific establishment slapping down a brilliant and innovative group of upstarts for reasons that are all too common in public discourse: to maintain the status quo. The status quo in this case may mean doing nothing in the face of impending disaster. That is the government's position. Individuals at risk need to decide for themselves.

To those inclined to buy the council's decision, I say, caveat emptor."

Herman Stackhouse posted a blog gloating about the NEPEC decision, calling it the St. Valentine's Day massacre. At one point he claimed that the government had validated what he, Herman Stackhouse, had been claiming all along, which made Carl wince and then chuckle over the fustian irony of the statement.

Fox News had a field day, showing the group photo from the student newspaper, referring to them as a "group of feckless scientists" and comparing the Cascadia prediction with the "cold fusion in a jar" episode as the latest example of science gone awry.

In a furious mood, Carl stormed around the house all morning. He came into Sally's studio looking angry enough to want to kick the cat. The potential target of his wrath gazed disdainfully up at him from the floor cushion where she was having her morning nap.

Sally, in an attempt to mollify him, put her arm around his waist and said, "My poor Cassandra, are we in a grumpy mood?"

That forced a wry grin from him. "Well, it is pretty damned annoying, you have to admit. What is really galling is all the cackling from Stackhouse and his gaggle of yammering yahoos."

"Bite your tongue, Carl; you may be speaking about some of our neighbors."

"This business has really gotten my back up. Sick as it sounds, it's actually started me wishing that the damned earthquake happens just to show the bastards."

"The gods are deaf to hot and peevish vows."

"What!?"

"Sorry, dear; I've still got Cassandra on the brain. That's one of her lines from *Troilus and Cressida*."

Portland

Margie Yamaguchi and Jackie Ahrens were having lunch at a Japanese restaurant in the Pearl District. They were discussing the NEPEC hearings and its repercussions.

Margie was saying, "I have to admit I don't understand the science all that well, but I found the story fascinating. And believable, too, you know. I think those people are serious scientists, not a bunch of kooks like some people are making out. It's a shame how Fox News portrayed it as being some kind of scientific hoax."

"What do you think about the NEPEC decision?"

"That was what I totally expected. It's the kind of decision you always get from a committee that's supposed to come to some conclusion about an uncomfortable topic. Believe you me, I've served on enough of them. There's such a pressure for consensus on committees like that. A group consciousness always makes itself felt early on so that conflicting opinions, if they appear at all, are apt to be so weakly expressed that they get easily swept under the rug. No boat rocking allowed. So after a lot of yada yada yada to satisfy everyone that the topic has been sufficiently aired, with an appropriate display of fairness and with everybody putting in their two bits' worth, the committee eventually arrives at the foregone conclusion. Afterward you think, 'what a colossal waste of time that was!' It sucks, really."

"I've been on some of those myself. So what happens now?"

"Well, as far as I'm concerned, it's over. Yesterday my boss told me that I'm not to work on preparedness for this earthquake any longer. He said that the order came down from above, implying the governor's office."

"I'm in the same boat. I'm told to work on other projects. My boss told me not to do anything that, quote, 'might increase public anxiety over this affair,' end quote. And of course, Fred Meyer Stores and Coleman canceled their promotions.

"So what are we supposed to do, spend the next six months twiddling our thumbs while all hell may be getting ready to break out? I can't tell you how uncomfortable I am about all this. My conscience tells me to do something about it. My job tells me to do something about it. But I'm paralyzed."

Seaside

Rick Ostreim was just wrapping up his report to the Emergency Planning Committee. "We're on schedule with the plan to erect and stock emergency supply sheds at three strategic locations at the assembly points of our tsunami evacuation routes. That job should be completed by May. However, there's another topic I want to bring up. According to the old native folklore, the last earthquake, in 1700, occurred in the middle of the night, so the tsunami waves overcame the people in darkness. They didn't know which way to run, and many of them perished as a result. The same thing might happen again if the next earthquake occurs at night, because the power would be knocked out and people would get lost trying to find their way to high ground. So I've been looking at guidance beacons that operate on backup batteries that could be placed at intervals along the evacuation routes. They would operate in a similar way as the lighting strips in airplane aisles that guide you to the exits in case of emergencies. I've found an Australian company—"

The mayor stood up. "Hold it. Hold it right there, Rick. This whole earthquake prediction business has been declared a fantasy by the US government, and the governor issued a statement saying the same thing. So I don't want to listen to any more of your plans about it."

"But Mike, we should—"

"No more, Rick. You can go ahead and finish stocking those sheds as we agreed, but I will not countenance any more spending of the taxpayers' dollars on planning for something that may not happen in the foreseeable future.

And that's final." With a dramatic gesture, he stalked out of the room.

Exasperated, Rick returned to his office. He couldn't stop envisioning what might happen in Seaside if the forecasted earthquake actually occurred. Most of Seaside was built on a low sandbar between the sea and the Necanicum River. He expected it to be entirely overwhelmed by any tsunami likely to be generated by an offshore earthquake. All their evacuation plans had been devised with the local residents in mind. They, knowing the drill and the evacuation routes, had a halfway decent chance to respond with sufficient dispatch to make it to safety.

He was much less sanguine about the fate of visiting tourists. Given the confusion that was likely to arise, he doubted that many caught on the beach at the time of an earthquake would make it to the safety of high ground, more than a mile away through a town badly damaged by the earthquake, in the twenty minutes or so before the arrival of the tsunami. He had spoken with Tommy Torgerson a few times about alternative plans, but they hadn't been able to come up with any options that would be able to deal with the kind of beach crowd they might expect on a sunny summer weekend.

MARCH 20

Corvallis

Carl asked for the check as Manny finished serving everyone in the back room.

"No, no. Pliz, Professor, no charge. This time is my pleasure. Is my honor to serve you."

After he left, Carl chuckled. "Well, one good thing about being publicly rebuked by the authorities: it seems to have elevated us in Manny's esteem." His quip didn't do much to alleviate the gloominess of the group.

"I have to apologize for not having prepared you guys for the likely outcome in Seattle. A friend of mine and an old USGS hand, Mitch Appleby, warned me way back at the AGU that it was pretty much a foregone conclusion that NEPEC would give us a big thumbs-down. It's a matter of their organizational purpose and history. They were originally set up mainly to throw cold water on the predictions of amateurs and various other nutcases promoting quasi- or pathological science. The only prediction they ever approved was promulgated by the USGS itself. It was for a magnitude six-ish earthquake that was supposed to occur near the small town of Parkfield in central California in the late eighties. At the time most people thought that it was a no-brainer. The USGS instrumented the hell out of the place and telemetered the data all up to Menlo Park. They developed a set of alarm protocols and a whole manual of notification rigmarole. Members of the prediction team were required to wear beepers at all times. Nature, however, is not so easily second-guessed. The earthquake eventually arrived in 2004, but that was long after the party had ended and the prediction had been formally retracted. It was a huge embarrassment for the Survey. So once bitten, as they say, this committee was unlikely to go for another pitch, no matter how persuasive we might have made it."

"But these people," Anastasia complained, "they are such stupeed ones. How they cannot see the danger of ignoring this warning?"

"There's no accounting for the mulish idiocy of committees," Mark commented with laconic irony. "It's simply the nature of the beast."

"Actually, the Japanese people are reacting very differently to this affair," Shuichi put in. "After the great 2011

Tohoku earthquake disaster, they became very angry at the government authorities.

"All seismic zonation in Japan was based on the history of the past 200 years of earthquakes. During that time no earthquake greater than magnitude 8.3 had struck the northeast coast of Japan, so the tsunami protection barriers were built to withstand tsunamis from such earthquakes, and critical engineering facilities such as nuclear power plants were also built according to those specifications. As a result they were completely unprepared for the magnitude 9 earthquake in 2011, which produced a tsunami that overwhelmed all their defenses. The authorities claimed the excuse that such an earthquake was unprecedented, but that was not true. Scholars studying old historic documents had found reports that the Jogan earthquake of AD 869. had produced huge tsunamis all along that coast that were much larger than had been caused by any modern earthquakes. In excavations in the Sendai plain, geologists found that the Jogan earthquake tsunami had washed more than four kilometers onshore, much farther than any historic earthquake since. In the same excavations, they found evidence for two older huge tsunami events in the last 3,000 years. So they knew that such giant earthquakes and tsunamis occurred every 1,000 years or so, the last one being in 869. These facts were reported as early as 2001. When this information was brought to the attention of the Japanese earthquake prediction evaluation committee, well before the 2011 disaster, it was ignored.

"So now the Japanese people don't believe the authorities anymore. The main Japanese newspapers, like *Asahi Shimbun*, and even commentators on the government TV station, NHK, are now saying that the American authorities are making the same mistake in the Cascadia case." He gave a diffident Japanese giggle, "And Carl's '*Shoganai*' comment has become a top hit on Japanese YouTube."

Everyone laughed, and the atmosphere in the room relaxed.

"Well, it's nice to know that somebody's on our side," Mark noted. "But where do we go now?"

"Indeed," said Carl. "And thanks, Shuichi, for that bit of perspective. One way to look at it is that NEPEC has taken from us the burden of responsibility for warning the public about this earthquake. That being the case, we should consider simply that we're in the middle of an ongoing test of our scientific hypothesis and proceed accordingly. The first thing on our agenda is to try to decode the SSE pattern. Shuichi, Kiersten, and I will proceed with that. Anastasia and José, why don't you join us? It looks to be a knotty problem, and we could use some additional input. We also need to start thinking about how to set up an observational facility so that we can look at all the GPS and seismic data in real time when the next SSE begins in August. Mark, could you look into that? Yes, Jason?"

Jason had been waving his hand from the back of the room. "I don't agree that you guys should just ignore your responsibility to the public. At the very least you should have a web page where you can post all your stuff just as things develop. I'd be happy to set it up and run it for you. I paid a lot of tuition bills in college designing websites for people, so no problem."

"That's a great idea, Jason. Does everybody agree? OK, Jason, you're on."

José called Carl aside after the meeting. "As you Americans say," he said, "the shit has hit the fan."

"Uh-oh. What happened?"

"After this latest news blast on Fox and all that, my chairman called me in and demanded to know if I was still working on this project. When I confessed that I was, he flew into a furious tirade. He accused me of insubordination, not following departmental guidelines, everything you can imagine. In the end he said that if I didn't cut my relations with this project immediately that when my tenure review comes up next semester he'll recommend against my tenure."

"Oh my God. What kind of a tyrant is this guy?"

"Oh, he's an asshole, no doubt about it. My big problem, which my chairman is fully aware of, is that although I've been in this country almost ten years now, I still don't have a green card. My wife is also Brazilian, and she's in the same situation. Even though both our kids were born here and are American citizens, we are not. I'm still on an

H1-B visa. If I lose my post, they'll jerk my visa, and we'll have to leave. This would be a big disaster for my family. We've made our lives here, and there's nothing left for us in Brazil. So I'm very sorry, Carl, but I have to quit the project."

"Don't apologize, José; I'd never for a second blame you. We actually owe you a great debt of gratitude for sticking it out for so long. You and Anastasia made very important contributions to the project, and for that I thank you. We'll be sorry to see you go."

"Me too. I've really enjoyed it." They shook hands. "And just to show that I take everything about our project seriously, I'm planning to take my family to Brazil for a holiday. For the month of August."

◆ ◆ ◆

Carl called Mark that evening. "Did you hear about José?"

"Yeah, poor guy. That's really disgusting. Talk about screwing somebody over their immigration status! His chairman ought to be fired, if not drawn and quartered."

"Yeah, I certainly agree. But I was wondering, Mark, what's your situation in all this hullabaloo?"

"Oh, there's no problem with me. A while ago my chairman asked me to fill him in on what we're up to. So I gave him the rundown. Although I'm sure he won't say anything publicly, he was pretty excited. Do you know what he said to me? He said, 'keep up the good work'! Anyway, unlike poor José, I got tenure last year. So I don't have to give a shit about what anybody says."

MARCH 22

Corvallis

Kiersten entered the apartment and dumped her laptop and rucksack on the hall table. David was sitting at the kitchen table tapping away on his laptop.

"Hi, honey; how was your day?" he asked.

"Exhausting. I'm beat. It was another long day of fruit-less drudgery over a computer screen. My eyes are about to pop out of my head. I hope you're cooking tonight."

"Better than that. I thought we'd go out tonight. I got reservations at Aqua Seafood."

"Wow, pretty fancy. What's the big occasion?"

"I just signed a book contract with Viking. They're going to send me a nice fat advance."

"Oh, that's terrific. Congratulations! What's it on?"

"It's on this. The Cascadia earthquake prediction story."

"What! You're writing a book about our project. How dare you?"

"What do you mean, how dare me? This is my baby. I broke the story, so I should be the one to write the book on it."

"What do you mean, your baby? It's our baby, me and Carl and Anastasia and the rest of us. It's our baby. We're the ones working our butts off on it while you laze around this apartment. What gives you the right to write a book about it?"

"But honey, this is my big break. This book will make my reputation as a science writer."

"Your reputation! All you're thinking about is your precious writerly reputation. Our reputations are the ones on the line here. All you're doing is hoping to profit from it. That's what you are, a profiteer, just like Halliburton in the Iraq war that you were always bitching about."

"That's not fair! I'm just doing an honest journalist's job. I'm writing the inside story on this business, trying to give the scientists' point of view. I'm surprised you aren't happy that I'm doing it instead of some hack. Somebody's bound to write a book about this, one way or the other."

"Inside story! That is some sick joke. You're sleeping with your primary source is what you're doing. What kind of a journalist does that make you?"

"Jeez, I didn't—"

"That's why you're always asking me about my work these days. I suppose you've been writing down everything

I've said for months. I suppose you're going to write about our sex life too."

"Oh, come on, honey; be reasonable."

"Reasonable my ass! Show me what you've been writing. I bet you've been keeping one of your journals on all this. Secretly writing down everything I've said for months. Show me your journal."

"My journals are my private property. I don't show them to anyone."

"That does it. I'm outta here!" She jumped up and stormed into the bedroom and began stripping her clothes off closet hangers and throwing them into a duffel bag.

He followed her into the bedroom. "Please, Kiersten, calm down. We can work this out."

"No, David, you can work it out. I'm leaving." She hoisted the duffel onto her shoulder, went to the front door, and collected her rucksack and laptop. "Go ahead and write your book, David. But you can do it from the outside like any other respectable journalist." She left, slamming the door behind her.

At the corner of the block, she stopped and thought for a moment. Then she took out her cell phone and made a call.

"Hi, Anastasia. It's me, Kiersten. I just broke up with David. I was wondering if I could stay with you for a few days."

APRIL 18

Corvallis

They had announced the meeting as a press conference, so a smattering of reporters had showed up and clustered at the rear table in Manny's back room. The prediction controversy had clearly dropped in the media priority rankings: it was not nearly the size of the press entourage that had attended the NEPEC hearings. There were two Japanese reporters, David, the owlish woman who Carl recognized from the AGU meeting and the NEPEC hearings and whom David had informed him was Joclyn Goodenow of the *Oregonian*, and a man who had introduced himself as a stringer with the *New York Times*.

Carl opened the proceeding by thanking the representatives from the press for attending. "As I said at our AGU press conference and again at the NEPEC hearings in

February, our team has been working on trying to improve our understanding of where the next Cascadia earthquake might occur. On those occasions we said that we were predicting that it would most likely occur during the next slow slip event in Cascadia. The time of that event is expected to be in the last three weeks of August, but we didn't know where it would occur, so we could also not say where the earthquake would occur. In the meantime we've been working on trying to decode the spatial pattern of past SSEs so that we might be able to predict the location of the next one. This would give us a midterm improvement in our predictions for the expected earthquake. The purpose of this press conference is to announce some encouraging results of that quest. I introduce to you now Professor Shuichi Kato, who has been leading our research on this problem."

Shuichi rose and gave a little bow. "Nice to meet you. I like to introduce my topic. Slow slip events propagate along a narrow strip of the plate interface at the base of the seismogenic zone. They occur quite periodically, every fourteen months, but each one does not run for the entire length of the plate boundary, but only for a distance of several hundred kilometers. Where they start and stop is pretty variable. Quite some time ago, Professor Strega asked me to help him try to determine the spatial pattern of their occurrence. I am not a seismologist, by the way. I am a mathematician, and my field of study is pattern recognition, so please don't ask me any questions about earthquakes. I never worked on any earthquake problem before, but this seemed like a problem of line segment patterns. This is a fairly typical problem in pattern recognition field, so I thought maybe I could help.

"We had the pattern of the last twenty years of SSEs, which by the way was provided by the work of Kiersten Lunqvist, a graduate student in the seismology group, who is seated over there." He indicated Kiersten, who interrupted a whispered conversation with Anastasia to give a little nod. "We tried many standard methods of line segment analysis, and even some nonstandard ones, but we could not decipher the pattern. Finally, as we were becoming pretty discouraged, Professor Strega suggested another approach. He suggested that we suppose that in equilibrium the sum of slip from SSEs in the transition strip must be equal at all points along the plate boundary. He said that this was a reasonable but untested hypothesis. With that assumption the regions that were the most lagging in slip could be supposed to be the regions most likely to have the next SSE. So we did this simple test and found a remarkable result, which I show in the first slide. Although the slip lag varied from place to place along the entire strip, there was one region that stood out from all the others in this lagging in slip. So we suppose that this is the most likely area for the next SSE. It is the area between approximately forty-four degrees and forty-six degrees north latitudes. That is in central to northern Oregon, which you can see is approximately between the cities of Florence and Seaside. So that is our conclusion I wanted to report to you. I will let Professor Strega explain what that means about the earthquake."

Shuichi took his seat, and Carl rose and strode to the front of the room.

"Thank you, Shuichi. Those who have been following our hypothesis up to now will know that we have predicted that the expected earthquake will nucleate within the region of the next SSE, which we now expect will be the region roughly between the latitudes of Florence and Seaside. At first we said only that such an earthquake would be of a minimum magnitude of 7.8 to 8.0. However, at the NEPEC meeting, Hugh Duckworth proposed an additional criterion that allows us to be more specific about the size of the earthquake. I have just put up the same slide that he showed at that meeting. By the way, Professor Duckworth is here today, so any questions regarding this argument should be directed to him." He made a slight gesture to indicate Duckworth.

"He showed that the prehistoric record shows Cascadia earthquakes fall into four types, as shown on the slide. He then proposed that this is a permanent condition, so that we can estimate the various possibilities of earthquake types from the position where the earthquake nucleates. So for an earthquake nucleating within the zone specified by Shuichi's analysis, there are three possibilities. The first is the magnitude 9 event that ruptures the entire plate boundary. The second is an 8.8 that ruptures from about Willapa

Bay, Washington, south to Cape Mendocino, California, and the third is an 8.6 that ruptures to the south from about Lincoln City, in the center of our nucleation region. So we now conclude that the expected earthquake will be in the magnitude range 8.6 to 9.0. Thus our minimum magnitude is now about eight times bigger than before. I am afraid that this does not eliminate too many possibilities, but that is just how things have worked out. Thank you for your attention. We will be pleased to answer any questions."

There were a series of clarification questions from the press, which Shuichi and Carl answered as appropriate.

At the pause signaling the end of the meeting, Hugh rose and cleared his throat. "I would like to make a statement, if you don't mind. I'm not a member of the research team that made this earthquake prediction, but I've followed their work quite closely as it developed. I admit to not being a theorist and to not being able follow many of the details of their model, but from what I know of the history of Cascadia earthquakes it seems to me that their proposal for a great earthquake to occur later this year is quite plausible. I was appalled at the NEPEC decision to reject it out of hand, because that is what I think they did. It would be one thing if they'd uncovered serious flaws in the theory, but that wasn't the case. So now I'd like to state my strong support for the seriousness of this group's prediction. In fact, if they'll have me, I'd like to join them in their continuing monitoring of the situation."

All the members of the group rose and applauded.

Carl clapped his arm around Hugh's shoulder. "Glad to have you with us, Hugh. Welcome aboard."

After the meeting broke up and people started to file out of the room, Carl remained at the front, in conversation with Mark. He asked, "What's with Kiersten and Anastasia? They seem to be quite pally these days. They used to be at each others' throats."

"Female solidarity, I suppose," replied Mark. "They've been living together since Kiersten broke up with David."

"What? This is the first I've heard of any of this. When did Kiersten and David split up?"

"About a month ago. Ever since David revealed that he's writing a book on the prediction project."

"Aha. She took it as an invasion of privacy, I suppose."

"I guess. Anyway, Kiersten and David became reconciled enough that he's still embedded with the group as our chronicler."

"I'm glad to hear that, anyway. David seems like the sort of fellow that'll do justice to the project."

◆　◆　◆

The following evening Joclyn uploaded a post onto her blog page.

"Media coverage of the prediction of a great Cascadia earthquake came to a quick end following the NEPEC committee's rejection of it two months ago. Nevertheless, Carl Strega and his research team are still hard at work trying to refine their prediction. Yesterday they announced what they claim as a major new development in their prediction. They now say that new improvements in their theory allow them to specify that the earthquake expected this summer will occur off the north coast of Oregon, initiating somewhere between Florence and Seaside. They also claim that the earthquake size will be from magnitude 8.6 to 9.0, much larger than they had originally specified. They had originally stated that a minimum estimate for the earthquake was between magnitude 7.8 and 8.0. Each two-tenths of a magnitude unit represents a doubling of the energy the earthquake packs. That means that the new minimum size, 8.6, is eight times larger than the old upper limit of their minimum size, 8.0.

"The team made their announcement at a sparsely attended news conference held in the back room of a coffeehouse in Corvallis. This has been the meeting place for the research group since it was forced off-campus by the university administration last December. Repeated queries to the university administration seeking the reasons behind the campus ban were answered only by the bland and entirely inadequate statement that the earthquake prediction work was not a sanctioned university research project. One wonders what political pressures led the university administration to so forcefully disavow the Strega project long before NEPEC made its own pronouncement. The student-run campus newspaper roundly criticized the administration at the time, arguing that the university was abrogating its responsibility to support research with potentially great societal impact. It is certainly unusual for a university administration to restrict academic research of any kind, as such an action threatens the very heart of academic freedom. Whatever the outcome of the Strega prediction saga, an inquiry by an independent body needs to be made into this sordid affair."

MAY 16

Seattle

Nick Singletree and Tom Mitkins were having a conversation about what to do about the Strega prediction in the latter's office in the subterranean headquarters of the Pacific Northwest Seismic Network (PNSN) at the University of Washington. They were interrupted by the ringing of the telephone on Tom's desk.

Tom answered, "Yes, I'll hold." He mouthed silently to Nick, "The director."

"Yes, Catherine, how are you? Everything's going well. Yes, no problems there. I see. Yes, I do too. Yes, we can do that. Sure, yeah." As Tom verbally bowed and scraped, he absentmindedly twiddled his spiked red hair and scratched his perpetual three-day beard, his idea of a fashion statement that only succeeded in making him look scruffy.

When he hung up, he said, "Well, speak of the devil! Although the USGS officially has disapproved the Strega prediction, we're to unofficially mount a full 24-7 monitoring operation for the next SSE period. Strictly on the qt. Costs to be covered by Reston."

"I see. Catherine is taking no chances. Well, that solves our problem doesn't it?'

"It certainly does. She said that this should be considered strictly a precautionary measure. But, and this really blew me away, she said that if at any time we consider it imperative to issue an early earthquake warning through the ShakeAlert system, we should first contact her for permission. She gave me her personal cell phone number."

Nick emitted a low whistle. "Wow! She certainly is taking this seriously, isn't she? But ShakeAlert? That wasn't meant for that purpose, was it? I thought it was designed to trigger on the first P-wave from an earthquake to give subscribers a ten- or twenty-second warning before a big earthquake. Isn't it just still just a prototype in testing mode?"

"That's no problem. We've got the ShakeAlert user group set up already, so if push comes to shove we can always send out an e-mail to that alias. We can also send out the warning to our subscribers of the Earthquake Notification Service. That should serve the purpose."

"So how are you going to man that kind of monitoring operation?"

"That'll be a problem. We don't have enough people in this office to man the situation round the clock. Hmm. Is there a chance that you and your students might volunteer to stand watch? Yes? Great; that'll probably just do it. I'll have to get in touch with Mark Weisenberg to coordinate with whatever they're doing in Corvallis. I'll have to clue in the PANGA people, too. Unofficially, of course. We don't want them scheduling any instrument servicing shutdowns during that period."

Corvallis

Mark and Jason had filled most of the blackboard with diagrams of their planned observation system. They would be getting real-time inputs of GPS data from PANGA and near real-time tremor and earthquake locations from PNSN in Seattle. The center of the system, and Jason's triumph, was an eighty-inch flat-screen HDTV monitor that he'd scrounged from somewhere and jiggered so that different data sets could be displayed simultaneously on different sectors of the screen, all controlled by his laptop. His unveiling of this system had brought enthusiastic applause.

The biggest applause, though, was reserved for Manny, when Mark announced that he was making his back room available for their observation center. He'd even volunteered to run a fiber-optic line in from the front of the café, which was also a Wi-Fi hotspot, so that they would have no problems with data feeds. He was planning to fit the back room with a lock and supply them with keys for it and for the front door so that they could have access twenty-four hours a day.

Carl rose. "We should all thank Manny for his generous support, and above all for his trust in allowing us access to this room after café opening hours." This brought wild applause.

Manny rose and gave several bows. "For me is a great honor. You are doing something maybe historic. To be a part of such a thing is more than my imagination. So is me who is thanking you."

Jason described a schedule for installing and testing all the equipment in June and July so as to have everything up and running by the beginning of August. "By the way," he said. "If no one objects, I plan to set up a Twitter account using the handle Quakewatch so I can tweet on our progress just as things happen."

Hugh Duckworth, who was now a part of the observation roster, made a suggestion. "The marine biologists have a buoy-tethered hydrophone array off Newport that they use seasonally to monitor the gray whale migrations. I was digging around our equipment warehouse and found a set of old navy surplus subchaser hydrophones that are tuned to the one-to-ten-hertz range. I think it might be possible to swap those out with some of the higher-frequency whale monitoring units. What do you think? Is it worthwhile setting that up just to give us some offshore monitoring capability?"

"It's worth a shot," said Mark. "If things start popping off Newport, we might just get real lucky with that. By all means, go ahead and set it up. Talk to Jason about what'll be needed for signal processing."

August 3

Corvallis

At the meeting to inaugurate the observation headquarters in Manny's back room, Mark was going over the equipment setup and procedures that he and Jason had developed over the past two months of work.

"Our main data display will be on the big screen. At the top left is the tremor map generated by the PNSN. That displays what the wags call the Wech-o-meter, after Aaron Wech, who invented the technique. It shows near real-time location of tremor events at *http://www.pnsn.org/tremor*. That display should begin to light up with red dots when the SSE begins and will continue to show tremor activity that delineates the current location of the areas that are actively slipping in the SSE. That display will show some activity every day. Most of that is from small local mini-SSEs that occur below forty kilometers and are too small to be registered on the GPS units. Don't be confused by that chatter. A larger, persistent cluster occurring at shallower depth that is also picked up by GPS will indicate a full-blown SSE. That's what we're looking for.

"Below that is the earthquake location map that also comes from the PNSN website, *http://www.pnsn.org/earthquakes/recent*. That's updated every minute. Those are computer locations, so the results for small events are available within about a minute. It takes a little longer for larger events to be processed because they often need to be checked manually. The right-hand side of the screen will be reserved for the GPS feeds from the PANGA website, *http://www.geodesy.cwu.edu/realtime*. Normally we'll be displaying the eight coastal sites that are most likely to pick up the SSE signal first. Those data come in once per minute.

"However, we'll have to keep track of about twenty other GPS stations in our region. Some of those have tiltmeters installed as well, and we need to keep track of those because in some cases they may be more sensitive than the GPS. Those additional stations will need to be monitored on an hourly basis with the other computer workstations that you see around the room. Any of those displays can also be put up on the big screen using the laptop. Jason will train everyone how to do that.

"There'll have to be at least two people on duty here twenty-four hours a day. We'll do it in eight-hour shifts.

I'm preparing a duty roster that I'll send out shortly. Any important observations or other problems are to be immediately reported to Carl and me. Our contact numbers are on the board. Carl will be staying in town for the duration, so one or both of us should be able to respond within a few minutes. An important issue is security. Keep the door to this room locked at all times. Manny has put a 'Closed, Under Construction' sign on the door, but please enter and leave the room as unobtrusively as possible. Manny is open from 7:00 a.m. to 10:00 p.m., so we don't want curious people barging in on us or wondering why all these people are going in and out of a closed room. And please don't disclose this location to anybody. We don't want our work to be disturbed by busybodies or reporters. David is the exception. He'll have a key.

"We'll be reporting our observations, as we get them, on our website. Jason will also be tweeting, but his tweets will have to be vetted by Carl or me. That's it for now. If you have any technical questions, please put them to Jason."

Jason took out his iPhone and tweeted @quakewatch: Cascadia quake monitoring is beginning 24/7 in undisclosed location #casquake.

Portland

Margie Yamaguchi stood in the driveway of her home shepherding her children, along with their pets, luggage, and vacation accoutrements, together with their father, into the family minivan. It had taken a morning's worth of packing, organization, and chivying to get everything and everyone into the vehicle and ready for their trip to spend the rest of August with her brother Alec and his clan in Bend.

After some serious thinking on the matter, Margie had decided that she believed the likelihood of the earthquake strongly enough that she wanted her family on the far side of the Cascades and well out of the danger zone for the critical weeks when the big one was expected. She wasn't worried about their house. Margie was trained as a geotechnical engineer and since taking her job at DOGAMI had specialized in the response of soils to seismic shaking. It was with this knowledge that she had picked out the Woodstock neighborhood of Portland as an area of the city likely to have relatively moderate shaking when the big one came. She had also carefully selected the house, a single-story wood-frame ranch, following the inverse three-little-pigs rule of seismic resistant construction. She and her husband, Bob, a consulting civil engineer, had also made a few minor but critical modifications: they had attached shear beams to the footings so that the house wouldn't be shaken off its foundation, and they had lopped the top off the brick fireplace chimney (which they never used) so it wouldn't collapse onto the roof or driveway. So she was confident that the family would be safe in the house during the earthquake. Her worry was about its aftermath, when they could expect several weeks without power, water, gas, communication, and dire shortages of everything else, in a chaotically disrupted city. It was better by far that they be spared the trauma of all that by riding it out safely in Bend.

But Margie was staying on in Portland. She had told Bob that her job required her to stay in town over the duration of the prediction. This was not exactly true: her office, following the governor's directive, didn't acknowledge the prediction. Margie thought otherwise. She wanted to stay, if truth be known, mainly because she wanted to experience the earthquake firsthand. She had spent years traveling to see the aftermaths of recent great earthquakes, in Japan, Chile, and Sumatra, and she was determined not to miss the big one on her home turf. She also knew that her services would be key to the post-earthquake recovery process, and in that effort the first seventy-two hours were the most crucial. So in spite of what her bosses thought, in all good conscience she couldn't be out of town when the earthquake hit.

Before getting in her car to go in to the office, she tweeted from her smartphone: @maryama: Sent family to safety in Bend. I'm staying in Ptld to see this thing out. #casquake

Crescent City

Kyle Lonnergan checked his iPhone after returning to his office in the Crescent City Fire Hall after lunch. He noted the quakewatch tweet and then clicked on the #casquake hashtag. He scrolled through those tweets, including Margie's, that were from the growing group of quakewatch followers who, in the informal ramifying manner of social networks, had begun calling themselves quakers. They were an anonymous group of people who, for whatever varied personal reasons, had been closely following events posted and tweeted by the group in Corvallis. Many of the tweets were comments reflecting growing feelings of anticipation that ranged the gamut from anxious dread to the excitement of experiencing one of nature's great paroxysms. Many described preparations they were taking to protect their families and property and traded tips about how best to do this.

Crescent City, a small fishing and logging port on the northernmost coast of California, was a particularly tsunami-conscious town. By some fluke of the bathymetry of the offshore seafloor, tsunamis generated by large earthquakes anywhere in the northern Pacific Basin became focused and amplified at Crescent City, which had experienced thirty-two tsunamis in the years from 1933 to 2011. Most of those had been minor and hardly perceptible, but the tsunami produced by the great Good Friday Alaskan earthquake of 1964 had arrived in four great waves over a one-and-a-half-hour period, each larger than the ones before, that had destroyed the port and the center of the city, killing eleven people and injuring hundreds of others. Kyle had been an infant during that event, and he had no personal recollection of it, but he had grown up with stories of the narrow escapes and adventures of his family and neighbors.

Everyone in Crescent City knew the story of the Clausons and their tavern, the Long Branch, in the '64 tsunami. Bill Clauson; his wife, Agatha; son, Gary; Gary's fiancée, Joan Fields, and three employees of the Long Branch had been at the Clausons' home celebrating Bill's fifty-fourth birthday when the tsunami hit. After the first wave subsided, they all went down to the tavern to empty the cash register, which had gotten wet. Since it seemed as though everything was over, they stayed on to continue their party. When the third wave arrived, it crashed through the rear wall, and the lights went out. They all climbed on top of the furniture as the water level quickly rose. The room filled until there was just enough headroom to breathe. After the wave crested and began to subside, everyone managed to climb onto the roof. Gary and another man swam to shore to get a boat. They returned with the boat and took everyone off the roof. While rowing to shore, they were caught by the fourth wave, which swept them into Elk Creek. One of the men managed to save himself by grabbing a hold of the Highway 101 bridge as they passed under it, and Gary, a strong swimmer, was able to make it to land. The other five perished.

No doubt about it, the '64 tsunami was biggest thing that had ever happened in Crescent City.

Since the advent, in recent years, of the modern tsunami warning system, the city had been subjected to several false tsunami alarms in response to large offshore earthquakes north of Cape Mendocino. Those earthquakes had turned out to be of the strike-slip variety in which the undersea movements were largely horizontal and therefore did not generate tsunamis. This hadn't damped the edginess of the local residents, however.

So it was that at dawn on the morning following the 2011 Tohoku, Japan, earthquake, sheriff's deputies went door to door in the low-lying areas of Crescent City to urge residents to go to higher ground. That morning, like many other townspeople, Kyle went up to the sea cliffs north of town to watch the arrival of the tsunami. After traversing the width of the Pacific Ocean, the wave was only an eight-footer by the time it reached Crescent City, but it was nonetheless impressive. In less than five minutes, the scene at the shore had changed from that of a placid low tide, with a wide expanse of exposed beach and offshore rocks, to a violent sea crashing against the base of the cliffs. Down in the fishing port, many boats were first left lodged in the mud by the initial withdrawal of the sea, then damaged or destroyed by the inrushing surge that followed. One man, who had gone to the mouth of the Klamath River to watch the spectacle, was washed out to sea and drowned.

Like many others Kyle had videoed the tsunami with his cell phone camera. Someone posted their video on YouTube, so by the next day most people in Crescent City had watched it.

Kyle, like a lot of people in Crescent City, was paying attention to this latest earthquake scare, as everyone was now calling it. It had become the talk of the town. Kyle was chief of the volunteer fire department and in that role would have a vital job to play in any earthquake disaster. Although there wasn't much he could do about a tsunami, he knew that most of the earthquake-induced damage in a town like Crescent City, built largely of wood frame buildings, would be from fires started by the deadly combination of ruptured gas and power lines. He was determined that his fire department would remain functional and effective enough to fight those fires after an earthquake. So he was paying particular attention.

Birkett Valley

Carl and Sally were having a last evening together before Carl moved down to a motel in Corvallis to join the others in monitoring the denouement of their scientific odyssey. Carl was in a somber mood.

"I have a very bad feeling about this entire business," he said. "I'm beginning to feel that I know what Oppenheimer was thinking when he quoted *The Bhagavad Gita* at Alamogordo. 'I become Death, the shatterer of Worlds.'"

"Don't be melodramatic, Carl. Oppenheimer built the bomb; you didn't make the earthquake."

"That's not the point. Oppenheimer foresaw the future and knew that he couldn't control it. And that was his fate."

He continued, "Through this whole miserable business, I've felt like an actor in a play. It was as if I were speaking lines written by another, and as a mere player had no power to influence the plot as it developed or to avert its tragic ending. Everything that has transpired seemed to come from an old script that is brought out on such occasions, like a Nativity play, to be recited anew as some sort of ritual. It was meaningless, all of it. We never seem to learn."

"What did you expect, Carl? It's an age-old story. Human society never seems prepared in the face of natural catastrophes. In our arrogance we like to believe we've tamed nature."

"Yeah, I know," he replied, with a tone of exasperation and querulous irony. "The rise of civilization comes at the price of a loss of respect for the power of nature. There's an interesting story about the Indian Ocean tsunami of 2004: the one that killed more than 200,000 people in Sumatra, Thailand, and Sri Lanka. Two strings of tiny islands, the Andamans and the Nicobars, sat astride the epicenter of that great disturbance. Several weeks after the disaster, a rescue ship visited one of those islands to investigate the fate of the local population: an indigenous tribe of Andaman Islanders living in Stone Age conditions. At first they could find no one about. They then conducted a thorough search and eventually came upon the entire population clustered in a tight group at the highest point of the island. It turns out that those people had immediately recognized, from their folklore, what the initial withdrawal of the sea signified, and they had immediately fled into the interior of the island. As a result none of their tribe was killed by the tsunami. What's even more amazing is that geologists have since found that such tsunamis occur in those islands only once about every 600 years. That is a cultural memory that we can no longer even conceive of having."

"That's the curse of modern life," Sally replied. "Nowadays we're inundated by such a glut of information, to say nothing about all the deliberate misinformation. Who can make heads or tails out of it all? Those island people are like the hedgehog: they know a few big things, and they know them well."

"You know, that story is not so unlike the L'Aquila one. There the old people, who followed tradition, knew best."

"In your case, Carl, things may turn out to be just the opposite. You guys are getting your message out on your website and on Twitter. For all you know, there may be a lot of people out there following those messages and taking precautions."

August 6

Corvallis

Jason and Mark had pulled the graveyard shift. It had been a long, dreary night spent staring at the big screen, cycling through the GPS feeds and tersely noting 'no activity' in the logbook. Just after 4:00 a.m., Jason noticed, with a start, a red dot that had appeared on the tremor map in the vicinity of Lincoln City.

He yelled at Mark, who had been nodding off, "Hey, we got some action here!" As they both stared at the display, a second red dot appeared, then a third, forming a little clump.

"Those guys are close to the coast, so they must be shallow. This must be it! The SSE has started," Jason exclaimed. "Look at that! It's right on the money. It's right smack dab in the middle of Shuichi's sector. How about that!" He jumped

243

up and down and high-fived Mark, who was startled into responding.

Mark stared openmouthed at the little red dots as a few more appeared. "By God, I believe you're right: it really is starting. This is the first time that it's dawned on me that what we are doing is actually for real. Before, I don't know, it didn't really click. I just seemed like we were doing this for drill—to carry out a kind of experimental procedure."

"Ha-ha," Jason hooted. "To be honest, me too. But I'm just a student. Up to now science for me has been something you learn from books and classes. I only just now realized that science is something you *do*. I mean, you can actually predict stuff? This is really hot shit, man!"

"Yeah, I know. Look, we'd better call Carl."

Carl arrived about twenty minutes later. He looked at the tremor screen where the dots had by then formed a red blob just below Lincoln City.

"Looks like it, all right," Carl said. "So let's look at the GPS. What's the closest station?"

Jason consulted the PANGA station map. "P395 is just inland from there." He put it up on the big screen. The trace was flat, like a dead EEG. He put up the other nearby stations, CHZZ and TILL near Tillamook and ONAB and P397 near Newport. Nothing was seen on those either.

Carl said, in a calm, matter-of-fact manner, "Let's keep monitoring those. We can't confirm the SSE until we see it on the GPS."

Just before 7:00 a.m., the first slight uptick appeared on P395. By eight o'clock it had defined a clear upward trend. The SSE was confirmed to have begun. The rest of the group arrived shortly thereafter and David a few minutes later. They all went into the front room of Manny's, took coffees, and began to talk excitedly.

Hugh wandered in a few minutes later. He looked closely at the map they had printed out and began to tell them about the location.

"That's a very interesting place. Just behind the dune ridge, there's a shallow pond called Devil's Lake. It's only about a meter above sea level, so every time there's a tsunami, it sloshes over into the lake and disrupts the finely layered varve deposits, so we can get very accurate dates on the tsunamis. It's one of our best locations for recording tsunamis."

Jason posted the tremor map and the P395 GPS record on the website. Then he tweeted @quakewatch: SSE began at 4:07 a.m. PST off Lincoln City. #casquake.

Mark sent a similar e-mail to Tom Mitkins at PNSN in Seattle, who forwarded it to Catherine Bisquette in Reston with a confirmatory note and the remark, "Score one for their team."

AUGUST 11

Corvallis

Anastasia and Kiersten were standing watch on the day shift. The SSE had been slowly propagating along the coast. It had reached past Newport in the south and Tillamook in the north and was now being registered on about a dozen GPS stations.

Anastasia had begun grumbling. "My God, this is *so* boring. Everything is happening so slowly. We just wait— wait and stare at the same data plots."

"I know," Kiersten replied. "It's about as much fun as watching grass grow."

"Ha-ha. Watching grass grow. Yes, is like that. Very funny, this expression. I like it. In Russian we have expression *а воз и ныне там*. Means 'things aren't moving.'"

"Well, let's hope things start moving pretty soon. I'm beginning to wonder if this thing is ever going to pop."

"What? You think it will not happen?"

"I have to admit I'm beginning to wonder."

"I think it will happen. You know, in physics we are often playing games with little models. See how they work. But we don't really believe it is the reality. But with Carl, I think is not a game."

"What do you mean?"

"When we got the first results at SETI, I was so shocked. I mean, the 2D results we had gotten earlier showed something interesting, like nucleation maybe. But I was not ready for what the 3D results showed. *Wow.* I was so shocked! Then later when we showed the video to the group, everybody also was shocked. Except for Carl. I was watching his face. When I showed the video for the first time, he just gave a little smile. *He knew.* I think he had the whole picture in his head before we did the modeling."

"You mean you think he knew everything from the beginning? Before all the work you and I did, he knew the answers?"

"Yes, I think so, but he didn't say anything. He wanted us to confirm it, independently."

"Well, I never! That's amazing. I mean, how could he?"

"Some people have deep insight into the physics. And they have a kind of intuition, too. A feeling that things must work in a certain way."

"Hm. You know, when I was first deciding about joining this project, I asked Mark for his advice. And do you know what he said? He said, 'Whatever else happens, if you follow Carl, it will be an adventure.' I'm beginning to see what he meant."

"Yes, it is adventure. For me is a great experience."

Portland

David Kenner had arrived at the DOGAMI headquarters on Oregon Street NE to interview Margie Yamaguchi. After depositing David's coat and bag in her cubicle, Margie took him to a large unoccupied corner office. Its large plate glass windows offered a panoramic view of the Willamette River bridges with downtown Portland in the background.

David was immediately attracted to the window. "What a terrific view!"

"Yes, I thought this room would provide the best vantage point for our discussion."

They arranged themselves in chairs on opposite sides of the only desk in the room, and David set up his tape recorder and took out his notebook. "Thank you for having me for this interview. As I told you over the phone, I'm doing an article on the ongoing earthquake prediction. I'm sure you must know all about it?"

"Yes, I've been following it quite closely."

"I imagine you must be. As part of the story, I want to get an idea of what damage Portland is likely to undergo if such an earthquake were to happen. I'm told that you're one of the experts to talk to about this kind of prognosis."

"Well, yes, we in this office, in cooperation with other organizations such as FEMA and the USGS, have made several damage assessments of the effects on Portland of a Cascadia-type earthquake. The bottom line is that we're rather poorly prepared for such an event."

"Oh, yes?"

"Yes. Unlike places like California and Japan, we didn't know until fairly recently that we even had a serious earthquake hazard in Oregon. Historically earthquakes in Oregon had been fairly small-magnitude inland events that caused only minor local damage. It wasn't until about thirty years ago, when geologists first began finding evidence of prehistoric tsunamis along the coast, that the threat of great earthquakes offshore on the Cascadia Subduction Zone gradually began to become apparent. So as a result, the first modern seismic resistant building code in Oregon wasn't enacted until pretty recently, 1993. A good deal of our building stock, and almost all of our major infrastructure, like the bridges and freeway interchanges that you can see from this window, were built well before that time. There's been some seismic retrofitting, but it's been spotty and far from adequate in most cases."

"That sounds not so good."

"It isn't. Most of the modern high-rise buildings you see across the river will make it through a major quake, all right. They'll lose a lot of glass; the elevators and other systems will be knocked out, and a lot of stuff will fly around inside, but structurally they'll remain pretty much intact. But many of the older lower-story buildings you see are of unreinforced masonry construction. They won't fare so well. Many of them will shed their masonry exteriors or collapse outright. Professionally, I'm more concerned with the major infrastructure elements, such as the bridges you see from the window."

"Yes, I noticed. It's quite an impressive display of bridges—every kind you can imagine. What's that bridge with the high arch over there in the distance? It's quite grand, isn't it?"

"Grand it may look, but it's one of the worst as far as earthquake resistance is concerned. That's the Fremont Bridge; it carries I-405 into the city. It was designed for .05 g."

"Come again?"

"Point-oh-five gee, five percent of the acceleration of gravity. A Cascadia-type earthquake will produce peak ground accelerations at least ten times that. Even worse is the duration of strong shaking. It'll last three to five minutes. That should be more than enough to take that bridge down. Its bridge-to-pier connections use rocker bearings, which have proven to be a very bad design element for earthquakes. So that bridge is likely to fail at its mountings and collapse."

As David gasped at this vision, she continued with quiet aplomb, "The bridges you see in the foreground all have moveable sections to allow river traffic to pass. So they're all operated with heavy counterweights that'll cause a lot of damage in an earthquake. That one with the high towers is the Hawthorne Bridge. It's a vertical lift bridge, operated by those huge counterweights you see in the towers. It's the oldest vertical lift bridge in the country still in operation. It'll act like a seismometer in an earthquake."

"How's that?"

"A seismometer consists of a mass that is delicately suspended from a platform, which in turn is rigidly attached to the earth. When the earth shakes in an earthquake, the mass, because of its inertia, doesn't move. The seismometer measures the relative motion between the mass and the platform, which then gives the motion of the earth. If you were to see that bridge in an earthquake, it would seem like the counterweights were swaying madly back and forth, but actually the reverse would be true. The counterweights would stay put, and the bridge would be moving along with you, the observer. No matter: their relative motions would most likely tear the bridge apart."

"So all the bridges into Portland will be destroyed?'

"Pretty much. They'd either be destroyed or put out of service for an extended period. And, of course, many will collapse into the river. So both land and river transport will be shut down. Power and communications will also be down. The Bonneville Power Administration estimates it would take seven to twenty-one days to restore power after such an earthquake. Recovery will also likely be slowed by a fuel shortage. All the fuel terminals and storage tank farms for this part of Oregon are in the northwest industrial district down the river from here. You can see them just off to the left if you lean a bit. That entire complex is constructed on landfill, which is likely to undergo liquefaction during a big earthquake. That kind of ground failure would destroy those facilities."

"Geez, the whole situation seems pretty grim."

"We measure things in the 3Ds: deaths, dollars, and downtime. Our estimate, which I think is actually almost a best-case scenario, is deaths, 5,000; dollars, 36 billion; and downtime, pretty much anybody's guess. The problem with the latter is that, aside from the local problems such as the bridges we just talked about, the whole I-5 corridor is likely to go down because of interchange collapses. Just out the window you can see the interchange between I-5 and I-84. That is likely to collapse, as are all the major bridge approaches."

"What about the tsunami? Isn't the earthquake expected to produce a big tsunami?"

"Oh, that's another matter. We've restricted ourselves to evaluating probable effects of the earthquake on the Portland metro area primarily from looking at an engineering analysis of foundations and structures. Nobody has attempted to guesstimate the losses from a tsunami. In that case the death toll would depend greatly on things like the season and the time of day. It basically comes down to how many people are at the beach on the fateful day."

"I see. In that case the Strega prediction for August doesn't bode so well, does it? That's in the middle of the summer beach season. Which reminds me, how seriously do you personally take this prediction?"

"Well, I work for the State. And, as you probably know, following the NEPEC decision, the State took the official position that the Strega prediction is not to be taken seriously. But I *can* tell you that I've sent my family to spend August with relatives in Bend."

"I see. Enough said. But you've stayed on. What are your plans?"

"If the earthquake comes, I plan to watch it. From this room."

"From this room! What a fantastic idea. It sounds stupid, but I plan to stay around for the earthquake too. Would you mind—I mean, is it at all possible that I could join you?"

"Officially, I am not supposed to be doing it at all. I haven't told anybody, but I've been sneaking food, water, and camping supplies into my office for the past week. When the time comes, I plan to camp out in this room and wait for things to happen. I don't know how it'll work out, but if it's at all possible, I'll try to sneak you in too."

"Oh, thank you so much. That would be great. I'm staying at the Holiday Inn. Here's my cell number."

"Do you have a car?"

"Yes, I do."

"Good. If you have a car with a tank full of gas and you happen to be on this side of the river when the earthquake strikes, you'd have a halfway decent chance of escaping from the disaster area in a reasonable amount of time. If you were on the other side of the river, car or no car, you'd be stuck in a disaster zone for a couple of weeks. That might be pretty grueling. I imagine that's a part of the story that you'd be happy to skip."

AUGUST 14

Corvallis: 3:00 a.m.

Jason and Mark were half asleep when the alarm buzzer went off on the control laptop. Jason scrolled down and found the message: *Alarm triggered, P367.* He clicked on the icon for that station, and the data stream appeared on the big screen. The slow rise in the data points for that GPS station showed an abrupt uptick. Jason zoomed in on the display: they saw a sharp rise, beginning at 3:04 a.m. Just then another data point appeared, continuing the rise.

"Oh my God, oh my God." Jason exclaimed. "It's the nucleation! It's really happening. *Holy* shit! We've got to call somebody—no, everybody."

Carl, who was staying in a nearby motel, arrived first. When he took off his coat, Mark noticed that, in his haste,

Carl had arrived with his pajama top tucked into his Levi's. Carl had a look at the plot.

"Yes indeed, it does look like it, all right. Just to be on the safe side, let's wait until we pick it up on another station."

The rest of the group trickled in over the next half hour. Everyone gathered in front of the big screen, watching it excitedly. At 3:56 a.m. the signal began appearing on ONAB, the GPS station just to the south of P367.

"OK, that confirms it," Carl said. "Jason, go ahead and send out the notifications.

Jason uploaded the two GPS records on to the website and tweeted:

@quakewatch: Nucleation began at 3:04 a.m. off Newport. WARNING: major earthquake expected within two days. #casquake.

He sent the same message by e-mail to Tom Mitkins in Seattle.

Seattle: 6:00 a.m.

Tom Mitkins's iPhone alert had woken him on arrival of the @quakewatch tweet. He called the rest of his team, had a coffee, and then headed into his office. He lived on Bainbridge Island but managed to get the first ferry at 4:45 a.m. and arrived at his office an hour later. Most of his staff was already there. He explained the situation to them, and they quickly pulled up from the PANGA website the real-time data for the GPS stations and confirmed the report from the Corvallis group. He organized his staff to monitor the situation and then retired to his office.

He composed a message, which he e-mailed to Catherine Bisquette in Reston with a cc to Alan Askew: "Sharp increase of displacement rate observed on two GPS receivers near Newport. It looks like the nucleation stage as modeled by the Strega group. According to their calculations, earthquake expected within two days. They have already tweeted this warning, so it is now public. This looks like it might be the real thing. Please stay in close communications contact. Will report as things develop. Mitkins."

He called Sue Garland into his office. "Shut the door, please, Sue."

He explained the full situation to her, including his earlier conversation with the director. "So I want you to set up ShakeAlert so that we can send out a warning on that system and also on the Earthquake Notification Service. I'll let you know when. I also want you to set up ShakeAlert so we can later put it on full operational status. When you do I want you to set it so that an automatic alert goes out when any station in the network registers a P-wave signal above threshold B. That'll give the user group a ten- or twenty-second warning before the main shaking arrives with the S-waves." She gave him an astonished look. "Yep. It's pins and needles time."

Portland: 6:00 a.m.

Margie Yamaguchi was also roused by her smartphone alert. She pulled on a robe and went into her small home office and turned on her computer. She checked the Quakewatch website and had a look at the GPS data. Then she called Jackie Ahrens, who answered after the sixth ring.

"Hi, it's Margie. Sorry to bother you at this hour, but it looks like things are poppin'. Have a look at the latest from quakewatch on Twitter." She waited a minute until Jackie picked up again. "OK, click on their website, and look at the GPS data they have displayed. Then click on their NEPEC talk, and have a look at slide number ten." Another pause. "So it looks like the real thing, doesn't it? Yeah, I'm going in to the office now. I think you should do the same. Yes, I do think you should call your boss. I know it's Saturday, but this could be the biggest day of our careers, to say nothing about our lives. Yes, I'm going to call my boss, too, but there's nothing *we* can do at this point in time. But you guys are in a position to do something. Your office ought to get into operational mode. Yes, of course, it's your decision to make. I've gotta go now. Call you later. Bye."

Then she called David. "Hi, it's Margie Yamaguchi. Looks like things are heating up. Can you meet me at the office in forty-five minutes? OK, see you then."

Margie met David at the entrance to the Oregon Street building and let him in through the front door. "Lucky it's a weekend; I can get you in without any fuss, and we'll have the place to ourselves for the big show."

She explained everything to David on the way up to the eighth-floor office. Once in the office suite, they went to the corner office.

"Let's get this desk and chair out of here," said Margie. "We don't want anything loose in here that could fly around."

When they had finished with that, Margie led him to a storage closet. "Help me with this." They dragged a chest-level office partition from the closet to the corner office. "That floor strip in the middle of the office is to anchor a partition. Help me line this up on it; then hold it there."

She went to her cubicle in the main room and returned with a rucksack. She pulled out a battery-powered screwdriver and a cloth bag of screws, with which she proceeded to attach the partition to the floor mounts.

"This'll give us something to hang onto when the time comes," she said. "It'll be like buckin' broncos in here when the earthquake hits, and we wouldn't be able to see anything if we couldn't stand up."

"Wow, you seem to have thought of everything."

"I'm not quite finished." She took a roll of fiberglass tape from the rucksack and proceeded to tape the windows in an X pattern. "This is to keep broken glass from flying around in here. That'd really spoil our fun."

"Oh, that's just like people do in hurricanes."

"Well, this'll be a lot different. Have you ever been in an earthquake?"

"When I was a kid I felt the Loma Prieta earthquake, down by Santa Cruz. We lived in Berkeley and felt the big rollers. And I saw what it did to the Nimitz Freeway down by the bay. Flattened it."

"Well, this one'll be a lot rougher than that, I guarantee you. In Berkeley you were a long way away from that earthquake, so you just felt the surface waves. Here we'll get hit by the body waves, the P and the S. The P isn't much, but the S will produce a lot of intense herky-jerky stuff. The surface waves, the big rollers, as you called them, will come in just behind them, but they'll be a lot stronger than what you felt. And it'll last a long time, three to five minutes. That'll seem like an eternity, believe me."

Margie dug around in her rucksack and came up with a tall thermos bottle and a large brown paper bag. "How about some breakfast? I don't know about you, but I'm starving."

Crescent City: 6:00 a.m.

Kyle Lonnergan checked his e-mail over coffee and then checked #casquake. He noted the quakewatch tweet with a grunt. He called his three crew bosses and told them to meet him at the Fire Hall at 7:00 a.m. He ate a hasty breakfast before departing himself. When he arrived only Kenny, the night man, was there. He told him to start moving the fire trucks out of the building into the tarmac yard in front; then he went into his office and made some phone calls.

Kenny was just finishing moving the last truck out by the time his crew bosses arrived. They gave quizzical looks at the trucks parked out front.

Mal Coons, the grizzled old-timer of the department who generally acted as their spokesman, said, "What's up, Chief?"

Kyle gave them a serious look. "You guys know about the big earthquake scare that's been going on. I've been following it pretty closely on the Internet. It seems they think things are coming to a head. This morning they sent out a warning that the big one should come in the next two days." The small group of men exchanged glances.

"If it comes, it's likely to start a lot of fires in town, so I'm taking some precautions to make sure that we're prepared for it. That's why the trucks are out front. The last thing we want is the quake to collapse the Fire Hall with the trucks inside."

Mel Coons broke in, "But what about the tsunami, Chief? If this big earthquake comes, we ought to get one hell of a tsunami right after. So what are we going to do about that?"

"I talked to Astrid in City Hall about it. It's her lookout to decide about calling for an evacuation or not. Our job is to make sure the fire department isn't caught flat-footed on this.

"Our main problem is going to be water. The quake'll likely break some of the major water mains in town, so we

261

can't count on any water pressure in the city system. So Rudy, I want you to go and check on all the cisterns in town. Make sure they're full and the valves are functional. Mal, go out to Lakeview Road as see if it's feasible to pump water out of Lake Earl from there. If not, scout out any other possible access points. Jim, I want you to take Kenny on down to the Six Rivers ranger station and pick up their tanker and bring it back up here. Yeah, the big tank truck they use for fighting forest fires. They agreed to loan it to us for a couple of days, so they'll be expecting you."

Cannon Beach: 6:00 a.m.

Mervyn Tomlinson arrived as usual at the office of The Breakers Motel at 6:00 a.m. and immediately turned on his computer. After checking his e-mail, he logged into Twitter and found the quakewatch tweet on #casquake. He read it over several times, then typed a message that he printed out on motel letterhead, made copies, and slipped them under the doors of his guestrooms, which were all occupied, this being the height of the season.

Dear Guests:

We have received information that there may be a strong earthquake in the next two days. There is no cause for alarm at present. Please go ahead and enjoy your day at the beach. We will be monitoring the situation carefully.

If we receive any more urgent information, we will fly a blue flag from the flagpole in front of the motel. If you see this flag, please return to the motel immediately for further instructions.

Any guest wishing to check out because of this warning, please come to the office. We will be happy to refund the unused portion of any prepayments.

Mervyn Tomlinson, Owner and Manager

Many of his guests came to the office later in the morning to ask about this notice, but only four parties decided to check out prematurely.

Corvallis: 7:00 a.m.

Kiersten and Anastasia were at the workstations monitoring all the data feeds. Just after seven o'clock, Kiersten gasped, "Something's happening on Hugh's hydrophones. Look: they're recording some kind of activity."

Jason toggled the laptop, and the hydrophone data appeared on the big screen. A series of small bursts showed on the record. They had begun about fifteen minutes earlier and were increasing in frequency.

"Looks like an earthquake swarm," Mark said excitedly. "Nothing shows up on the earthquake plot though. They must be too small to be located with the automatic picker. I'd better call Mitkins."

Mitkins picked up the phone right away.

Mark said, "Hi, Tom. Glad to see you're up and at 'em. Yeah, we are too. You read that correctly. We're pretty excited down here. Listen, Tom, we've got a hydrophone array working off Newport that we've been monitoring. About fifteen minutes ago, it started to pick up what looks like an earthquake swarm. Your automatic earthquake picker doesn't seem to be registering anything, though. Could you check your seismic stations in the vicinity to see if they're picking up any of this stuff? Yes. Yes, it would be nice if we could locate them. OK, get back to me as soon as you've got anything."

Then Mark phoned Hugh. "Your hydrophones are popping. Looks like an earthquake swarm is starting up off Newport. OK, see you in a bit."

Seaside: 8:00 a.m.

Mike Tilson was furious. "Just what do you think you're doing, Ellie?

"What does it look like I'm doing? I'm packing the car. I'm taking the kids to Martine's."

"You can't go to your sister's today. Today is the day of the big Tea Party Rally. We're expected to be sitting on the speaker's platform as the host and hostess."

"I told you before; I'm not going to that thing, and I think you oughta cancel it. I got a call from Alice Davis earlier this morning. She told me that the scientists are now predicting that the big one is going to be today or tomorrow. She said lots of people are gonna leave town and get clear away from the coast. And that's what I'm gonna do, too."

"Don't tell me you believe those scientists' malarkey? Jesus, Ellie, the experts shot down that nutty idea months ago. And I'm sure as hell not going to cancel the rally. George Westerly and I spent months on this. We made a big effort to convince the Tea Party to have their rally at Seaside to help make up for all the business we've been losing because of this damn earthquake scare. This'll be a big weekend for Seaside, and there're a lot of important people coming, like Sheldon Silk. His wife Dorothy particularly asked if you were coming. She doesn't want to be the only woman on the platform. You can't let her down."

"I don't care, Mike. Martine and Bill think we should take this warning seriously, and I'm sure as hell not going to take any chances with the kids. I'm getting them good and hell out of here. If you had half a brain, you'd come with us. And to hell with that stuffed shirt Silk and his snooty wife."

"Oh, sure, no doubt Martine and her tree-hugging husband would believe that crap! It's just like them to side with those lefty scientists."

"Leave my sister out of this. And fuck you, Mike! Everything isn't political. The forces of nature don't give a flying fuck about you and your politics."

She turned and shouted, "Come on, kids; let's go!"

Mike stood at the end of the driveway as they pulled away, shouting, "Go ahead, leave, then. Damn you, Ellie! And don't bother to come back anytime soon!"

◆ ◆ ◆

Rick Orstreim looked through the latest tweets on #casquake on his iPhone over his morning coffee on his deck. He noticed the warning from quakewatch. He walked into the kitchen, where his wife, Katie, was fixing breakfast.

"Listen, honey, the Corvallis people put out a warning this morning," he said. "They're claiming the big one will occur today or tomorrow. Let's play it safe. I want you to keep the girls home today."

"But they've got soccer this morning at 10."

"Yeah, I know, but cancel that. I don't want to take any chances. We're high enough here that a tsunami won't reach the house, and I don't want them running around somewhere where we can't track them down in a hurry. I'm going to call my mom and dad and get them to come over here to stay until this is all over."

"Aren't you jumping the gun a bit? There'll plenty of time for them to get to high ground if anything happens, won't there?"

"No, not if this thing goes, I don't think that at their age they'd be able to evacuate to the Cove in time. I'll phone them from the office. I've got to go down to there to wait this thing out. No, I'd better skip breakfast. Talk to you later; bye."

In his City Hall office, he made another cup of coffee and called his mom and dad to explain things to them. It took a while to convince them, but they finally agreed to go over to stay with Katie and the kids.

He ruminated about the situation. *It couldn't be a worse time for an earthquake*, he thought. Tommy Torgerson had told him that he expected 7,000 or 8,000 people on the beach today, what with the Tea Party convention and the usual hordes of tourists and day-trippers come over the hill from Portland to enjoy a beautiful sunny day on the coast.

Corvallis: 10:00 a.m.

They had just finished the breakfast Jason had brought in from a nearby fast food joint. They were studying the epicenter map on the big screen. The PNSN people had succeeded in locating some of the small earthquakes in the swarm detected by the hydrophones. They now appeared as small yellow circles offshore of Newport. Suddenly the building shuddered and creaked and began to shake.

"Earthquake! Get down! Get down!" shouted Mark. Everyone scrambled under the tables.

It was all over in ten seconds. As they crawled out from under the tables, Anastasia emerged with wide eyes and hands covering her mouth as if to stifle an incipient scream.

Then she blinked, lowered her hands and said, "Was that it? Was that the whole thing?"

Mark replied, "No, no; at least I don't think so. That wasn't nearly big enough." Just then a big red circle appeared on the epicenter map next to the cluster of smaller yellow circles marking the swarm. Mark came closer and read the inscription below the map. "It was a magnitude 6, just off Newport. Looks like part of the swarm."

A few minutes later, after studying the GPS data streams, Carl remarked, "It looks like the nearest GPS stations recorded a small coseismic offset from that event. But," he said after another moment, "they're continuing on their upward trends. So it looks like the nucleation is proceeding on track. So that little shock wasn't our baby, after all. I'd call it a foreshock. Jason, send that interpretation to Mitkins and to your Twitter followers. How many are there now, by the way?"

"Over 5,000, plus those following the #casquake feed. They've begun to call themselves quakers. I've no idea how many of them there are, but there're a lot of tweets appearing on that thread."

Carl went on, "This situation is not so unusual. A foreshock is a premature instability during the nucleation for a large event. It's kind of a false start. The 2011 Tohoku earthquake in Japan was preceded by a magnitude 7.3 about a day and a half before the mainshock. So, hang on, everybody; I believe the big one is still to come.

"By the way, all this stuff going on off Newport reminds me, where are the university's research vessels, Hugh?"

"Why, they're in port. In Newport, as a matter of fact."

"Don't you think you ought to get them out of there? You don't want them in port if there's going to be a tsunami."

"Oh, Christ! I hadn't thought of that! Shit! I've got to call the port captain and see how quickly we can get them out to sea." Hugh went to the corner of the room and had an animated conversation on his cell phone. He put it back in his pocket and made for the door. "Sorry to leave. I've gotta get out to Newport right away. Bye." Without waiting for a reply, he rushed out the door.

Seaside: 10:00 a.m.

A speaker's platform had been set up on the beach just opposite the Broadway entrance. It was decked out in patriotic bunting and had a large backdrop, over which was displayed the banner: Oregon Tea Party Election Kickoff Rally and Brunch Picnic. At a long table on the dais was arrayed an assemblage of dignitaries. The local Tea Party chairman, Douglas Martinelli, took center stage, flanked by the two main speakers, Herman Stackhouse and Sheldon Silk, the Republican candidate for governor. An array of other Tea Party–supported election hopefuls was seated along either side. Mayor Mike Tilson and Chamber of Commerce President George Westerly represented Seaside. The latter was engaged in an amiable conversation with J. Gordon Parkington, representing the Tourism Association, who had come over from Salem for the occasion. The audience of party loyalists, some 4,000 strong, was spread out on blankets and beach chairs in ranks running across and down the beach for a hundred yards or more. Huge speaker systems were erected on platforms on either side of the dais.

Martinelli gave the welcoming address. He introduced Tilson and George Westerly, who had served as cochairmen of the local organizing committee. "It's appropriate," he declaimed, "that we are having our election kickoff rally here in Seaside, a fine city that, as you will all well remember, was the victim, as were all the ocean communities in

270

our fair state, of a vicious earthquake scare campaign by a group of radical scientists, which, had it been successful, would have destroyed the tourism economies that they so depend on to support their admirable way of life."

Cheers and catcalls and loud drones of vuvuzelas and blasts of horns erupted from the enthusiastic crowd.

When the din abated, he continued, "It is our gesture of wholehearted support for Seaside, and indeed for all our ocean communities, that we're having our rally here. It's also appropriate that our first speaker is the man who first exposed that socialist plot and called the world's attention to it. I give you our illustrious pundit and journalist, Herman Stackhouse!"

More cheers and shouting commenced as Herman rose and waved his arms with Nixonian clenched hands, as if in victory.

Herman was about five minutes into his tub-thumping delivery, stirring the party faithful into a partisan frenzy, when the waves emanating from the shock off Newport began shaking the beach at Seaside. There was a stunned silence, followed by shrieks and shouts, people jumping up and stumbling, falling down again, clutching at each other, a flailing of arms and legs, a crablike scrambling, and a general confusion as incipient panic began rising among the throngs on the beach.

Herman looked about in terror, grasping the lectern, which rocked back and forth. Then the waves passed by, and the shaking ceased. He regained his composure, and seeing parts of his audience beginning to bolt for the sea-wall separating the beach from the town, shouted into the microphone, "Hold it! Hold it! Calm down, everybody! Calm down, it's all over." Then he boldly took back control of the situation. "That was just a piddling little tremor, people. It's nothing to get excited about. So much for the great earthquake those pointy-headed scientists have been talking about! It seems the laugh is on them," he exclaimed. "Their great earthquake prediction turned out to be a great big dud!"

◆　◆　◆

Rick Orstreim's contemplation of the situation was interrupted by the shaking from the Newport earthquake. His coffee cup went flying as he ducked under his desk.

When it was all over, he gingerly crawled back out, totally unnerved. He had thought for sure it was the big one, and in the few seconds it had lasted, his mind had been overloaded with a rush of disaster scenarios. After he pulled himself together, he called Tommy, who was on beach patrol. Tommy told him how the crowd had reacted and how Herman Stackhouse had calmed them down by saying that the minor temblor had shown the scientist's prediction to be a false alarm.

"Well, for once I hope that gasbag is right about something," Rick replied.

Rick went out before noon, picked up some lunches, and brought them back to eat with Chief Newhouse at the police headquarters across the city office complex. As they ate the chief was telling him that some people had already begun to leave town.

"There are rumors going around on Twitter," he said. "It's just a trickle so far, mainly residents and a few of the time-share people. If it gets any worse, though, I'm going to post some officers to direct traffic downtown and at the lights on 101."

Crescent City: 10:00 a.m.

After the call from Kurt Lonergan, Astrid Winslow, the Crescent City city manager, had mulled over the situation. The city had recently, at considerable cost, installed structures designed to make the port tsunami resistant. But they were designed only to withstand a ten-foot wave, of the type expected from a distant circum-Pacific earthquake. She knew that a local Cascadia megaquake would produce a tsunami two or three times that high. So if what Kurt had warned about was true, they provided a false sense of security. What to do?

When she felt the faint but distinct shaking from the Newport foreshock, 250 miles away, she made her decision.

Within minutes deputy sheriffs began spreading out over the downtown area to warn people to evacuate to higher ground. Somewhat to their surprise, they found a downtown Crescent City that was eerily quiet for a sunny Saturday morning. The *#casquake* tweet had been seen by the unusually large number of *quakers* in the town, and accounts of the early morning actions of the fire department had been widely circulated, so talk of a coming tsunami had spread like a hot rumor through the already tsunami-spooked populace. The deputies found that people were already in the midst of evacuating.

Those who lived in the higher districts to the north of town had avoided going down to the low-lying business district, and by early morning the people who lived down there had began evacuating to higher ground. The evacuation had started as spontaneously and mysteriously as a migration of lemmings and gradually took form as if it had been planned all along. Those who had no mountain cabins or relatives to go to gathered on the grounds of the high school, which was on higher ground, where a makeshift encampment was formed. Most businesses closed by midmorning. Groups of volunteers formed to help relatives move the sick and elderly to high ground. Those boats of the fishing fleet that were locally owned and crewed were hastily put out to sea. This was all improvised. Sheriff's deputies and firemen were mustered out to direct traffic, but the exodus was largely impromptu, as though the residents had been long waiting this day to band together in the face of their long-feared collective threat.

Newport: 10:00 a.m.

As he mowed the lawn in the back of his house on the bluff overlooking the harbor, Red Finnegan mused on his new endeavor at commercial salmon fishing. His first few trips had been successful. The Coho were running strong, and he had made sizeable and profitable landings. The new crew he had picked up was for the most part working out satisfactorily. He had kept his old shipmate Franco on and made him mate. The Mexican hands, Juan and Fernando, had proven to be reliable and hard workers. He would probably have to get rid of Eddie, a local man who had turned out to have a nasty habit of going on drinking binges as soon as they reached port and disappearing for days on end. He would turn up again for the next scheduled trip but would be pretty useless for the first day out.

That pleasant line of thought was interrupted by the onset of strong shaking from the earthquake just below and offshore the town. He was knocked to the ground by the force of it and stayed there in a state of shock until it was over. He ran to the house and opened the kitchen door to find his wife, Mary Kate, standing by the kitchen sink with a dazed look on her face. The kitchen was littered with pots, pans, broken dishes, and various provisions that had been toppled and tossed out of the kitchen cabinets.

He ran to her and took her in his arms. "Are you OK? Are you OK?"

She said, "Jesus, Mary, and Joseph! Did the house blow up or what?"

He looked around. The house seemed intact enough. It was just a mess because everything loose had been thrown around.

"I guess it must have been an earthquake, Mary Kate," he said. "You know, what they've been talking about on the TV. They were saying there was supposed to be a big one this summer."

Red walked around the house, checking everything. There didn't seem to be any serious damage. He turned on the TV, found a local news report, and sat down to watch it. After a few minutes, Mary Kate joined him. They were showing cell phone videos sent in from various locations around town. The damage seemed to be minor: the biggest thing was the brickwork over a few stores downtown that had come down onto the sidewalks. There were some scenes of broken windows and goods tossed off the shelves of a local drugstore and strewn in the aisles. There didn't seem to be any serious injuries.

An on-scene reporter interviewed groups of excited people. The studio reporter was giving a running commentary. "According to the USGS Seattle office, the earthquake was a magnitude 6, just off the coast of Newport. This was a moderate-size quake, according to their spokesperson, Sue

Garland. It was not the 'big one' that had been predicted by the Corvallis group, and no tsunami warning has been issued for this quake. According to the website of the Corvallis group, this earthquake was a foreshock. Their claim, which is controversial, is that the big one is still expected to occur off the north Oregon coast within the next two days."

The mention of a tsunami startled Red. He had gone out to see the Japanese fishing dock that had washed ashore at Agate Beach a year after the big Japanese earthquake and tsunami. He'd been greatly impressed by the spectacle of the stranded dock, all sixty-six feet and 160 tons of it. It was a huge thing to have been swept away by a wave and washed all the way across the Pacific. Seeing it he felt a more immediate sense of the power of the tsunami than he had felt when originally watching the TV coverage of the disaster in Japan. Afterward he had returned home and searched on his computer for images of the tsunami. He saw videos of unimaginably huge waves sweeping over seawalls and destroying harbors, of huge trawlers swept far onshore and deposited on top of buildings and crushed against bridges, of whole towns destroyed.

He turned to Mary Kate. "Listen, honey, I'm going to take the *Yaquina Belle* out to sea. If this here big one comes, I want to be in deep water where we can ride her out. I don't want to chance getting her caught in port with this tsunami maybe coming on. She's my new darling, and I don't want to lose her."

"What about me? What am I supposed to be doin' with earthquakes and all happenin' with you away taking care of your new darling?"

"Don't worry," he assured her. "We're on high ground here. Go out and stock up on food and water and flashlight batteries and such like. The house'll be OK. If the quake happens, just remember to turn off the gas afterward. You can get out the Coleman stove and lanterns from the garage. That'll get you by, camping style. I'll be back as soon as it's over."

He got on the phone. "Franco, get the crew together and meet me at the dock pronto. Yeah, it shook pretty good here, too. They say there might be a big one coming with a tsunami. Yeah, that's right; we gotta get out of Dodge before the big one is a comin'. You're damn right about that. Pick up some groceries on the way." He grabbed his sea bag, kissed Mary, and headed out the door.

Down on the dock an hour later, they were getting the *Yaquina Belle* ready to put to sea. The whole crew was there, except for Eddie, who had been seen tying one on the night before and couldn't be found all morning.

Armando Louros, leaning over the side of the *Cisco Catcher*, the big albacore troller moored at the next berth, shouted down to Red, "What're ya doin', Red? I thought you brought in your quota two days ago."

"They say there might be a big quake comin'. That one this morning was just a little tickler. I don't want to be caught in port if there's a tsunami comin'."

"What? You're talking about that prediction nonsense. That's a lot of hooey, ain't it?"

"Just you look across the bay, there. That big ship is the *Grampus*, the university's research vessel. It's already got a head of steam up, and look at 'em running around the deck. You think they're not trying to get the hell out of port? The little one, the *Skawitz*, weighed anchor a few minutes ago. You think they might know somethin' that we don't know?"

Armando had a good look. "Holy shit, you're right." He pulled out his cell phone and began calling his crew.

◆　◆　◆

A half hour later, just across the bay at the university's dock, Hugh Duckworth raced up the steps to the port captain's office and burst in without knocking. Art Zimmer, the port captain, was speaking into a microphone at his bench overlooking the yard. He turned and waved him in.

"There you are, finally. I was about to send out search parties. We're about ready to set sail."

"Sorry I'm so late. It took me close to half an hour to convince the dean to sign the ship release forms. Here they are." He passed over a sheaf of paper.

"Fine," the port captain said as he shuffled through them. "Everything looks shipshape. The *Skawitz* left port about thirty minutes ago. I released her on your say-so that the paperwork was on the way. I sent her out with a four-man crew, which is shorthanded but should do for a few days if the weather holds. I managed to put together a skeleton crew for the *Grampus*, basically using every hand I could find who was still in the Newport area. She's about ready to sail."

"That's great. Did you inform the Coast Guard?"

"That I did. But the commander of the Coast Guard Station says he can't evacuate the harbor unless he gets an official warning from the USGS. He phoned their office in Seattle, and they told him they weren't issuing one at this time. Same thing happened with NOAA. Their port captain says he's not authorized to send out his vessels without blessings from Washington, which amounts to the same thing. Just the same there's been a number of fishing boats leaving the harbor across the bay. Word is they've been warned by some Twitter messages or some such.

"I've advised our crews of the situation, so they've been able to warn their families to move to high ground. I only had one desertion over that. Young feller said he couldn't locate his girlfriend by phone and took off."

"OK, then. I'm going to go on board. Are you joining us?"

"Might as well. There's nothing left for me to do here except watch the tsunami come in, and I'd just as soon miss that, all things considered."

Seattle: 10:30 a.m.

The PNSN headquarters was a beehive of frantic activity. The entire crew had been called in, and all workstations were being manned. Sue Garland and her little band of public outreach personnel were trying to keep up with an overload of incoming telephone calls. Nick Singletree and Tom Mitkins were having a heated discussion behind the closed door of Tom's office.

Nick was arguing, "I still say there's no way you can tell a priori if it's a foreshock."

"What Carl is saying," Tom replied, "is that the nearest GPS stations recorded the offset from that earthquake and just kept on climbing. So he's saying that the nucleation was unaffected by it, which means the big one is yet to come.

"I'm buying that argument," he continued. "All the GPS stations from Florence to Tillamook are showing rapid uplift. I mean, they're screaming. We've never seen that before in any SSE. What else could it be but the nucleation phase that those guys have been predicting? Look," he said, passing over a figure from Strega's NEPEC report. "That's the uplift that was seen just before the 1944 earthquake in Japan. It looks pretty familiar, doesn't it?"

While Nick mulled over the figure, Tom clicked on Twitter. "Look at this activity on the #casquake feed. It's gone viral. People all over the state are freaking out. They've been flooding us with calls. What is Sue supposed to keep telling them—not to worry? We have no choice; we've got to make some sort of public statement."

He leaned back in his chair. "I'm going to pull the plug on this. I'm going to call the director and request that we send out an alert."

Nick looked at the computer screen. #casquake was now trending on Twitter. "Yeah, I see the problem. If ya gotta, ya gotta."

Tom called the director on her private line. She picked up quickly.

"Catherine, it's Tom Mitkins. Things are turning nasty out here. No, I can't wait for you to call me back. Get out of your meeting. This is more important. Go out in the hall then." There was a pause. "OK, listen, Catherine. We had a magnitude 6 off Newport half an hour ago. Strega is publicly calling it a foreshock. Yes, on his website and on Twitter. They've got thousands of followers—they've been flooding us with calls. Yes. Well, I'm inclined to agree with him. We've got rapid uplift on a dozen GPS stations over 150 kilometers of coastline. It looks just like the nucleation modeling they showed at NEPEC. Yes, that's right. Yes, I think we should issue a warning. Immediately. Oh, no! Yes, I understand. Please get back to me then as soon as possible. I can't sit on this forever." He hung up and made a face at Nick. "Fucking bloody hell! She says she has to pass this by the secretary of the interior. She says that he's been getting a lot of flak about this from various conservative fat cats on his golf circuit. He made her promise to contact him before she takes any action on this matter."

"What are we supposed to do in the meantime?"

"I guess we are supposed to sit on our bums and whistle a pretty tune whilst thinking nasty thoughts."

Nick chuckled. "Can you do both at the same time?"

Tom gave him a sardonic look. "Of course I can. I'm British."

Seattle: Noon

Tom was stewing in his office. Steaming, in fact. After waiting an hour and a half, he had called Alan Askew in Reston to find out what the delay was. Askew had told him that the secretary was on a junket to the Northern Marianas and that it was the middle of the night there. Tom had erupted in indignation, asking him why the fuck they didn't wake him up, for Christ's sake. Askew explained that there had been a reception the previous evening and the secretary had had quite a bit to drink, and his aides didn't want to wake him until it was a decent hour. Tom's reply was unprintable. When he hung up, he felt like screaming and pulling his hair out, and he probably would have too, had there been enough of it to grip.

"Bloody fucking politicians," he muttered to himself.

The call finally came in at 12:15 p.m. He snatched the receiver in midring. "Mitkins here. Yes, Catherine. Oh, thank God. Sorry to put you in such a spot. Yes, we'll do it right away. Thank you again; bye."

He raced out of his office and found Sue Garland in the outreach office. "OK, we've got approval. Yes, the director had to threaten to resign if the secretary didn't go along with it. Send out the alarm on ShakeAlert and the Earthquake Information Service, both e-mail and Twitter. And when you're done, don't forget to reset ShakeAlert to automatic trigger, level B. Yeah, what a way to debut the system, isn't it? I hope everyone has it turned on."

Portland: 12:30 p.m.

Margie and David had been relaxing all morning on yoga mats in the corner of the office. Margie had called her husband in Bend and told him the latest news: that the big one was expected in a day or two, but not to worry, she was well prepared for it. She assured him that the house was all buttoned up. Yes, indeed, she had turned off the gas, electricity, and water, and gotten rid of any food that would spoil. Then she called her boss and informed him of the situation. She told him not to bother about coming in. She would stay in the office to tend the phones if anything happened.

She turned to David. "If my boss showed up and saw how we've rigged this room, he'd have a cow."

They were having lunch from yet another container that had appeared from Margie's rucksack when Margie's smartphone made a donking sound. She clicked on the screen.

"Well, I'll be; the USGS has just put out an official alert: major Cascadia earthquake expected within two days. They must have pulled some strings to get that approved."

She retweeted the alert with the hashtag #casquake and forwarded the e-mail to her earthquake responder contact list. Then she called Jackie Ahrens.

"Jackie, it's Margie. Check your e-mail; the USGS just issued an official alert. Yes, they're saying about the same thing that the Strega group has been claiming. Oh, boy. Sure. OK, go for it. Talk to you later."

She hung up and turned to David. "Her boss was pissed at her for phoning him this morning, but after the Newport quake, he grudgingly came into the office about an hour ago and has been bitching at her ever since. But now that she has the USGS alert, she has all the authority she needs to start putting the emergency service organizations in the city on full alert status."

"Great!"

"Yes, it could be a real lifesaver. Let's hope they have enough time to get ready."

Seaside: 12:30 p.m.

Rick's phone alerted him to Margie's retweet of the USGS alert. "Have a look at this," he said, shoving the iPhone across the desk to the chief. "It's official."

They looked at each other. "I think we should activate the reverse nine-one-one system," Rick said. "I'd better call the mayor." He spoke hurriedly and heatedly on the phone for a few minutes. He hung up and turned to the chief. "He's down on the speaker's podium. He says Silk is in the middle of his campaign speech and he can't interrupt him, but I got him to reluctantly agree to activate the system."

They went down the hall to the communications center. At the phone console, Rick scrolled through a series of pre-recorded messages until he found the one he wanted. It told people that there was an official earthquake alert for the next two days. It said that an evacuation was not yet being ordered, but that everyone should get prepared for one. They activated the reverse 911 system, and it began robocalling the message to every residence and business in Seaside.

The chief said, "I have a feeling my trickle is soon going to be a flood. I'm going to set up those traffic details." He went over to the dispatcher and gave her the orders.

Portland: 1:10 p.m.

Margie's phone emitted a loud beep. "Whoops, the ShakeAlert just triggered! Quick, get a good grip on the room partition and brace yourself. It's going to be rock-and-roll time in about ten seconds!"

They braced themselves as Margie counted down. At the count of five, the building shivered, and the windows began to rattle as the P-wave train began passing through. Ten seconds later the S-waves arrived with a jolt, and the building began to shake violently. David held on for dear life as the building swayed erratically back and forth while simultaneously jerking and twisting.

Out the window everything was swaying in a hodge-podge blur of dizzying motions. There was a rushing, booming noise, multitudes of car alarms went off, and screeches and screams were heard from outside. The great arch of the distant bridge swayed side to side and then crumpled at one end, dropping down as if kneeling and then slowly keeling over sideways and disappearing from view. One of the MAX Red Line commuter trains had just entered the Steel Bridge. The bridge swayed and twisted, and the rear car of the train, protruding from the end of the bridge, was shaken like a rag doll in the mouth of a playful puppy. The high towers of the Hawthorne Bridge, with their massive counterweights, seemed to lurch back and forth in great arcs until suddenly the bridge broke apart, accompanied by screams of torn metal, and collapsed into the river. To David's terror, spider webs of cracks slitted across the windows just in front of his face. He flinched, expecting to get it full in the face, but the strands of tape held, and the shards of broken glass shivered there in space. The room partition he was clinging to was buffeting him like a jackhammer. And the shaking went on, and on.

Across the river in downtown Portland, tall modern office towers swayed and jerked like drunken marionettes, their vitreous facades losing their adamantine luster as their great glass curtain walls shattered, turning milky with cracks or sheeting in great fragments off into space, leaving dark voids behind. Older buildings collapsed or shed their brick facings, disappearing in billowing clouds of dust that sprouted up all over the cityscape. Just below them a huge freeway interchange cracked and crumbled, then collapsed in a thunderous roar, sucking cars and trucks into an abyss of exploding rubble. And the shaking went on.

After what seemed an eternity, the waves passed by, rolling on to the northeast, and the shaking stopped as suddenly as it had begun, leaving a great silence as the sounds of destruction ceased. David, dazed and bruised by the buffeting his body had taken against the partition, gradually released his clenched grip on its frame.

In a small, tremulous voice, he said, "I never could have imagined what that was like. Not in a million years. It was terrifying, awesome. But it a strange way it was thrilling, too."

Margie consulted her watch and clicked the stopwatch switch. "Just over three and a half minutes," she said. "It was a biggie, all right, but it wasn't the whole shebang. They said that would be five or six minutes." Turning to him, she said, "Yeah, but if you'd been in downtown Portland, you wouldn't have thought it was too thrilling."

"Let's have a better look," Margie said, walking to the windows. They gazed out at a scene of widespread, but oddly patchy, destruction. Whole sections of the city on both sides of the river were cloaked in dust clouds. Crazily cocked and twisted skeletons of buildings, bridges, and other structures presented a macabre skyline. Smoke was beginning to rise from fires here and there. Other sections of the city, of mainly low-rise buildings, appeared unscathed. The seawall fronting the downtown had collapsed into the river, taking several bridges with it and allowing the river to flood into the downtown area. Of the Willamette River crossings, only the Marquam Bridge, carrying I-5, seemed intact. Down the river huge fireballs billowed into the sky.

"That must be the fuel depots going up." Margie said. "Their soil foundations must have liquefacted, just as I had expected. They would have turned into mush, busting up everything sitting on them. Look at the Marquam Bridge: it looks like it rode it out just fine. That's the only bridge that was seismically retrofitted. That's gratifying—something worked right!"

Margie went over and flicked the light switch. "Yep, the power is out." She checked her cell phone. "Dead, no signal. No phone, no Internet."

David, still wrung out from the most terrifying experience of his life, watched in amazement as Margie matter-of-factly checked out the situation, item by item. He was greatly impressed by her unflappable professionalism.

"How can you be so calm," he asked, "after witnessing all that horror? I mean, did you see what happened to that commuter train? And those cars disappearing into that collapsed interchange. I'm just imagining what happened to the people inside."

"That's for the EMS people to worry about. I've got to stay focused on the engineering problems. I didn't set up this observation position just to watch the spectacle. I'm part of the emergency response team responsible for getting this city up and running again. My work is just beginning."

Margie went over to the far corner, where her rucksack had ended up after flying about the room. Picking it up, she fished out a road map.

"OK, David, I've got to get to work, and you've got to get out of town. I brought you this road map because the GPS in your car won't be working. You need to go south to get back to Corvallis, but you'll have to avoid the direct route on I-5 because most of its interchanges will be down. You want to pick up Route 26 here and follow it east. It'll take you east of the Cascades and out of the damage zone. It may be rough going at first; traffic lights won't be working, and you may have to make some detours, but stick with 26. Ignore the aftershocks—they'll be scary, but they should be pretty harmless once you're out of the high-rise area. When you get to 97, you'll be safely behind the Cascades—turn south. As soon as you get somewhere where the phones are working, please call my husband, Bob, at this number. Tell him that I'm OK and will be staying in town to help with the recovery work. Tell him he should stay put with the kids until services are restored in Portland. That may take a few weeks. In case the phones aren't working anywhere, here's his address in Bend where you can leave the message. From Bend you can take Highway 20 back over the hump to Corvallis. Good luck."

◆   ◆   ◆

After Jackie Ahrens got the call from Margie, she checked her e-mail to verify that the USGS had indeed sent out an official alarm. She printed it out, took it to the next office, and slid it onto the desk of her boss, Hugo Montero, who was leaning back with his feet propped up, reading the sports section of the newspaper. He was startled, and his feet slipped off the desk and almost unbalanced him out of his chair. Regaining his composure, he picked up the e-mail and began reading. His eyes widened.

"Holy Jesus, this is the real deal, no?"

"Sure looks like it. We'd better get to work."

Returning to her office, she immediately sent priority e-mails to all emergency medical services, fire, and police departments in Portland and Multnomah County, informing them of the situation and putting them on disaster standby alert. She taped a message for the Emergency Alert

System and sent that out to be broadcast on the radio and TV stations assigned to the system.

When she had finished those duties, she gazed out at the view of downtown Portland from her office in the glass-sheathed Congress Center at Fifth Avenue and Salmon Street, wondering how this bustling, modern city would fare in the major earthquake that to her astonishment seemed just on the threshold of becoming reality. Even though her professional life had, for many years, involved preparing the city for this disaster, she had never imagined actually experiencing it herself. So it was with a surreal sense of inner disbelief that she tried to come to grips with the meaning of the USGS alert. Trying to get back in focus, she went to a filing cabinet and removed a thick three-ring binder that contained the city's earthquake response plan that she had helped draft several years before. Flicking through it, she found her post-earthquake assignment: she was to assist in organizing a triage center at Pioneer Courthouse Square, an open plaza two blocks from her office.

In this conflicted state of mind, the abrupt onset of shaking caught her off guard. She ducked under her desk and covered her head with her arms, just as she had taught in the innumerable drills she had given at schools: Drop–Cover–Hold On! Those feeble defenses were no match for the intense shaking that ensued—she was quickly deprived of the protection of her desk as it went skittering across the office and slammed into the opposite wall. Her empty grasping hands found a pipe protruding from the floor, which she desperately clutched onto to keep from being thrown about.

With a screeching wail followed by an explosive report, the floor-to-ceiling glass wall next to her shattered and disappeared into space, leaving her poised on the brink of an open void six stories above street level. Panicking at her sudden exposure to falling from such a height, she scrambled desperately toward the interior of the room, crawling over an upset bookcase and getting tangled up with a light fixture and chair and a jumble of other flotsam. The next few minutes went by in a blur as she was tossed this way and that with the rest of the contents of the room, as though tumbled with a load of lumber in an industrial clothes dryer with faulty bearings, all the while struggling in terror to distance herself from the gaping open hole at the end of what had formerly been her office.

When the shaking subsided, Jackie slowly extricated herself from the wreckage and examined herself for injuries. She was bruised and scraped but luckily had no broken bones or major cuts. She looked with despair at her hands: the sight of her nails broken off at the quick and her fingers scraped raw and bleeding vividly brought back her frantic scrambling to reach safety.

She struggled, limping, into the next office. Hugo was nowhere to be seen, but she could hear moaning from beneath a jumbled pile of furniture. Getting down on hands and knees, she looked under a toppled bookcase and found him pinned beneath it.

"Hugo, can you hear me?" He moaned louder and uttered some guttural curses in Spanish. "Can you move, Hugo? Hugo, I'm going to try lifting the corner of the bookcase. Try to crawl out when I've got it up. OK, ready, go!" She lifted; Hugo heaved and managed to squirm a foot or so before she had to let it down again. After three tries he was free.

When Hugo regained his dignity and stopped cursing, he thanked her for rescuing him. He appeared to be unharmed except for a bruise and bleeding gash on his forehead that he stanched with a handkerchief. He checked his cell phone.

"No signal," he muttered. He looked around at their trashed offices. "No point in sticking around here. We'd better get to our emergency stations. I'm supposed to go to City Hall to the communications center. What about you?"

"Courthouse Square. I'm to help set up a triage center."

They left their suite and joined a parade of equally dazed people descending the usually deserted stairs to the ground level. The revolving glass doors in the lobby were jammed shut, but someone had cleared a passage through a broken plate glass window that allowed access to the sidewalk. The street scene was nightmarish—the twenty-three-story glass tower had shed its skin, and the corner of Fifth and Salmon and half a block on either side was covered in glass shards of all shapes and sizes. Victims of the falling debris were lying here and there, some struggling to rise. Just in front of the door lay the body of a man that seemed to have been sliced almost in half by a flying lance of glass. Other people were staggering around streaming blood from wounds. A brick building across the way had collapsed, leaving a gaping facade and a talus pile of bricks strewn across the street, burying cars and people and erupting a billowing cloud of masonry dust. There was a growing crowd of stunned people disgorging from buildings and from cars left stalled in the street. One man gunned his car up onto the sidewalk, frantically trying to escape the scene. Survivors scattered, trying to avoid his careening car, which finally was stopped by colliding with a lamp pole on the corner.

While Jackie and Hugo stood there, stunned by the gruesome scene, a strong aftershock rattled through, shaking down a new shower of loosened glass from above and causing people to scream and run this way and that, holding jackets over their heads and seeking cover beneath any possible shelter.

In a daze Jackie parted company with Hugo and made her way through a continuous trail of destruction and carnage for the two blocks to Pioneer Courthouse Square, where she sank down on a bench and waited for the EMS vehicles to arrive.

Corvallis: 1:10 p.m.

The stately old four-story red brick commercial building took up half a block of downtown. As part of the city's renaissance, its old loft spaces had been reconfigured into spacious apartments, and its long derelict ground floor was now occupied by a row of trendy businesses. For the first twenty seconds, it seemed to withstand the strong shaking. Then it gradually began coming apart, as though its component parts wanted to disassociate themselves from the structure in which they had been for so long architecturally conjoined. Pieces of cornice work fell from the elaborate parapet, crashing onto the sidewalk below. A latticework of cracks zigzagged up its brick front, storefront windows shattered as their frames bent and twisted, and angles of the building became oddly skewed and twisted. People began bolting out of its doorways, first from the shops, then from the stairways leading down from the apartments, all scrambling for the seeming safety of the open street.

The central front of the building bulged outward, then buckled and toppled into the street with a roar, splattering bricks in all directions. Apartments and stairwells were momentarily exposed in a state of embarrassed undress until the roof collapsed and took everything with it on its descent into a rubble pile that overflowed the basement. The end walls were the last to go, hesitating for a moment as if surprised by their sudden lack of support and then toppling outward. The northern of these collapsed into a narrow

yard that separated the building from a low wooden structure that housed Manny's Roasting Hut. The avalanche of
bricks pitched outward, staving in the rear wall of Manny's
and punching it into the interior.

The scientists occupying Manny's back room were cow-
ering beneath the tables when the rear wall came in at them.
The room became filled with a thick cloud of masonry dust
and bits of old insulation infused with the choking stink of
old mold. The group was trapped in a dimly lit triangular
cavity between the rear and front walls, buttressed in by
the tables. Jason found a crevice where the wall corner had
sprung open that left just enough room to allow the group to
crawl past a row of exposed nails to the outer room—which
seemed relatively unscathed except for the central barista
serving area, where the massive Italian espresso machine
had come adrift and was hanging by several bent pipes and
the floor was littered with broken cups, glasses, and other
utensils. Several customers were crawling out from beneath
the booth tables along the side and front walls.

Amid this wreckage stood Manny, staring at them with
wide eyes and a crazed grin.

In a dazed voice, he murmured, "It has come true. All
what you predicted has come to happen. How can it be? Are
you the new oracles? Forgive me, for although I supported
you, I doubted you."

"You aren't the only one, Manny," Anastasia wailed in
a voice quavering on the fringes of hysteria. "Mostly the

people they did not believe us. So our work was for nothing. For nothing. We failed." She began to weep silently.

Kiersten took her into her arms and gently rocked her as she sobbed and shuddered in an effusion of pent-up emotions.

Jason suddenly jerked, as if coming out of a trance, and began whooping and leaping up and down.

"We did it!" he shouted. "We did it. We nailed the sucker! Holy shit, I can't believe it."

Mark grabbed him by the shoulders. "Calm down, Jason. Take it easy. This isn't the time or the place for it."

In the ensuing silence, they heard a distant wailing of sirens, people screaming, and, from somewhere nearby, plaintive cries for help.

Carl, who had appeared as stunned as everyone, appeared to pull himself together. He said, "Don't be so sure of that, Anastasia. Plenty of people were following Jason's tweets, so we may have done more good than we realize. And Jason is right; our prediction was as successful as we could possibly have hoped. Although it may sound ghoulish to say so in the present circumstances, think about the future, when the method we've just seen proven may well be instrumental in saving countless lives. Maybe it didn't help too many people this time around, but we should be proud of what we've accomplished. I want to thank everyone for a great job done. You, too, Manny; your support was heartening to us all.

"Now I think we need to get out of here and try to find our various ways home. That may not be easy. The going's likely to be pretty treacherous out there."

Three of Manny's patrons were frantically and fruitlessly trying to open the street door, which was firmly jammed in its twisted frame. At the far end, Shuichi was wielding a chair, methodically poking out shards of glass that remained in the frame of the once impressive plate glass window that, inscribed with ornate gold lettering, had announced Manny's establishment to passersby. Carl grabbed another chair and pitched in, and soon a passage was cleared that allowed everyone to exit over the low sill onto the sidewalk.

Cannon Beach: 1:10 p.m.

Mervyn Tomlinson had been monitoring #casquake all morning. The growing number of people following that hashtag were becoming anxious; quite a few tweeted that they were already evacuating coastal towns. When some of his guests arrived back at the motel for lunch, they kidded him about the minor quake of the morning. He told them that things were becoming serious and to stick around the motel. A group of them were gathered in the lounge, talking nervously; several went to pack their bags.

When he received Margie's retweet of the USGS alert, he immediately went out and hoisted the blue flag. He returned to his office and beginning calling the guest rooms, asking anyone who answered to come down to the lounge.

He anxiously waited as his guests straggled in from the beach. He was just counting heads against his guest list when the earthquake struck. He shouted for everyone to get down and cover their heads.

When the shaking subsided the tsunami warning sirens began wailing.

Mervyn stood and shouted above the din, "Everybody up! Follow me. We have to evacuate; a tsunami is coming."

When he had gotten everyone regrouped outside, he glanced quickly along the shore. He saw hundreds of people way down the beach, milling about in confusion. *Those poor souls*, he thought, *will never make it*.

"Now listen up!" he shouted. "Follow me, and step lively. We don't have much time."

He led them out onto the main drag, Hemlock Street, and turned south. People were piling out of houses, restaurants, shops, and motels from every direction, some running, some walking, some limping, some streaming blood from wounds. As they moved down Hemlock Street, the thickening crowd began to stampede as people panicked and those in the rear tried to force themselves ahead, creating jams that perversely slowed the pace to a crawl.

Mervyn separated his group from the milling mob and led them on a shortcut past City Hall onto Spruce Street, which was less crowded. They quickly reached the evacuation assembly point at the top of the Spruce Street hill.

A crowd had formed there and, turning, looked down the steep road to its base, where the frantic crowd from Hemlock Street had just arrived and was trying to jam its way up the narrow road. People, eyes wide with fear, broke loose from the front of the crowd and bolted up the steep hill. Five minutes later, the first of the great waters swept through the town and snatched away the screaming throng at the base of the hill. Where a moment before there had been a crowd of frantic people, there remained only foaming, seething waves.

Gold Beach: 1:10 p.m.

Angelo Bregas was starting up a barbecue in his backyard grill. His wife, Manuela, was relaxing nearby on a chaise longue. Their two children were playing on a jungle gym set on the lawn beneath the Chinese elm they had planted when they moved into this place, their first home. All they noticed at first was a whispering sound from the rustling of the leaves of the elm. When the strong shocks arrived, Angelo was barely able to leap aside as the grill was upset. He landed heavily on his back on the deck. The children began to scream. In the heavy shaking that followed, Manuela somehow managed to crawl across the lawn and gather the terrified children into her arms.

When the shaking ceased, Angelo rushed to them. After checking them for injuries, he crouched next to them and said, "Manuela, there's going to be a tsunami. Take the kids to the trail at the end of the road, and follow it into the hills. Don't stop. Just keep climbing. I have to take the boat out to sea."

"Angelo, no! Leave the boat. Come with us. Please, Angelo."

"I've got to save the boat. It's all we have. Don't worry; I'll be OK. Just go. Now!"

He ran to his pickup and, quickly reversing out of the drive, gunned it down the street. He humped it onto Highway 101. Cars and trucks were stopped in odd positions all up and down the highway. A gasoline tanker was tipped on its side, a pool of gasoline spreading from it. On the other side of the highway, he turned right and headed for the marina. In a short distance, he came to an area of broken ground, lique-facted by the mighty shaking. The road had collapsed, disap-pearing into a crevice. Huge sections of ground had broken into blocks that had rotated into great jumbles. People were running out of houses that were tilted at crazy angles, only to find gaping holes or high mounds where their front yards used to be. Angelo abandoned the truck and ran through this obstacle course, jumping gaping cracks and scrambling up and down fresh cliffs of soil and rubble.

When he got to the pier, Nestor was already there, wres-tling with the mooring lines of *The Sea Dancer*. The pier had sunk with the land, and *The Sea Dancer* was canted over, pulled down by the hawsers that attached her to the bol-lards of the pier. Angelo leaped aboard and grabbed a fire ax and threw it to Nestor.

"Cut the lines with this, Nestor!" He checked the controls and had the twin diesels running by the time Nestor had freed the boat and leaped aboard.

He slammed the throttles down hard and steered the boat out of the small marina into the Rogue estuary, where he pointed it toward the river mouth and the open sea beyond. Ahead he could see two other boats that were also making a run for it. They had just reached the breakwaters of the channel. Then he saw their masts jerk back and forth and their hulls lift up and tilt back, their decks exposed.

"Oh, shit, it's already coming!" He cranked the wheel hard to the right, and *The Sea Dancer* heeled over and turned sharply to starboard. "Hold, on, Nestor. We've got to make a run for it up the river."

They barreled up the wide river estuary, engines flat out.

Nestor, in the stern, shouted, "It's coming! It's catching us!"

Angelo looked back and to his horror saw the huge wave just a few hundred yards behind them. It was cresting in the estuary—one of the fishing boats was caught athwartships in the curl of the wave, the other tossed almost vertically. Angelo watched helplessly as the wave rapidly overtook *The Sea Dancer* as she ran at full throttle up the channel.

When Angelo felt the boat tilt forward and begin to lift, he fought at the controls to try to maintain steerageway. As the great wave slid under them, the boat rose higher and higher, and in the immense power of the flood, Angelo lost all control over the boat, which became a mere projectile, hurled along like so much sea wrack in the roiling, turbulent flow. He looked forward through the windscreen and with terror saw the highway bridge looming up before them.

"*Merda!* Nestor, hold on! We're going to hit the bridge!"

The Sea Dancer slammed into the concrete arches of the bridge. The pressure of the oncoming flood pinned her against them. The fiberglass hull collapsed around one of the arches, and when the first wave receded, she was perched there, wedged into the bridge superstructure.

Angelo crawled out of the wreckage of the cabin. Nestor was lying in the stern tangled up in broken rigging, his leg canted at an unnatural angle.

"Nestor, can you move? We've got to get onto the bridge." He started to make his way down the steeply inclined deck toward Nestor when the second wave swept over the boat. Angelo grabbed a stanchion and hung on as the wave engulfed him. When the wave receded, Nestor was gone.

Angelo made his way onto the concrete arch of the bridge and crawled up through the superstructure until he was just below the roadway, where he clung, spent, unable to manage to climb over the overhang onto the road. Some time later he heard voices above him, and stretching out and looking up, he saw a man's head looking down at him. He had on the familiar blue Smoky Bear hat of a highway patrolman.

"Are you OK, buddy?" he asked.

They lowered a rope and hoisted him up onto the road surface, where he stood, bent from exhaustion of mind and body.

Moments later Manuela ran down the span of the bridge, leaped on him, and wrapped herself around him.

"Angelo, Angelo. *Graças a Deus!* Angelo, you're alive! Oh, Angelo, we saw the whole thing! From the hills we saw it take the boat. It was so horrible. Horrible. We thought you would be killed. Oh, Angelo, the whole town is gone." She broke into violent sobbing.

Seaside: 1:10 p.m.

Rick Orsteim and the chief were in the communications center when the ShakeAlert arrived. The chief activated the tsunami warning sirens before he ducked for cover with the others.

Shortly after the shaking ceased, leaving an uncanny reverberating stillness, a message was received at police headquarters that the Broadway Bridge over the Necanicum River downtown had collapsed. Rick and the chief waited long enough to send out a text message ordering the tsunami evacuation, and then, following long-established procedure, they abandoned their posts and joined a stream of people hurriedly making their way up East Broadway, following the evacuation route to the eastern hills.

◆ ◆ ◆

Officer Anthony Durko was directing a growing traffic jam at Columbia Street and Broadway, a block from the beachfront Promenade. When the sirens went off, he turned around, puzzled. He felt some vibrations in his feet, and the overhead traffic light began swaying. Then came a jolt that knocked him off his feet. In the next three minutes of intense shaking, he manage to alternatively crawl and be half hurled out of the center of the intersection to the far curb, where he grasped one arm around a signpost and wrapped the other around his head. Face to the ground, he listened to the sounds of buildings grinding against each other, glass shattering, and the crashing and banging of innumerable unknown flying objects. He cringed and held on.

When the shaking ceased, he struggled to his feet and beheld a hellish scene before him. People were screaming and shouting, car horns were blaring; the sirens wailed on. The street was strewn with glass and debris. His radio buzzed. He pulled it out and saw the text message:

TSUNAMI EVACUATION
BROADWAY BRIDGE COLLAPSED
USE 1ST STREET

He looked up Broadway and saw people piling out of shops and cars, walking, then running, away from the beach up Broadway on a route to safety that they would soon find blocked by the collapsed bridge. He turned and made his way through crowds of running, panicked people to the Turnaround plaza, where Broadway joined the Promenade. He stared in amazement. The beach had disappeared. The ground had sunk six feet, and where there had once been 200 yards of sandy beach, the sea now lapped almost at the edge of the Promenade wall. Throngs of people were struggling through waist-deep water trying to get to the new shoreline. Directly in front of him, the twelve-foot-high Tea Party speaker's platform was now a heap of rubble; it had pancaked into its scaffolding, and the tall loudspeaker towers had collapsed on top of it. He could hear screams from within the pile of bent tubing and tangled planks that now lay in two feet of water.

He was jerked back to attention as Tommy Torgerson pulled up in his beach patrol jeep and started shouting at him. "Durko, get down to the Trendwest parking garage. We've got to direct people into that structure."

He turned and saw crowds trying to push their way into the entrances of the nine- story Wyndham resort and the five-story Shilo Inn across the street. Huge bottlenecks were developing as more and more people tried to shove their way into the narrow doorways. Durko ran down the street to the five-story parking structure and began blowing his traffic whistle and waving his arms to get people to move that way. Torgerson stayed at the Turnaround to direct people toward the garage, where the wide car ramps provided quicker access than the narrow hotel entranceways.

As the crowds surged his way, Durko stood at the entrance ramp, shouting, "Move! Move! All the way up! Don't stop! Move! Move!"

Streams of panicked people, some carrying or dragging screaming children, ran up the ramps and stairways to the top of the parking structure. Durko stayed at his post, yelling at the people to move, until he saw the rising surge of the sea moving across what remained of the beach. He turned and ran up the ramp just in front of the rapidly rising waters.

When he got to the top, he ran to the side and watched the first wave, as high as the third parking level, rush through the town. Five minutes later the second wave crested at the top of the fourth level. This wave was followed by a prolonged ebbing, a sucking back, the waters rushing swiftly back out of the town to the sea. They took with them great rafts of jumbled wreckage. Suddenly, with a horrible realization, Durko recognized bodies entangled among the floating debris—hundreds of them. He vomited over the side.

◆ ◆ ◆

At the top of the hill, Rick and the chief joined hundreds of other evacuees looking back down at the town, where they saw the tsunami, like a gigantic flash flood, sweep through the town, carrying before it houses, cars, trees, and myriad other chunks of wreckage, large and small. It raced across Highway 101, through the city government complex, and then over a half mile of fields before it crashed against the foot of the hill below them.

Some people wept and whimpered, and a woman began shrieking in hysteria for her children, but most of the small crowd stood mutely in shock. No amount of talking about tsunamis had prepared them for this.

Takonda Cove: 1:15 p.m.

The old man lay on the floor of the cabin, beside his toppled rocking chair. The air was full of dust and ashes from the wood stove. He shook his craggy head, clearing the mental detritus that cluttered his brain. He looked around and then crawled over to his bed. He pulled out a wooden box from beneath the bed. Still crawling, he dragged the box to the doorway, where the door stood ajar, hanging from one hinge. He struggled with it out onto the porch, where he managed to sit himself upright on the top step. He reached into the box and pulled out a bottle of Jack Daniels.

For twenty years the damned doctor forbid me to touch the stuff, he thought. *Lucky I stashed a supply away in case the right time might come along. And this is surely it.*

He uncapped the bottle, took a long pull, and let out a satisfied sigh. He rummaged around in the box again and fished out a ceramic jar, which he uncorked, and extracted a long cigar. He struck a match and lit up and took a deep drag, coughing a bit from its long forgotten bite. He took another swig from the bottle and settled back to wait for the wave.

Crescent City: 3:00 p.m.

When the great tsunami arrived at Crescent City, it swept through the low-lying downtown, utterly destroying it. That part of the fishing fleet that had not fled to deep water was also destroyed, like all the other fleets along the coast. Boats were either sunk at their moorings or dashed and wrecked upon the shore. The fire department survived intact and successfully controlled the many fires that had been started by the earthquake.

It would later be said that it was miraculous that there were so few casualties in Crescent City. But that would be missing the point.

EPILOGUE

The great South Cascadia earthquake, a magnitude 8.7, ruptured the southern half of the Cascadia Subduction Zone. Starting off Newport it propagated bilaterally, ripping south to Cape Mendocino and ending in the north at a point about thirty miles past the mouth of the Columbia River. Because the northern part of the subduction zone was unaffected, Seattle and Tacoma were spared major damage, and the tsunami that entered Puget Sound was moderate in size. In Hawaii the tsunami caused local devastation at coastal points on the Windward Coast of Oahu, such as Kailua, which was overwhelmed. On the Big Island, major damage was wreaked on the port and waterfront of Hilo.

More than 21,000 people were killed by the great Cascadia earthquake, most of those by the tsunami, with the beach towns of Seaside, Oregon, and Ocean Shores, Washington, suffering the brunt of those losses. This made it the deadliest natural disaster to have stricken the United States, greatly exceeding the old record holder, the Galveston hurricane of 1900. It was also among the costliest, with something over $100 billion in damages, putting it in the same class as hurricanes Katrina and Sandy. It took more than a year for Portland to regain its footing as a functioning city. To this day most of the coastal towns remain scarcely recognizable remnants of their former identities. The fishing industry on that coast was almost entirely destroyed.

The value of the Strega prediction became a political football. Recriminations were thrown back and forth. The various political factions maintained positions just as divergent on that issue as on many others in the American cultural divide.

In the background of this political bickering, a grassroots nonpartisan movement arose that celebrated the Strega group as lifesavers. This community was primarily made up of those thousands who called themselves quakers. They had first come together on the Internet to share their experiences of the earthquake and tsunami and how they had benefited by being forewarned by following #casquake. Among the most fervently grateful were the residents of Crescent City. This diverse group became organized with their own website, quakersurvivors.org, and became a potent force in delivering the message that tens of thousands of people's lives had been saved by the Strega prediction. David's book, which he ended up coauthoring with Kiersten, was rushed to print and quickly became a national best seller. As a result of these efforts, the Strega group became heroes in the minds of the public. They were pictured on the cover of *Time*.

There was also considerable debate within the scientific community, but in the end the consensus was that the Strega prediction had been the first successful science-based earthquake prediction. The actions of the USGS and its director, though belated, were also applauded as playing an important role in saving many thousands of lives.

That winter the entire Strega group, including Manny and José, was invited to the White House, where they were personally thanked by the president for their actions in saving the lives of tens of thousands of people. The president used that occasion to authorize an emergency spending measure to bolster scientific monitoring and earthquake preparedness for the northern Cascadia region. In his statement he said, "The earthquake that was predicted by the Strega group ruptured the southern half of the Cascadia Subduction Zone. Professor Strega has convinced me that this earthquake has now stressed the adjacent part of the plate boundary, which makes it all the more likely that another earthquake of similar size is imminent for the northern half of Cascadia, which includes the greater urban areas of Seattle and Vancouver. With the new prediction capability that the Strega group has given us and more vigorous mitigation efforts, we can now be more prepared to meet the challenge of the next 'big one'."

Acknowledgments

The great magnitude 9 Tohoku-oki, Japan, earthquake of March 11, 2011, and its attendant tsunami were a shock to everyone, particularly to those of us in the various professions concerned with seismic hazards. How was it that an advanced country like Japan, with its very long and well-studied history of damaging earthquakes and tsunamis, was so unprepared for this latest catastrophe? In particular, how was it that the Fukushima nuclear power station was not designed to withstand the 2011 tsunami?

This was not due to scientific ignorance. In 2001 a report on historical and geological investigations showed that the Jogan-era earthquake of AD 869 had produced a tsunami that had penetrated much farther inland and over a much longer length of Japanese coastline than had ever been produced by any of the more recent and well-known earthquakes upon which seismic hazard estimates of Japan were based. Excavations further revealed that two earlier events of similar size had occurred in the previous 3,000 years. And so it could have been concluded at that time that such a giant earthquake and tsunami should be expected about once a millennium and that one was just about due. This information, published in the open scientific literature, did not make it up to the proper level in the Japanese seismic risk assessment system, where it might have been acted on. Once again, the resistance of society to inconvenient news is the real tragedy behind a great disaster.

These things were very much on my mind during a visit I made to Oregon that same summer. The reason for the trip was to visit my sister and her family in Medford, but along the way I spent a week driving down the coast. I couldn't help thinking how the coastal towns I visited were vulnerable to tsunamis. The tsunami evacuation route signs one sees here and there did not reassure my mind's eye, which could envision the great waves overwhelming the beaches and the coastal resort towns. The Cascadia coast, which extends from British Columbia to Northern California, is the site of one of the world's great subduction zones, the same tectonic feature that produced the Tohoku-oki earthquake in Japan. In Cascadia the next great earthquake and tsunami are, like the Tohoku-oki case, about due, although just as in that case, the uncertainty in the time scale is longer than a human lifetime. This uncertainty seems to belie the urgency for preparedness for such a disaster—which, on the other hand, could occur at any time. Such paradoxes in reacting to uncertainties are a matter of everyday life. So how might we, as a society, react if this uncertainty were suddenly reduced? That is the germ of the idea that led to this book.

Over that winter I researched the science behind the book, and the following summer I traveled back to Oregon to gather information on scenes that needed to go into the telling of the story. For that I am particularly indebted to Yumei Wang, Richard Mays, Mark Winstanley, and Chris Goldfinger. I also thank Einat Aharonov for an early reading and encouragement and Roger Jellinek for many helpful comments during the writing and editing process.

About the Author

Christopher Scholz is a professor of geophysics at the Lamont-Doherty Earth Observatory of Columbia University. His specialty is the physics of earthquakes. He is the author of a scientific monograph, *The Mechanics of Earthquakes and Faulting*; a memoir, *Fieldwork: A Geologist's Memoir of the Kalahari*; and more than 250 scientific papers.

Made in United States
North Haven, CT
14 May 2023

36576048R00200